A CRIME NOVEL

THE MEMORY OF THE BEACH

Printed in Australia

Cover and internal design by Luke Harris

www.workingtype.com.au

First printing: SEPTEMBER 2024

Paperback ISBN 978 1 9231 7240 1

eBook ISBN 978 1 9231 7252 4

Hardback ISBN 9781923172647

A catalogue record for this work is available from the National Library of Australia

We acknowledges the traditional owners of the land and pays respects to the Elders, past, present and future.

A CRIME NOVEL

THE MEMORY OF THE BEACH

G R ARMSTRONG

To the lost ones

No Light Amongst the Darkness

Australian Summer 1967

ERIC RAN AS IF his life depended on it. If they caught him, they might do anything. At the last corner, his friend Ian had disappeared into a side alley. He hoped he had gotten away. He risked a glance back down the street; they were still behind him. He dug deeper.

Obstacles, people walking slowly, cars waiting in line, he dodged them all. A woman glared at him as he ran past. She yelled something at him but he'd gone by in a flash and missed it. Now he was out on the main street and the obstacles became moving metal monsters. A few of them honked at him as he ran between them, trying to put distance between him and his chasers.

It hadn't been his fault. He hadn't started this. It had been of Caruso's making, his third friend. Eric had no idea what had happened to Caruso. Maybe he ran the opposite way. Or maybe he stayed to fight. That would be something Caruso would do. Even if the odds were against him, and they were.

He was getting tired. His heart thumped with every step. He knew he couldn't last much longer. He would have to stop soon and take in some air. If he could just make it to the tram station he might reach some semblance of safety. He would need luck though. He looked up; a tram was just coming to a stop at the terminal. That luck might have just arrived.

'Stop, you little turd. Stop right there. Spike wants to talk to you, you little shit,' one of the chasers yelled as Eric leapt over the tram guard rail. He looked back at the three youths. He knew with absolute surety that if he stopped, the three hoons would beat the crap out of him. He'd seen them in action; Spike's henchmen, thugs, all of them.

No, he couldn't stop.

The tram had come to a halt and its doors were wide open. His white sandshoes pounded against the footpath. His heart threatened to pop out of his chest. Just a few more paces. The last of the passengers climbed aboard. With sweat smearing his vision, he saw the doors close. He stumbled over the tram tracks as it began to slowly take off. He reached the side of the tram and touched it lightly.

He was shattered. He looked up and saw someone staring back at him through the window. He must have looked desperate because at the very moment he gave up his chase, the door of the moving tram opened and an arm reached out and pulled him inside.

He looked back at his three chasers and watched as they scrambled down the tracks after him, yelling and cursing as the tram moved away. Eric smiled and gave them the two-fingered salute.

'Why were they chasing you?' asked his rescuer. A girl stood, holding a leather strap that hung down from the rail above her head. Eric gripped the back of a seat as the tram rocked from side to side.

'It's no big deal. One of my mates said something about the guy who runs everything at the carny. I guess they didn't like what he said. Er, thanks for, you know. Thanks for opening the door.'

She smiled.

'Jody,' she said, sticking out her dainty hand. He looked at it. It hung there a moment before it struck him that he was supposed to shake it.

'Er... it's Eric, but you can call me Rick. Everybody does.'

Of course, this was a lie. No one called him Rick. He didn't even know why he told her that. He just thought it sounded cooler than Eric.

His face went red. He wasn't used to talking to girls. He wouldn't have said he was shy but he went to an all-boys college and the only girls he knew were sisters of his fellow students.

The tram's wheels ground against the metal tracks as it slowed. A conductor was headed their way. He had no ticket. He began to panic, his hands went clammy and then realised that he still had her hand in his. He pulled back and went for the door.

'We come to the beach every day during the holidays, my brother and sister.'

Eric looked over her shoulder and saw a young girl and an even younger boy sitting on the bench seat, staring at him.

'We always go to the reserve to meet friends,' Jody said, reaching into her colourful handbag, and taking out three tram tickets. 'You should come. That is if you can manage to avoid those hoods.' She laughed.

Eric went red and mumbled a tongue-tied thanks.

He stood on the platform and watched the tram pull away from the station. He could see Jody looking back at him. She waved. He waved. Then the tram was gone.

He felt an ache in his stomach. What was that all about? He was twelve and he had only really spoken with one girl before. He was just glad he was in one piece. He hoped his friends Ian and Caruso had also escaped.

*

The storm came upon him unexpectedly. From a drop here and there to a light drizzle then to driving rain. Then it got as dark as night. He skirted around the areas he thought the thugs might come from. This meant a long meandering walk through the back streets of Southway. He looked for familiar road signs but in the wet, they were not easily seen. A car raced past, sending a torrent of slush and dirty water all over him. He braced himself as another car threatened more of the same. But this one slowed as it approached. He shielded his eyes as the sedan's headlights hit him.

He stood at the kerb and waited for the car to pass. It stopped alongside him and the passenger's window lowered. The driver of the car reached across his seat to open the door invitingly.

Eric looked into the opened door.

'Looks like you could do with a ride home, my boy.'

The rain got heavier. Then hail. That's all he needed.

He could see the dark outline of a man behind the steering wheel.

'Get in, that rain ain't gunna get any lighter.' The man laughed. 'Come on, I haven't got all night. Things to do, people to see.'

The inside did look inviting.

'I've got a heater, you'll be dry before the end of the road,' the man said. His voice took on a low soothing whine. 'Don't you wanna be safe and warm?'

Eric put his hand on the door and lowered his head to look inside. Warm air wafted from the vent inside the door.

Tiredness overwhelmed him. Hell, he had just run a marathon getting away from those thugs. He looked at the warm soft seat and almost gave in. Then he smelt something. Something was not quite right. He looked at the driver. A man with a shock of blond hair that flopped down over his face.

Then the voice in his head told him to run.

Eric took hold of the door, slammed it shut, spun around and took off.

'Hey kid, wait.' The voice had a twinge of desperation.

As he reached the corner, he slipped sideways and nearly collected a giant elm tree. He heard the roar of an engine as a car took off at speed. He glanced over his shoulder and saw the headlights bouncing up and down. The car was coming right for him.

He ran as fast as he could. The car was gaining on him. He needed to get off the road but all he could see were high fences. Maybe he could scale a fence? Not enough time. The car was almost on him. The roar of the engine was getting louder with every step he took. He looked ahead. To the right was a dissecting street with not much cover. To the left was a dark opening. He went to his left. An alleyway. Maybe he would get lucky and the car would give up on him. No such luck. The car swerved and headed towards the alley. He kept running.

The alley was a dead end.

'Shit,' he said out loud.

In the distance, he heard the screaming of a police car siren. The headlights stopped in the middle of the road, then reversed and disappeared around the corner.

The rain kept coming down.

*

Two days later the sun was out. The reserve was packed as usual. Every inch of the grass was covered with towels, rugs and baskets. It seemed that half of Southway was here. Eric put his arm up to block out the sun and slowly scanned the reserve. He saw them by the rotunda.

Jody smiled at him as he approached. She held out her hand and he took it and pulled her to her feet. 'You came.'

'One of my mates, Caruso, is working the carny with his brothers. I came with him.'

'I think I know him. Is he Italian?'

'He likes to pretend he is. He was born right here in Southway, his folks are I-ties though so I guess that makes him half and half.'

Jody turned her head and nodded. 'This is my sister Hilda, and that…' she said, pointing to a blond-haired boy of about six who was squirming on a towel trying to put on a mask and snorkel. He wasn't succeeding. 'Is my brother, Peter.'

'Hey, come on, Sis, you promised this time we'll go off the jetty,' Peter yelled as he finally got his mask over his head and onto his forehead.

'Hilda is going to take you.'

'Do I have to?' Hilda chipped. 'He's a pain. He can't swim and I have to hold his hand.'

'I can swim. I learned it last year,' Peter whined.

'You nearly drowned last year,' Hilda said.

Eric got the impression that Jody was thinking of something else. She gazed at the road.

'I have to wait, you two go ahead.'

Hilda picked up a towel and took Peter's hand. 'She don't wanna go, she wants to meet her special friend, her special male friend,' Hilda whispered loudly as if it was a big secret.

Eric looked at Jody. She went crimson. 'I don't have a special friend. He's just someone that we met down here. I just told him that we might come today. He was going to bring his new car, that's all.'

'He's old,' Peter said, 'but I like cars. Can I stay and see it?'

'No,' Jody said. 'Besides, he might not come.'

'He'll come. He comes here every day,' Hilda said.

'He's kinda like a friend of the family,' Jody said in a low voice so her brother and sister couldn't hear.

Eric squirmed quite a lot talking to girls. He knew one thing about them. They always liked someone else. Someone cooler.

'They didn't catch you then,' Jody said, bringing her attention back to the boy in front of her. Eric shook his head.

'Got away, thanks to you. My mate Ian wasn't so lucky. He spent the night in the hospital. They stretched his arm up behind his back so hard they broke it. He wears a cast now. He thinks it's cool though.'

He gazed back towards the carny. His fingers twitched. They always did when he was nervous. 'I'll probably just head back to the dodgems. Caruso will be finishing soon and then we can walk home together.'

She reached out and touched him on the arm.

'You could come back later?' she said with a shy smile.

He looked at her and slowly nodded.

*

He waited for Caruso by the carousel on the foreshore. The day was getting older and hotter by the minute. He stepped back into the shade as the sun crept across the sky, burning everything in its path. 'A real stinker' his dad called them days. He reached in his pocket for sunscreen but only found the empty bottle. He threw it into a nearby bin.

He shielded his eyes and looked back at where he'd left Jody waiting for her 'friend'. A twinge of jealousy coursed through him.

A car pulled up on the far side of the reserve. His heart did a little skip. It was the car that chased him the other night. A man slid out of the front seat and strode over the carefully cut grass towards him. A tall blond man, the very same man who had attempted to pick him up. For a second, Eric hesitated. Had the man seen him? Should he run? He was sure the man was up to no good. He'd heard of men like him before. Men who picked up children. Hell, his father had warned him about such men. And now he was coming towards him.

Eric was just about to run when the man suddenly swerved to his left, then honed into a girl sitting on her towel.

Jody turned towards him and smiled. The blond man laughed then flopped himself down beside her. He took her by the hand and lifted it to his lips.

He kissed it.

Eric's heart lurched. He wanted to yell out a warning but his voice wouldn't work.

He backed away a few steps. As he did, the man looked up and saw him staring. The man's grin turned to a sneer as if he was saying, 'She's mine, kid.'

Two weeks later Jody, her sister Hilda and her little brother Peter went missing.

They were never seen again.

1

The Memory of the Beach

Forty Years Later

IT WAS AS IF the beach had memory. Memory of children playing on its white sands. Memory of life and loss. And then there was the memory of the soul. The memory of the missing was also not far from its thoughts. It was what brought him back. As Rick watched the surf, he zipped up his black raincoat and brought his focus from the jetty to the beach. He wondered whether it was at this spot his father died. Maybe a little further down. An old lady with a wooden stick drew symmetrical circles on the beach. They were perfect. Each circle was drawn with dexterity and accuracy. Three small children, an older man and two fishermen watched from the jetty.

The sun was shining but still, it was cold. Not bitterly cold like he had remembered it but cold enough to wear his ski jumper and beanie. He appeared unaware that people were watching him. They were talking about him. The sea breeze blew against his face, gently freezing the end of his nose. He shook his head and stretched his fingers out. He had picked the middle bench to sit, away from others. It wasn't because he was unsociable; he could talk when needed and given the right situation. It was just he was usually a solitary man, a man comfortable with his own company.

The beach was the same as he remembered. The jetty not so much – the old one had blown away. The Arch of Remembrance was still there. He recalled the old jetty and the days when he would dash down its length barefoot on its tarred wood. The heat underfoot was not just uncomfortable but damn near unbearable. He would sprint down the length of the jetty and throw himself off the end before swimming back to shore. He couldn't imagine doing that now.

He stared out to sea. A surfer made the bold decision to stand against a broken wave. For a moment, it looked like he would make it until the three-footer wave began to break up under him. This was not a beach for surfers. This was the beach for swimmers. The ones who put in the big strokes, like his father. As a boy, he would watch him wade out into the deep and then make his slight frame swim against the tide. He would make the biggest and slowest strokes imaginable. Many times, the boy thought his dad would go under due to the lack of speed. But in the end, he would get to where he was going turn around and come back at a snail's pace.

He looked back down at where his dad had died and was struck by a deep sorrow that his mother had to witness his death. And although he missed his father, there was something in the adage that he had died doing something he loved. Not for him to go through the pains of old age or dementia or cancer. A good old-fashioned heart attack would do it on the beach he loved so much.

Nowadays, there were more dogs than he remembered before. Big, small, trendy and the occasional plain mutt. He watched as they overran the beach, dipping into the surf when their masters, brandishing some sort of ball tosser, would fling it casually into the water. He wondered when the beach had become trendy. Probably after the new jetty had been built, he mused, and when had the dry cleaner and bait shop become a place to get coffee and tiny pastries?

The walk down the length of the jetty was a ritual. He had made this walk several times on his return. He used it to think. He would clear his mind and walk with hands in his pocket to the end where he would pause, lean over the edge and look at the water for a while then turn and walk back. It was calming.

He had been back in Southway for only a few days. This was his beach. This was the beach where he had met his first love. This was the beach where he discovered rock and roll. And of course, the beach where his father died.

The circle woman finished her work and looked up at him. She shrugged her shoulders and ambled away. He stared at the concentric circles and wondered if they had any meaning. No, they were just drawings. But they were so compelling. The longer he looked, the more he thought that she had drawn it for him.

He watched a couple walking hand in hand on the boardwalk. He wanted to smile at them but couldn't. Not that it was hard for him, no, that wasn't it. He thought deeply about why he couldn't smile. In the end, he guessed he just wasn't having a good day.

The wind blew colder in his face.

He glanced at two old ladies sipping their cappuccinos under the awning of the Esplanade café. The building loomed large in his memory. But for now, those memories were well back in the recesses of his mind. If he had known the two old ladies were talking about him maybe he wouldn't have stared so much.

*

The next day the circle woman was back. He thought it seemed slightly odd that she picked the same spot each time she drew her designs. Perfect circle after perfect circle were scratched out by a long stick. Not just any stick. From his seat on the Esplanade, he could see it was decorated along the shaft. It fit perfectly in the old woman's hand. She hardly even looked at the fine white sand as she etched her masterpiece. He sat watching closely as the drawing evolved from simple circles to complexities that had to have been planned. Occasionally, she would pause as if to reconsider her options. She glanced up at him and glared.

Something was tugging at his mind. Something he was meant to remember but what was it? He frowned. The old woman had finished her drawing and had disappeared.

Suddenly, she was behind him.

'What are you looking at me like that for?' she said.

He spun around. The woman looked curious, harsh lines etched a frown on her liver-spotted face.

'Just admiring your work, I guess.'

She shook her head violently. 'No, you were spying. I can tell the difference.'

'What, you think I was stealing your ideas, do you?' He smiled to himself.

'Could have been. You could be a stealer.'

'A stealer?'

'Yeah, someone who steals souls.'

Ah, he understood now, she was a kook. It made sense, drawing on a beach, with a stick – that was real kooky stuff.

'That's ridiculous.'

'Not so, it's been done before.'

He looked at her again and noticed she didn't have her stick with her. Before he could wonder where it was, she sneered.

'You don't think I would bring it up here, do you? I had it nicked before, nearly killed me, it did.'

'It's just a stick.'

She laughed at him. 'That's what they'd have you believe. That's what they told me when they stole it last time, said it was a weapon.'

She spat on the ground when she uttered those words.

'I'm not going to steal your stick.'

'Well, I don't know about that.'

'You're crazy.'

As soon as he said it, Rick regretted it. Who was he to say she was crazy? He should be elsewhere but he kept on coming back here. Now that was crazy.

She didn't seem to mind being called crazy.

'Those circles you draw.'

'What about them?'

'Well, do they mean anything?'

The old lady looked at him to see if he was playing her. She must have decided he wasn't.

'Everybody wants to know that.' She glanced down at the beach as if seeing her artwork for the first time. 'Life and death. That's what it's about. Lots of people die on the beach.'

A shock shot up his spine. Did she know about his father dying on the beach right about where her circles now decorated the white sand? No, she couldn't have. That was more than forty years ago. He looked at her; she was certainly old enough to have been around at that time but what were the odds? Pretty high, he thought.

'Children too,' she said.

He stared at her. How had she known that? Could she read minds?

'Children, what do you mean?'

It had been the stuff of his nightmares, ever since those dark days. The nightmares had not softened with age. They had grown. The old woman looked at him and nodded knowingly. For the first time, he could see that she wasn't all that old, maybe younger than he was. Yes, she had lines around her eyes but her face was animated. There was no way she could have been around when his father died… he looked down at the spot right in the middle of her 'crop circle'.

'My circles are just what other people see in them. Just something for people to smile at,' she said. 'Do you see anything special in them?'

Her green eyes bore right into him.

'Not really.'

She laughed. Not uproariously, just a confident laugh, as if she knew he was lying.

'Why do you draw in the same spot all the time?'

'I draw all over the place.'

'I haven't ever seen them before and I've been to a lot of beaches,' he said. Yes, he had been to a lot of beaches but mostly overseas.

'Not enough,' she said with confidence. 'I pick out a spot where I get a feeling and then I draw. Sometimes it's where bad things have happened, sometimes not.'

He glared at her but she was unfazed, she was used to having to explain her motives.

'You seem sad,' she said, watching the man shift from one foot to another. His favourite bench seat facing both the sea and the jetty was suddenly too crowded for his liking. He leaned over the railing and looked ahead, trying to ignore her.

'I'm fine.'

He wasn't. This was getting uncomfortable. In his mind, he saw his father doing the Australian crawl just to the side of the jetty.

She knows, son.

He pushed his father's voice out of his mind. He had no right to be there after all these years. He had gone far too early. He missed him.

'If you could just let me sit here in peace, I'd be a lot better.'

'You started this.'

She waved her hands in resignation then stomped away. He knew how to make friends.

Then again, friends were yet another reason he was here now. Or in particular, two friends. Both of whom had been there with him all those years ago. The nightmares were still there but had become more pointed and darker with age. Had he done enough back then? No. He knew that was true. But what could he do now? Probably nothing. But he had to try. That much he knew. The rock and roll world that he came from, combined with the alcohol and occasional drugs, no longer did the trick. First thing was that he needed to find Ian. Then he could at least concentrate on what happened to those children. The missing children! The ones who had never been found. That horrified him still. How could those who had taken them never be brought to justice?

'But how the hell do I do that?'

He didn't know why he said it out loud. It just flew out of his mouth. A flash of the horror of what had happened all those years ago hit him. The surroundings had made it more prevalent. It was as if the beach was trying to tell him its secrets.

He stepped through it the way he always did with problems.

Finding Ian should be easy. They had kept in casual contact over the years and Ian had become, and probably still was, a corporate lawyer. Somewhat easy to find. And Caruso was dead. A few months ago. It hadn't been unexpected. Out of the three of them, Caruso not only had all the vices but it had also sent him in and out of prison with regularity.

He reached into his pocket and pulled out a letter. He read it again and then put it back. A feeling of hopelessness swept through him. He had let those children down. He should have done something on that day. Instead, he had done nothing. He'd been scared. Hell, he'd only been twelve years old when it had happened.

It wasn't his fault. He thought about the children who had gone missing. Jody, Hilda and Peter. He patted his pocket and gritted his teeth. If the letter was right then there might be an outside chance to find some answers. Could he put things right? Could it stop his nightmares?

Of course, he had been a child himself when it had happened but that did not excuse him from all those other years when he'd been older. He hadn't looked for them; instead, he disappeared, joined a band and travelled the world, blocking out all that had happened to the three of them back on that Australian beach all those years ago.

The beach made remembering easier for him.

He looked towards the road leading down to the jetty. Nothing was open yet.

But he had all the time in the world. Nobody was waiting for him anymore. Rick sighed and looked out to sea.

2

'Watch Out for Sharks, Son.'

RICK WAS THINKING OF sharks. Australian waters were full of them. Even more so in the southern waters where he came from. And then there were the other kind of sharks. The ones his father warned him of.

It was two days later. This time, he was at the end of the jetty, leaning over the side, watching the churning waters below. The weather was keeping the people away and that was the thing he liked the most, solitude and silence. He put his hands to his ears – they were cold! So cold his lobes were sore. His life thus far had been so, well, loud for one thing and complicated for another. So many people depended on him. Or they had. That felt like a million years ago.

He scratched his head. The scars were still sore, both literally and figuratively. It had been a few years now since the accident that caused the scars but they still itched and throbbed at times. He tugged his beanie down lower and turned his head against the bitter wind. Some said he had become reclusive. He didn't mind that, as long as they left him alone! Boom-Boom! He smiled at his joke.

He looked for the old lady but she wasn't around. Too cold for the old. Only old fools. He smiled again. He was both old and foolish. Had he regretted anything in his life? Many things, too many to list. But there was one that stood out. One that was the hardest for him. This memory he always struggled with. He had buried it deep but it forced itself to the surface.

His face was frozen.

'Shit,' he said, slapping his face to wake it up.

He realised too late he had spoken out loud. The one and only fisherman standing at the end of the jetty thought the question was directed at him.

'You talking to me?'

He was an older Asian man.

'Nah, mate, just thinking. I grew up here,' said Rick.

He didn't know why he was talking to the man. He was just as mad standing out in the wind freezing his bollocks and cheeks so hard they hurt. The Asian man was catching nothing. He had two lines and three crab nets on the go.

'No bloody good today,' he said angrily. His clipped accent was somewhat hard to hear.

'Too cold for the fish?'

The fisherman stared at him as if he were mad.

'You're no good at jokes, mister,' said the fisherman.

He grinned; this man kinda made sense.

'I let my childhood sweetheart go.'

The man seemed to consider this. He flung out his line again.

'Plenty more fish in the sea,' said the fisherman.

He didn't know whether the man was taking the piss or not.

'One of my friends died a few months ago. I only just found out. And I haven't seen my other friends for years,' he said.

The man seemed distant. He was concentrating on the growing waves.

'They understand,' he said finally, 'true friends do.'

Was he the smartest man he'd ever met? Maybe yes, then again, he caught no fish, how smart was that?

'You ever caught a shark here?'

'Sharks don't come here. Never seen one,' said the fisherman.

'They used to.'

'That musta been a long time ago. No bloody sharks here, mate,' said the fisherman.

He leant on the railings and watched as the fisherman pulled up his nets, reset his bait and flung them back out into the ocean.

'It was a long time ago.' He watched as the fisherman sent out another line.

*

He looked through the window and then tapped lightly on the door. He looked at the name of the store. Molly Muggins. Rick smiled. The caricature drawn on the window showed an amply proportioned woman with a wild look in her eye carrying a tray of coffee. Underneath the tray it said:

Purveyor of fine coffee and cakes.

He hesitated then pulled up his coat collar. Could he do this? It had been such a long time. The letter in his coat pocket told him yes.

There was movement behind the counter. A man wearing a white apron shuffled towards the door.

The door opened.

'Well, if it ain't the superstar himself,' said the silver-haired man. He rubbed his hands on his apron and stuck out his hand. Rick stared at him then smiled and slowly took the man's hand in his.

'Good to see you, Vince. It's been a while.'

Vince had already turned his head to the rear of the shop.

'Hey, Molly, we've got a visitor.'

A slightly less voluminous version of the caricature drawn

on the window appeared from the dark recesses of the café. She shrieked and ran at Rick, wrapping her arms around his body and hugging him as a grandmother would.

'Eric… you've gotten bigger,' she said almost as an afterthought.

'Hi, Molly. No one's called me Eric for a very long time,' Rick said, extracting himself from the bear hug that she currently had on him.

'I'm sorry but I can't quite get used to that. Eric Donahue was a very respectable name. I'm sure your parents wouldn't approve if they were still alive.'

'He's a rock and roller, Molly. Rock and rollers have to have a rock and roll name. Eric Donahue doesn't cut it but Rick Deal? That's rock and roll,' Vince said with gusto.

'Not rock and roll anymore, Vince. I gave all that up a couple of years back.'

'I heard that. So, what have you been up to since then?' asked Vince.

Rick shrugged. 'A bit of this and a bit of that.'

Molly smiled. 'Don't hassle him, Vince. He's probably sick of everybody asking him.'

'Actually, Molly, I came back because of the letter.' Rick patted his pocket.

'What letter?'

Vince looked slightly embarrassed. He went into retreat mode and lifted his hands in defence.

Molly turned on him. 'You didn't?' She was red-faced. 'I told you to leave it. Eric doesn't need that anymore. All that happened years ago. You're dragging up the past.'

Vince was speechless.

'It's okay, Molly. Vince was only doing a favour for an old friend,' Rick said.

'An old friend? Caruso was a crook. He did some terrible things and now he's dead. Suicide,' Molly said, 'and those poor children. They're going to drag all that up again. The poor parents.'

'I heard they were going to, even on the east coast it's big news,' said Rick.

'Do you think it'll make any difference now? I mean, it's been forty years, what evidence could they possibly have now? It's all a political witch hunt if you ask me,' Molly said.

'Political or not, the parents have a right to know what happened to their children,' Vince said.

'Still, you shouldn't have sent that letter, Vince, Rick doesn't need to be reminded of what happened all those years ago,' said Molly.

'I had to tell him that Caruso had died. He was Rick's friend, Molly,' Vince said.

'Do you still think Caruso knew what happened to those three children?'

'I'm not sure, Molly. Maybe,' Rick said.

'I know you all were friends. I remember when they took you all in for questioning, it was horrible,' said Molly.

'I knew Jody, the eldest, and I was there the day they got taken. There's not a day that goes past when I'm not reminded of what happened. Maybe if I'd been more aware that day, maybe if I'd stopped them getting in that car.'

'Lots of maybe's, Rick.' Molly threw her hands up in the air and retreated to the coffee machine.

Rick tried to break the mood a little.

'How did you find me? I mean, to send the letter?'

Vince looked like he didn't want to say.

'Sally gave me an address. She kept in touch with your mum along the way. And before your mum died, she went to see her at the nursing home. I think your mum was worried about you then, said she hadn't been able to get in touch with you. She said your wife left and you gave up playing with the band. I think she kinda thought that maybe you and Sally would get back together…'

'Vince, don't bring all that up. Rick doesn't want to hear it.'

'That's okay, Molly,' Rick said. 'I was still living over the east coast. Had an apartment at the beach. So, when I got your letter, I thought I would come back home for a while, see Mum and Dad's graves and generally see how things have changed over here. But things are much the same as they've always been.'

Molly handed him a cappuccino she'd just brewed.

'In the letter, you mentioned that he left something for me?'

'I was going to send it but I wasn't sure the letter would get to you so I kept it here,' Vince said, moving behind the counter. He rummaged around.

'Ah, here it is,' said Vince. He dragged out a small cardboard box and placed it on the counter. It was still sealed.

'Caruso came looking for Sally. I didn't recognise him straight away. He was as thin as a rake and his hair was greyer than mine. I told him that Sally had taken a job down south and that she wasn't here anymore. He sorta looked at me like I was a stranger. Then he asked if I would give you this. I told him that I hadn't heard from you for years, not since, well, not since you and Sally were together. I told him I didn't have an address for you. He looked a bit lost. He asked if he could leave it here anyway. I told him fine. Then he said something weird.'

'What?'

'He asked if I knew where the cop that was part of the investigation lived. You know the guy, Murphy, I think.'

'The cop? Why would he want to know that?'

Vince lowered his voice. 'You don't think that it has something to do with those kids, do you?'

'You didn't open it?'

Vince quickly crossed himself. He was catholic to a tee. 'No, of course not. To be honest, I forgot all about it until I heard from Ian that Caruso had died. He told me he might be able to get a message to you. So, I sent the letter and kept this just in case.'

Rick picked up the package. On it, it read.

To Rick, my friend, from Caruso. 'Everything can find a way home.'

He fingered it for a few moments, transferring it from one hand to another. It was light. He shook it. Something rattled. He pulled at the cardboard and it came apart easily. A cloth with two rubber bands, one at each end, held the contents in place.

He unwrapped the cloth and a large bronze key rolled out onto the counter. Rick picked it up and stared at it closely. He looked in the box to see if there was anything else. It was empty.

'Wow, I haven't seen one of these for years. They used to be everywhere, most of the old houses around here had one for the back door,' said Vince. 'Why would Caruso take the trouble of sending it to you? Mean anything to you?'

Rick stared at it. He ran his fingers over the words Caruso had written.

'What do you think it means? Everything can find a way home?' Rick said.

'Dunno, but knowing Caruso it probably has to do with something illegal. I wouldn't touch it,' Molly said from behind the counter.

Something triggered in Rick's mind. He lifted the key and stared at it. The past. It was always about the past.

'We had a treehouse,' he began vaguely. 'At the back of my family home. We built it in some almond trees.' Rick knew he was rambling but he kept going. 'We used old wood we found down the back streets. I remember the three of us gathering every bit of material we could find to build the damn thing.' He flipped the key over and over in his hand. It was old. Encrusted with rust, it looked like it hadn't been used for a very long time.

'You used the key on your treehouse?' Vince added, a little confused.

Rick shook his head. 'No. If I remember correctly, Ian and Caruso found a chest in someone's rubbish. We used it for a desk, and to put things in. It was lockable.' He rolled the key over in his palm. 'And if I'm right, this was the key.'

'And what happened to it?'

Rick considered the question. 'No idea. We all used the treehouse for a couple of years but when we got older, it sorta fell into disrepair. In the end, it was too dangerous to climb. I remember coming home one day and the treehouse was gone. I didn't even think of it again. The old man pulled it apart.'

'So, you don't know where the chest went?' Vince said.

Rick turned and looked out the window. He tried to think. 'The old man might have put it in the shed. More likely he would have chucked it. When he died, Mum sold the house. It was too big for her. Dunno what happened to all the stuff from the shed.'

Vince sighed. 'Well, somehow Caruso must have gotten hold of it and kept it. Pretty weird, don't you think?'

'So why send it to me now?'

'Do you think he kept the chest all these years?' Vince said.

'Might have. If he wanted me to have the key, he must have the chest somewhere.'

'So, what would he have kept in the chest, Ricky?' Vince said.

Molly harrumphed in the background.

'Nothing pleasant, I would guess,' she said.

The back door slammed and a girl came running through the café. She stopped when she saw Rick standing at the counter.

'Oh, I didn't know you were already open,' she said coyly.

'That's alright, sweetheart. This is an old friend of ours. He's been away for a long time,' Vince said sweetly. He took her by the hand and pulled her into a hug. 'He's also a friend of your mother's.'

She looked at Rick and smiled. 'Hi, my name's Sophia. What's yours?'

'My name's Eric but you can call me Rick.'

He put out his hand. She grasped it and shook it up and down.

'You know my mother?' Sophia said.

Rick gave Molly and Vince a glance then nodded. 'We were very close a long time ago.'

Then it twigged in her mind.

'You were her boyfriend? Why did you break up? Did you know my father?'

Rick smiled again.

'I think you ought to move along, young lady,' Molly interrupted. 'You're going to be late for school and besides, your mother might not like her twelve-year-old daughter asking personal questions.'

'I don't mind, Molly. Yes, I was her boyfriend and we broke up because I wasn't any good for her and no, I didn't know your father,' said Rick.

'They divorced when I was a child so I don't know him. He was a musician, a good one,' said Sophia. 'Were you a musician too?'

Rick laughed. 'Yes.'

'A good one?'

Before he could respond, Vince led her back to the rear of the shop. 'Your ride will be here soon, missy, we can't have you late again,' Vince said as they disappeared around the back.

'Sweet kid.'

'She's a lot tougher than most. After Sally separated from her husband, she found it hard. That's why we're looking after Sophia. Sally's got a job down south. She thought that Sophia would respond well to this place. She loved the beach and the jetty and the shop. She loved you too, Rick,' said Molly.

'I know,' Rick said. 'Sally was lucky to have you both as parents.'

Molly stopped her cleaning and eyed Rick.

'Why are you really back, Rick?' asked Molly.

That was something Rick couldn't answer. He stared at the key then wrapped it back up in the cloth and slipped it into his coat pocket.

3

Finding Things

RICK STOOD OUT THE front of his old family home. He remembered when his father came home late one night and told them that he had bought a house near the beach. Something he had always wanted to do. He was a swimmer. He was a beachcomber. Like father like son.

The old house hadn't changed much. A new coat of paint and a new front fence. The old one was a hedge, this one a wrought iron monstrosity. How many years had it been? More than a few, less than a lot.

Ever since he had arrived back at the beach, he'd been feeling a little lost. If truth be known, when he'd heard that the case of the missing children was being looked at yet again, he had a deep feeling that if he returned it might help him excise from his heart what happened all those years ago. It was a long shot. He thought about that day. He thought about Jody, her sister and younger brother. Could he have made a difference? He'd been twelve at the time. Not many twelve-year-olds could defy a monster, could they? He had gone over that day a thousand times, no, more than that. Every time he had those thoughts, he would save the day and become a hero. But the sad tragic facts were that nothing could save those children from the monster that lurked.

The monster he knew as Whitey.

'Everything can find a way home.' Caruso's words rang a bell. But not loud enough for him to recall. Home! What home did he have? What home did Caruso have?

Rick sat on the curb and stared at the old red-bricked house that had once been his home. Not only was it his home, but it had also been where the three of them, Caruso, Ian and the young and naïve Eric, congregated in those long hot summers. They spent most of their time in the treehouse and backyard. Every day during the school holidays he would have an early breakfast and then scoot down to the treehouse. He would be there to answer the knock and ask for the password before allowing entry. Caruso would be there first and Ian would always be dragging the chain. When they were all gathered, they would religiously empty their pockets and combine whatever money they had. Almost all the time, Caruso had none and Ian had some. Rick himself was usually skint but on occasion, like birthdays or Christmas, he might have some money. These times were special because they could afford to go to the carny or better still, to the flicks.

Nowadays the back fence was less imposing than the front wrought iron. Made of corrugated sheets of metal, it was easily climbable. He swung himself up and over before he knew what he was doing. He dropped into a yard that was completely familiar to him. Even though it had been forty years, everything was as it had been. The trees, minus their treehouse, still occupied the back half of the property. He could see a light shining through from the main house. He knew he could make all sorts of noise and still be unheard. He stepped over to the almond trees and looked up. The long craggy branches swept up, its canopy full of leaves and burgeoning growths of almonds. A sense of home swept over him.

Nothing much to see here. The overgrowth told him that nobody had accessed the rear of the house for some time, possibly years. The shed still stood minus a few shingles on its side and roof. It seemed smaller than in his youth. He remembered the day when his father had managed to hook power up to the shed. He proceeded to 'borrow' his father's record player. It was in this shed his joy for music emerged. It was here he learnt how to play the guitar. His father had once said, 'Son, legends will be born of this shed.' He knew his father had been joking but, in a way, he had been right. This is where rock and roll lived for him.

Thoughts of Caruso invaded his mind. Everywhere he looked, a memory came back to him. The door was jammed shut but he put enough elbow grease into it and it started to move. He put his hand inside and felt for the light switch. He found it but it didn't work. This didn't surprise him at all. He slipped the torch out of his pocket and shone it into the gloom.

He stepped into his past. The ceiling was gabled about four feet over his head. The ground was covered with dirt and growing its version of weed. Clumps of those weeds made a barrier between the makeshift door and where the record player once had stood. On one side of the shed, flat timbers were stacked in layers and at the furthest point, an old four-seater couch complete with patchy cushions made it a less-than-inviting scene. As he shone his torch around the shed, he noticed something odd. Behind the couch, hidden was an old bed roll and behind that, an inflatable rubber beach raft lay with one solitary pillow at its top. An ashtray with a thousand butts stood on a small table next to the bed roll. It looked like someone had used this place to doss down. A place out of the rain, almost undetectable unless you knew where to look.

Who had stayed here?

Bits of paper and magazines were stuffed along the ground where the woodwork met the floor. They had been used to keep the wind out. Back in the day when the wind roared outside, it would get bitterly cold inside the shed. Almost too cold to bear. In the far corner was a stack of old jumpers. Maybe whoever stayed here had use of these woollen moth-eaten jumpers too.

He sat down on the couch and shone his torch over the inside of the shed. From his sitting position, he could scan the whole of the interior. Still, in his mind, he didn't quite know why he was here. It just seemed right. He patted his pocket. It was like he needed to make sure the key hadn't disappeared into thin air. If he was right then the chest was here somewhere and Caruso had meant for him to find it. But why? What could he possibly have wanted him to have after all these years?

He kept looking.

A long spider web swept up from the metal rafters of the shed. Rick traced it in his beam. It went from the roof to the main joint down to the wooden frame and back up again. It zig-zagged all over the roof until it hit the corner. He flashed his torch in one area and then another.

Then he saw it. The outline of something large sitting on the wooden ceiling truss. He looked around for something to stand on. The small table was too short and the couch too unstable. He pulled over a wooden crate that was propping up a stack of old paintings in the corner. He dragged it to the middle of the room and then tentatively knelt on it. It held his weight as he carefully got to his feet. He was a few feet short of the ceiling. He took hold of the object. It was a heavy box. He dragged it to the edge of the ceiling space and then let it go. It crashed to the ground with a thud he thought would wake the dead. He listened for a while. Nothing. Not a cracker.

He got down and surveyed the mess. The box had split apart and several pieces of it landed on the couch. He shone his torch inside.

He pulled out a rectangular metal chest the size of a large toolbox. He placed it on the bedside table. It was the one from the treehouse.

He sat on the couch, a little stunned at his finding. He'd only half suspected he would find anything in this place. A place he hadn't been in for nearly forty years. The fact that it was there made him realise that maybe Caruso had been the user of this place. A safe place to doss down. Maybe he used it when he didn't have a place to stay. It would make a good haven.

Anxiety swept over him as he fumbled the key from his pocket and its plastic wrappings. His hands shook as he picked up the key and tried it in the lock. He half expected that it would not work, after all, it was both rusty and the key slot was as crumbly as the chest itself.

It went in with a bit of effort.

He was back in the treehouse. The three of them pondered on what to put in their newfound treasure box.

'I've got some comics we can put in,' Ian quipped.

'Comics? You're joking. Comics aren't worth shit – nobody wants to save them for the future,' Caruso said.

'But they might be valuable in the future. I've got an early Superman.'

They had been debating on what they would put inside the chest for safekeeping. The trouble was most of their stuff wasn't worth keeping.

'It's gotta be something that increases in value the longer we keep it.'

'Marbles!' Eric said.

'Don't be daft,' Caruso whined. 'Come on, think. We've gotta have something of value between the three of us.'

Rick stared at the chest. For the life of him, he couldn't remember if they had come to any consensus about what to put in there.

His hands began to shake just a little as he held the torch in one hand and twisted the key anti-clockwise.

Rick lifted the lid. There was something inside. A large plastic bag was wrapped around an object. It was sealed shut. He tore at the opening and slid it out onto the table.

It was a handbag.

A colourful handbag.

A handbag he had seen before.

He placed his fingers at the clasp and opened it. He tipped it over and a small piece of paper fluttered out. There was nothing else. On the inside were small splotches of red on the lining.

Was it blood?

His hands shook as he placed it back in the plastic bag.

The piece of paper had a name and address. It looked like Caruso's handwriting.

*

He had to clear his mind. His first thought was to go to the police. He hesitated. Why was he waiting? If this handbag was what he thought it was, it could be the only piece of evidence anyone had found on the missing children. Could he be wrong? Was it the one he had seen Jody with? He tried to remember. He was running away from the thugs. He was watching the tram take off, always just beyond his reach. The doors closing. Then his sudden change of luck. The door opened and a hand helped him inside.

He closed his eyes. He saw her wearing a white top embroidered with blue tassels and a pair of faded denim jeans, her handbag draped over her shoulder.

There was a difference.

He picked up the plastic bag and stared at it. The handles were gone, torn off. The one he had seen on the tram had slung over her shoulder. Which meant the straps had been quite long. Was this the same handbag? And if so, how had Caruso come to have it?

He had no idea.

He couldn't go to the police with such flimsy evidence.

Or could he?

He took out his phone and googled the missing children. Jody, Hilda and Peter. There were hundreds of websites set up with varying amounts of fact, fiction, theories and blatant sensationalism. There was the iconic photo of the three of them staring into the lens of their father's camera. No one seemed to have anything new and none of them mentioned a handbag of any kind.

He did see an interesting story about a cop being sanctioned about the case.

The picture on the web saw the officer in question standing out the front of the Reserve Police Station. He did not need to know his name.

He held up the piece of paper that fell from the purse.

Written in Caruso's scrawl of a hand. Detective Joseph Murphy, Number 4 Scott Street, Riverside.

*

Number 4 Scott Street, Riverside was an old bluestone cottage. Rick stood at the gate and looked at the front yard. It looked slightly unkempt. A narrow path wound its way through the garden to the front door. He hesitated. To continue meant that he was ready for it and he wasn't.

'You looking for someone?' said a voice from beyond the path, closer to the side fence. A man, bent over with a set of shears in his hand, got to his feet, slowly wiping the dirt from his trousers. He stretched his back, then groaned. 'The back's not so good these days.'

Rick had his hand on the gate. He wasn't sure he could explain all this.

'You selling something? If you are, I've gotta tell you that I'm on a pension now. Don't have much cash to splash around.' The man laughed then stopped in mid-laugh. 'You're not from the church, are you? Because, although my good wife Sarah had time for you people, I've gotta tell you, I'm not much of a fan. God didn't help her when she got the cancer the second time. But I guess she was a believer until the end.'

'I'm not from the church,' Rick said, jolted from his inaction. 'I'm, well, I'm not exactly sure why I'm here. Are you Detective Murphy?'

The man placed his shears on the porch of his house.

'Listen, it's just Joe Murphy now. Retired a few years ago. Thought it might help if I was home when she got sick. Didn't help really. I was just a burden.'

Rick realised that he hadn't moved an inch. His hand was still on the gate.

'You wanna come in?'

Rick looked at the man. He could see the young constable's face in this older one.

He nodded.

'I can scrounge us up a cup of tea or instant coffee if you prefer. Don't have the fancy coffee machines they have these days. I'm afraid it's just hot water on a tea bag or a few grains of coffee,' Murphy said, opening the front door of his quaint cottage.

'I only pretend to keep the garden thing going. My wife was the one with the green thumb. I'm afraid my thumb is just a bit black. Hence everything's dying,' Murphy said as he held the door open for Rick.

The inside was as quaint as the outside. Mismatched stools huddled around a table that had seen better days. Murphy used one arm to sweep up some used breakfast plates.

'Here, sit. Don't mind the cat. He knows he shouldn't be sleeping in here.'

A mangy black cat took one look at Rick, hissed then leapt to the ground and sped out the back. 'So, what are you selling?' Murphy asked as he poured boiling water into two mugs.

Rick was stuck for words. He felt the plastic bag sitting uncomfortably under his coat.

'Not selling anything. I got your address from the local police station,' he lied. 'They didn't want to give it to me as they said you'd retired but the guy on the desk sorta recognised me. He also told me you weren't a constable anymore but a fully-fledged detective. I told him a little lie that we were related. Sorry, but I needed to find you.' Rick wondered whether he had blown it right there. He was starting to ramble.

Suddenly, Murphy stopped pouring. His face turned bright red. He put his hand to his head as if he had the beginnings of a migraine and his left hand started to shake just a little.

'I thought you looked familiar,' Murphy said, then stopped and started again. 'It might be better if you just left, okay?'

Rick saw a newspaper spread out next to the sink. He could see the headlines from where he sat.

'POLICE TO OPEN MISSING CHILDREN CASE.'

Rick's face grew warm. He realised his mistake in coming here. This guy didn't want to be dragged back into a case that had probably haunted him for forty years. But as he weighed up his options, he looked at the man in front of him. He'd gotten old.

Joseph Murphy stood and turned his back on the younger man. Rick could see the man's shoulders slightly tremor. The former police officer gripped the edge of the sink.

'I'm sorry, I didn't mean to intrude but I thought you might be able to help me,' said Rick, stumbling for words. This was not the easiest conversation for him.

Murphy stood, clutching the faded laminate of the sink for a second or so. Then he pushed himself upright.

'Don't have time for old cases. Not even that one. The stress was just too much. Can't get myself involved in all that again. It ain't good for my health.'

Rick said nothing. If anything, his old man had taught him all those years ago to be patient.

He waited.

'We were going to have children ourselves back in the day. First when I made constable but we were young and thought we'd have plenty of time. Then those kids went missing and I was right in the middle of the investigations. I guess I kinda got narrow-minded and focused too much on it. Anyway, before we knew it, my Sarah got her first cancer. It hit us pretty hard. She recovered but we didn't talk about having kids anymore. There was something wrong with her plumbing. The docs couldn't work it out. I told her that we didn't need kids. We'd be together, always.' Murphy paused then picked up the paper. 'Then all this started again. Seems to happen every ten years or so, when the press doesn't have a big story to plaster over their papers. They drag it up again with headlines like this. Always the same, always saying things like, "We owe it to the missing children's parents, to find out what happened to them." Shit, we know that. We want to find them but it's been forty years and they're gone, kaput, nothing left. Not even a shred of evidence that anyone took them. Even the guy we think took them is dead.'

'Whitey?'

'Died about ten years ago. We couldn't prove a thing back then and nothing has come up since.' Murphy was out of breath. He took a step and then pointed to the door. 'So that's the story. You lot come out here after forty years and ask for help. I got no more help to give. I'm all helped out.'

The look on the former detective's face told Rick that maybe he should just back away now. Anyway, what good could come from it now? Something twigged in his mind.

'You said "you lot". Has someone else been to see you?' Rick asked. Murphy looked him in the eye and hesitated. Finally, he sighed and let out a breath.

'Guess it doesn't matter much now but yes, I had a visit from someone, an old mate of yours, Gino Caruso. Doesn't matter much now as…' Murphy paused and Rick finished his sentence.

'He's dead.'

'Yup, afraid so. A few weeks after he came to see me, I got a call from an old colleague. He'd been found in some old hovel, shot dead, suicide.'

'How'd they know to ring you? I mean, it was a long time ago.'

'Funny thing, that. They found a letter on him, had my name and old police station phone number on the back.'

'A suicide note?'

Murphy grew defensive Rick could see it on his face.

'Look, it doesn't matter. Whitey is dead, end of story. Maybe we should have done more to convict the guy but no matter how hard we tried, no evidence turned up. So now, years later, your friend turns up with some cock-and-bull story and you expect me to jump to it and get right back into the hole. Not this time,' said Murphy, getting up a head of steam.

'What cock-and-bull story?'

Murphy looked at Rick as if he didn't want to get started down this path. He sighed deeply and turned to look out the window.

'Look, just piss off, will you? I don't need this shit. Fairy tales.

Everybody thinks they know what happened to those kids. But I gotta tell you, they're gone and it doesn't do anybody any good, least of all me, to drag it all up again.'

Rick could see it was no use.

He didn't know how the former detective would react so he just did it. He opened his coat and pulled out the plastic bag. He carefully poured its contents out on the kitchen table.

It was like he'd poured a bucket of excrement on the table. The dirty cloth the purse was wrapped in came apart and the purse lay exposed on the table. Two things struck Rick as he watched Murphy's reaction. First were the red stains on the latch. He hadn't noticed that before in the dark. The light streamed through the kitchen window landing right on the front of the purse. The second thing he realised was there seemed to be some grubby finger marks on the frayed strap as if someone had yanked it from somebody's arm.

For a moment, time slowed. Murphy, silent and brooding, stood defiantly as if nothing had changed.

'It's hers. It's Jody's,' Rick said quietly. 'I know it because she had it when I first met her.'

Murphy gave a stifled laugh.

'What's so funny?'

Murphy sighed. 'If you knew how many times I've heard that over the years, you'd laugh too. If I were you, I'd forget all this. That purse proves nothing. You don't know it was hers. You're only guessing. Oh, sure, it might look like it is but let me tell you evidence like that doesn't just turn up forty years after the fact. So, if you don't mind, I'd like to be left alone.' Murphy paused then looked down at the purse. He couldn't help himself. He had to ask. 'Where did you get it anyway?'

For a moment, he didn't want to tell him that it was from Caruso. But he gave up. There was no point in keeping it to himself.

'The junkie. He sent it to you.' Rick knew it was pointless going on.

Murphy glared at Rick as he rewrapped the purse and put it back under his jacket.

'If you won't help, maybe the cops will listen to me,' said Rick under his breath.

'Don't hold your breath.'

He didn't.

Murphy was right. No one wanted to know about the colourful purse and the stains on the leather strap remnants.

<h1 style="text-align:center">4
Persistence and Old Haunts</h1>

THE NEXT DAY WAS still bitterly cold. The carny was long gone. Taken apart piece by piece by a council that wanted quiet rather than the uproar a thousand children on holiday made. Rick wondered whether the disappearance of Jody, Hilda and Peter had something to do with it. The mix of rides, pinball machines and food stalls can mean dodgy people involved in dodgy things wanting to make money was a common goal. People in charge liked control and by that, it somehow took the fun out of places like this. Rick thought it looked plain now. A large expanse of grasslands fronted a swathe of giant holiday apartments. This was today's look, not the look of his childhood. He searched for something he recognised. There it was.

He sat on a bench near the rotunda. He felt under his coat for the purse that nobody seemed to want. He eyed a nearby bin and for a second, he thought about dumping it.

Then came the image of Jody standing with the purse draped over her shoulder rocking gently as the tram wound its way to its next stop. He couldn't do it.

'Thought I might find you here.' Murphy stood next to the bench. 'Mind if I sit?' He sat down without a nod of approval from Rick. 'They called you Eric, back in the day. Eric Donahue, wasn't it? Sorry about before. I was rude.'

'I was just some kid.'

'You're not just some kid now. Big rock and roller, they tell me. Rick Deal.'

'Didn't know you were a fan.'

'I'm not but even old farts like myself can use the internet. In other words, I googled you.'

'So now you believe me because I'm not just some random kid?'

The wind dropped.

'Should I call you Eric or Rick?'

'No one's called me Eric for a very long time, Detective.'

'Likewise, Rick, just plain Joe now.'

Rick glanced at Murphy. He wore a long dark trench coat that had seen better days. He hadn't noticed before but the former detective had aged badly.

'I've been retired for near on ten years.'

Ragged and craggy would be a good description for him. Tall and thin also. Rick glanced at him then turned away sharply. He wasn't in the mood to be polite.

'So why are you here?' Rick said, 'I thought you made it perfectly clear you didn't want any part of this.'

Murphy looked at the jetty and gave a gruff laugh. 'As I said. I was rude back at the house. I just wanted to apologise, that's all.'

'How did you find me…?'

'Had a friendly call from one of my former colleagues at the station. He said that you'd come in with some wild-eyed story.'

'Yeah, he didn't believe me either. Said that there wasn't any mention of a purse, et cetera, et cetera. Didn't want to know.'

'But he was still concerned enough to call me. Thought I'd wanna know that a former rock and roll star had come in. He thought it was particularly brave of someone in the public eye to come forward like that.'

'But he still didn't believe me.'

'Yeah, but that don't mean he wasn't impressed. He thought I'd wanna know as I was always so close to the case,' Murphy muttered.

'So did you come just to tell me I was a fool for believing this purse was hers?'

'Maybe, maybe not. I got to thinking last night. I was so caught up in my grief. I sorta blamed myself for Sarah dying because for all those years I was caught up in that case. There was never a week that went by without me going on some wild goose chase. People came up with some mad stuff and I would always believe them. I would believe that I was on the verge of solving the case. I abandoned her when she needed me. Of course, she never said that. She was always encouraging me to go after the leads. But it never came to anything. All those leads, all those clues amounted to nothing. And then she died…' Murphy looked down at his shoes.

Rick was silent. What could he say?

'So maybe I was just a little harsh before. That's all,' Murphy said with a touch of reluctance.

'That's all?'

'Pretty much but I was thinking that maybe I could run the purse through my guy.'

'Your guy?'

'Yeah, my guy, he does a few things for me. He works in some government laboratory. Sometimes, just sometimes, he helps me with projects.'

'Projects?'

Murphy shifted uncomfortably on the bench. 'You know, when I want to get something checked out, maybe a DNA test here and there, that sort of thing.'

Three children ran onto the rotunda and started hollering as if they were in an echo chamber. Their voices reverberated to Rick and Murphy seated against the far wall of the ancient structure. The expanse of lush green grass spread out like a carpet all the way to the beach.

'So, you think it might be hers then?'

Murphy was still reluctant. 'I still think you're putting too much store in your old mate, Caruso. I mean, he didn't actually spell it out for you. And memories are a funny thing. Everyone has a different angle.'

'My memory is fine. I remember Jody having this purse.'

He handed the plastic bag to Murphy then looked back over the reserve. The years flooded back. He was a kid again standing on the rotunda, trying to get a little shade from the ever-present sun. He shielded his eyes.

Murphy took a deep breath. 'Look, it might help if you told me exactly what you remember about that day.'

Rick looked sceptical. 'I told you guys everything I knew. I told you about Whitey and the other guy. Both Caruso and Ian told you too. You wrote it down in your fucken little book.'

Murphy glanced down at the bulge in his coat pocket. His little notebook made quite the lump.

'Listen, I'm not sure where this will take us,' Murphy said, holding the plastic bag, 'but if you want me to help it can't hurt to refresh things. You know, there might be something we overlooked back then, I dunno, I'm clutching at straws here, help me. I mean, you knew Jody well,' Murphy said.

The wind picked up its tempo.

'Tell me again what happened that day. You saw, Whitey, a.k.a. Speedo man, real name, Anthony Rutherglen. How did you know it was him?' Murphy prompted.

'I can't remember,' Rick said, staring at the green expanse that stretched to the frontage of the new apartment blocks.

'Well, why don't you just start with what you do remember of that day,' Murphy persisted. 'What did you do when you got to the park that morning?'

Rick stared out at the sea. Somehow the memory of the smell of old wet canvass flooded back. Of course he'd been with his friends, Caruso and Ian. They had got there early so that Caruso could introduce them to his new boss, Spike. Rick recalled Ian being a little suspicious of Spike. So, when Caruso took them to a shabby marquee Ian lingered at the entrance.

Murphy took out his notebook and casually flipped to a blank page. Rick's eyes narrowed. Remembering was hard. And remembering fact from fiction was even harder.

'I remember Caruso getting angry when Ian wouldn't go into Spike's tent.'

'And Spike was the go-between for Whitey?'

'Spike was the boss of the carny workers. He would allocate jobs and organise labour if the stallholders needed any muscle. That kind of thing.'

Rick cast his mind back.

*

'Move yer arse or I'll move it for ya,' Spike scowled at them.

The marquee was dark and dingy. Water had seeped through tiny holes in the corners, staining the walls and delivering a stink that went through everything.

'Who ya got here, Spike?' said a deep voice.

A tall heavyset man in a blue singlet and severely torn jeans stood with arms folded. Three more roustabouts or carny men as they were known, stood in the corner amidst the haze of cigarette smoke.

'Whitey needs a kid,' said Spike.

This brought laughter from the gathered.

'Whatever Whitey wants, Whitey gets,' said the heavyset man.

The marquee was sweating. It was so hot outside that the condensation quickly gathered under its eaves. Muggy!

'You boys thirsty?' The voice came from behind. At first, they didn't think he was talking to them. Spike and his gang were not exactly pleasant and this voice seemed friendly.

They heard the fizzing of a bottle being opened and a gurgle of contentment as the contents were devoured.

'Got three more bottles here,' said the friendly voice.

They turned. A man was standing near the opening of the marquee, balanced in his right hand between his fingers, three bottles of Coke.

The heavyset man sniggered and then spat on the ground. 'Spike says you need a kid,' he said with a leer.

'No need to be uncouth,' said the friendly voice.

The heavyset man stopped sniggering immediately. He knew when to shut up.

Eric went rigid. He recognised him straight away. It was the man from the car.

The man walked up to the three boys and handed them all Cokes.

'Do I know you?' Whitey said as he stood in front of Eric.

He was tall, 6'2", slim with a head full of white hair – not just white, it was whiter than white. The strange thing about the man was that he was wearing a pair of Speedo bathers and a pair of rubber thongs on his feet. It was an odd thing to see a man of his age stripped to the barest. Odd man, odd attire, odd mannerisms. Normally you wouldn't think a man like this would be seen around a gang of carny men but they all seemed to fear him – odd again.

Eric looked at the bottle in his hand. For a second, he couldn't respond. The hairs on his arm stood to attention.

Eric shook his head to Whitey's question. 'No,' he managed to get out as he gripped the bottle in his hand.

'Go on, drink!' he told them in a high-pitched voice, 'and be merry.'

Well-spoken and highly educated, another couple of odd things about the man.

The three boys gulped politely at their Cokes, all the time watching the strange man as he circled them.

'I need someone to help me with a small problem. It's nothing. I have some things that I need to be loaded in my car, that's all.'

'What things?' Ian looked inquisitively at Whitey. 'Why do you need us?'

For the first time, the man's demeanour changed just a fraction. His face went a crimson colour and his lips pursed as if deciding whether to explode or not. In the end, he simply laughed and slapped Ian on the back. He was not used to being questioned.

'I'll do it,' said Caruso. He stepped forward and handed his empty bottle back to Whitey with a smile. He looked at Caruso as if seeing him for the first time. Putting his hand to his jaw he cocked his head to the side looking Caruso up and down.

'Yes, you'll do,' said Whitey.

*

'And are you sure it was the same person? You know, the one who tried to pick you up in the car?' Murphy said, glancing at his notes.

Rick looked sideways at the detective. Now he remembered why he had clammed up all those years ago. He hated being put on the spot. Maybe that was the start of his rebellion. Maybe all that drove him into his rock and roll career. Something for him to think about.

'Absolutely. It was the same guy.'

He was as sure as he could be being it all happened close to forty years ago. He remembered the shock of seeing the children's picture in the newspapers the following day.

The headline banner said it all. MISSING CHILDREN.

At that stage, no hint of them being taken – only a vague reference to them being last seen with a blond-haired man. The story made headlines in every paper.

He read their names.

Jody Milburn, aged twelve; Hilda Milburn, aged ten; and Peter Milburn, aged eight. That headline had been a shock back then.

Rick looked at Murphy. The former cop had his head down staring at his scruffy shoes.

'So, you'll help?'

Murphy looked at the plastic bag he was carrying. 'I must be crazy to get back involved in all this. But I think my Sarah would want me to help. She was a good woman. Maybe your friends could help too.'

Rick felt a pressing weight of sadness drift over him. He looked at the detective and grimaced. He had a feeling that this conversation was going to end badly.

'I have no friends.'

'You did then,' Murphy said, 'there was another kid.'

'You mean Ian.'

'Yeah, he ended up a lawyer. I ran into him a few times when I was a cop.'

'The three of us were inseparable. We did everything together back then.'

'A lawyer, a junkie and a rock and roller, what a trio.'

Rick looked sideways at him to see if he was serious. He was. He watched as the former cop took out his notepad and scribbled down a few lines.

'They were both with you on that day. Gino and Ian.'

'Caruso, his name was Caruso. He didn't like Gino. Anyway, it doesn't matter now.'

'The coroner's report was pretty conclusive,' Murphy said slowly. He tapped three times on his notepad. It seemed like an old habit.

The suicide had been no real surprise to Rick. People who mixed with the wrong kind tended to end up dead. Both Vince and Ian had sent him a message when it happened. Ian's brief note read, 'Caruso passed away.' At the time Rick assumed it had been the drugs. He hadn't responded. He wasn't in a good place himself.

Murphy glanced down at his notes. Rick noticed that his hands were shaking just a little.

'You stayed on the case for a long time.'

'I always said to myself that all it would take to break the case wide open was one piece of evidence, or that someone would remember one crucial bit of information but nothing ever came. Maybe this is it,' Murphy said, holding up the plastic bag.

Rick looked over to where the carnival had once stood. He imagined Spike and Caruso leaning over the railing of the dodgem cars.

'You said he came to see you,' said Rick, still immersed in his reverie.

'He said he had something to tell me,' Murphy said. 'I told him I wasn't a cop anymore and if he had any information he should ring Crime Stoppers.' Murphy paused. His face reddened. 'I was an arsehole. I should have listened but I'd just lost my Sarah and I was feeling like shit. He was the last person I wanted to see.'

'What did he tell you?'

Murphy grizzled. 'Some bullshit story.'

Rick looked at the former cop. 'What bullshit story?'

'He told me that he'd seen Whitey recently.'

'Impossible, Whitey's dead. He must have been wrong. I remember seeing it in all the papers. I can't remember what he died of though.'

'Car accident. Ten years ago. I was still a cop. I was assigned to go to the funeral. It was a pretty low-key gathering. The family wanted it that way. I remember having some difficulty in getting into the church.'

'Was there a coroner's report done? I mean, don't they do it for all accidental deaths?'

'Yup, nothing much to report. They only recovered the charred remains. The car took fire and went over the edge at Devil's Reach. It was all pretty conclusive.'

'Did they ever find the car that we saw him drive back before the children went missing?'

Murphy shook his head. 'Never appeared. That was the one thing we were hanging our case on. Getting hold of that car. Some in the department thought he got rid of it sometime after the children went missing but we couldn't prove anything.'

'So, the case went cold.'

'Colder than the Antarctic.'

'So why do you think Caruso said he saw Whitey?'

'I have no idea. He was your friend. Would you have believed him?'

'I knew him a long time ago. I guess I thought I knew him when we were kids but now after all these years and what we all went through? I'm not so sure.'

'If I was playing devil's advocate, I could put up a case that he believed what he saw.' Murphy kept talking. 'I remember when he turned up. I was in the garden. At first, I didn't recognise him – he looked pretty bad. Then he told me who he was. And then there was the story. He'd seen Whitey, in a supermarket of all places. Well, I guess I doubted him but when he died soon after, well, I was curious. They found a note on his body.'

'The suicide letter?'

'Kind of,' Murphy said. He fumbled around in his coat top

pocket. 'They called me when they found it. Here it is. I took a copy when my colleague called me.'

'Why did they call you? I mean, if you are retired and all.'

'They found my card with him. One that I'd given him a very long time ago.'

Rick took the piece of paper and read.

'I know that I have not lived a good life. My parents were not proud of me. My brothers and sisters turned their backs on me a long time ago. I have not seen or heard from my friends since I became a thief. I was a drug user and I did not treat my friends very well. I stole from them and they couldn't rely on me. I have been having dreams ever since that day when I saw … A monster. I blocked him out all these years. I feared him in the dark, around the corner and every time I opened my eyes. For a time, I blocked it all out until a week ago when I saw him again.

Please understand that I cannot live like this.'

'It doesn't sound like something Caruso would write. He wasn't that literate. He might have written it but it kinda sounds like an apology letter. It actually sounds like someone wrote it for him.'

'Too well written?' Murphy said, shrugging his shoulders. 'It was a long time ago you knew him. He might have gotten an education.'

Rick looked at him. 'Maybe. Still doesn't sound like him much.'

'One thing I will say. I think he knew more about what happened to those kids.' Murphy gritted his teeth and stared ahead.

'He told the cops everything back then. He told you all about Whitey and the other guy. All about the car and everything. You just didn't believe him.'

He paused again.

'And for that, I'm sorry. If I could change all that, I would.

The trouble was most of my colleagues never believed any of it. And when we did bring in Whitey, he had a rock-solid alibi and nobody could prove anything.'

Rick stared out into the sea. 'I need a drink.' He hadn't partaken for ten years now. The giving up of the smokes had come a few years later.

'You spend a lot of time at the beach, don't you,' Murphy said. It wasn't a question.

Rick thought for a second. 'It helps.'

Murphy seemed to understand. His gaze shifted from the condos towards the sea.

'Listen, the way I see it is it doesn't matter if Whitey is dead,' said Rick. 'We need to find out what happened to those kids. Caruso probably saw an old man who reminded him of Whitey, that's all. It doesn't mean we can't get some payback for those kids.'

Murphy looked at Rick and sighed. He was hooked yet again. He held up the plastic bag.

'Maybe the purse will prove something. If the bloods don't do it, maybe the parents will recognise it.'

'You know where they are?'

'I had access to them over the years. The mother is in care but the father is still living in the same house. I might be able to get to him.'

Waves broke and spread white foam everywhere. It was calming.

'So, what do you want me to do?' asked Rick. 'How can I possibly help?'

'First things first, we have to go through what happened on that day again. We build evidence and a case. We find out who is responsible.'

'We know who is responsible. Whitey.'

'Then we find proof.'

'Even if he's dead.'

'Even if he's dead,' repeated Murphy. 'It will be an answer.'

Murphy fiddled with his notepad. His whole body suddenly shivered from the cold. He put his well-chewed pencil between his teeth and bit down. This could be a long session.

5

Waves of Another Kind

RICK FOUND A CAFÉ that did take away. He took a slug of decaf coffee and screwed up his nose. He had to stop drinking this crap. Murphy, on the other hand, gulped his coffee down without so much as a quiver. He was used to drinking crap.

'You think Caruso told your other friend, Ian, something about the kids?' Murphy asked.

Rick slowly shook his head. Nothing had made sense, not then and certainly not now. 'No. Not that I can recall. I'm pretty sure that if Caruso knew anything he would have told me.'

'He didn't tell you about the purse,' Murphy said quietly.

There was that, Rick had to admit.

'Maybe if you spoke to Ian again, he might remember something.'

Something was niggling at the back of his mind. 'Tell me something, Detective. I'm having problems remembering. When did the police find out that the kids were missing? I mean, I remember the headlines after the first day. It didn't mention that they had been abducted – it just said they were missing.'

Murphy took his dark sunglasses off and wiped them down. Hell, he didn't need the glasses today, it was a force of habit he had them on.

'The children's dad came into the police station at about five o'clock. They were meant to be home by about three. He got home from work; his missus told him they hadn't arrived so he jumped in the car. He cruised around a bit before he came to the counter. By that time, he knew something was up. Bloody heartbreaking

53

it was. I was on duty, a junior constable, in my early days. My first case. Didn't know it'd last all my life.'

Rick paused. 'How long did it take when you thought something bad happened?'

Murphy cast his gaze to the beach.

'I had a gut feeling. Kids went missing all the time but for some strange reason, my gut told me this was not good. The dad showed me a picture of his kids. The oldest, Jody, was in the foreground. The photo was in colour. Her eyes hit me straight away. They were…'

'Green, her eyes were green.'

They both went silent. Then Murphy started talking again.

'We started getting reports about a tall blond guy in a pair of Speedos hanging around some children. Well, my gut got a lot worse.'

'So, the cops knew about Whitey even then,' Rick said, his face going a shade of red. He was quick to anger these days. 'So why did it take so long to bring him in?'

'We didn't have a name. We were getting a lot of people coming up with little bits of information. We had to sift through the info carefully. I guess in retrospect we took too long. By the time we looked into that particular piece of info, it was too late. He had an alibi,' Murphy said.

'So how long was it before you brought him in?'

Murphy looked embarrassed.

'By the end of the first week, we'd picked up a few suspects but I reckon it wasn't until the end of the second week we had an actual name. Anthony Rutherglen.'

'I don't remember the papers saying anything about him then.'

Murphy recalled that day. 'He turned up at the police station one day, with his lawyer. Said something glib like, "I hear you boys are looking for me." Then he produced his alibi. It was from a very prominent person.'

'Who?'

'A judge. A very senior judge. Someone so senior that we had to drop him like a hot cake. I wanted to dig deeper but my bosses at the time shelved the whole thing. We were hopeful about this guy as a suspect and then! Nothing. We had to let him go. Not even so much as an interview. It was depressing at the time.'

'You brought him in again later. Why?'

'Later when the pressure ramped up for a result, the senior bosses thought we should at least interview the guy. So, we brought him in. He came in with his lawyers again and this time we were able to get a few details from him but nothing to make it stick. He was an arrogant son of a bitch – that much I remember from being around the interview room. I was only a constable then so I was relegated to making the coffee. He laughed a lot. Joked with his lawyers and generally, I got the impression that his suit was made of Teflon; nothing would stick no matter how much shit was thrown.'

Rick's nose twitched when he got angry. Murphy gently berated him.

'No point in getting angry. The son of a bitch is long dead.' He paused. 'Tell me again what happened on that day. Try and remember anything.'

Rick scratched his head and tried to bring it all back.

*

He was standing with Caruso and Ian on the reserve. The sky was void of clouds. A blue sky to go with their perfect day. He looked up at that moment to see three children on the far side of the reserve.

It was Jody and her siblings. They were with two men. He shaded his eyes to see but the glare from the sun momentarily blinded him. But just as he looked away, the cloud drifted over the sun and everything became clearer. Jody had a towel that she was trying to put down so Peter could lie on it. She was scowling at him as he had decided that he didn't want to waste his time lying down. Whitey was standing staring back at him. A second man, with his back to Whitey was talking to the children. He could tell that he was laughing. His shoulders went up and down. A real belly laugh.

*

Murphy stopped him there. 'You told the cops about Whitey. What about the other man you saw? Try and remember something else about this guy.'

'He was older. Well, he dressed more like an older person.'

Murphy was scratching at his notepad. He flipped over a new sheet, licked the end of his pencil and scribbled a few lines. 'You also said in your interview that the car was a Holden, blue and white sedan, licence plates unknown. Anything else while I've got my pencil out?'

'I remember it because it was the one he was driving when he tried to pick me up. It was a big car. I didn't catch the licence plates.'

'But you said that Caruso might have gotten closer, didn't you? I mean, he helped Whitey put some stuff in the car.'

'Sure, but if he didn't say anything he probably didn't remember the plates either.'

'Maybe he did but just didn't tell us? After all, he was working for Whitey, and he was a j…' Murphy trailed off.

'A junkie, I know, but he wasn't one then. He was my friend.'

Rick watched as Murphy's hands shook a little. Murphy placed one hand on the other to stop the tremble. He said nothing about his affliction.

'We checked every Holden we could find especially the blue and white ones. Couldn't find it. Disappeared for a long time until...'

'I know. You found a burnt-out Holden buried on some bikie's property in the country. Twenty years too late. I read that in the paper,' Rick said.

'Maybe if we'd had the plate number it would have helped.'

Rick glanced at Murphy. Was he having a dig at him?

Murphy's pencil scratched as he wrote furiously in his notebook.

'So did anybody tie in that burnt-out Holden with Whitey?' Rick asked finally.

Murphy shook his head. 'When we found it, I spent a week in the Department of Licences and Registration trying to find the link, but I found nothing.'

'You guys seemed to have failed on a lot of points back then.'

Murphy couldn't argue with that.

*

They had agreed to meet at the scene of the crime. The reserve. Rick got there first. Murphy figured Rick's memory might improve at the place where it happened.

Rick stood on the rotunda and looked out at the marina. Row after row of million-dollar boats jammed together all bobbing up and down in rhythmic progression. Things had certainly changed since the heady days of his youth. Huge holiday apartments almost blocked out the sun. The tiny shards of light filtered through the buildings giving the grassy area an ethereal feel. Back in the day, every piece of grass was taken up by bathers who would bake out in the midday sun. He tilted his sunglasses up and leaned back on the rotunda's railings. Two children ran around the perimeter playing chasey. It put a smile on his face.

'You look different when you smile. For a moment, I didn't recognise you,' Murphy said.

'Yeah, well, I've been known to smile, occasionally.'

'The place has changed a bit since those days. See that pylon over there?' He pointed to the far side of the reserve. 'That's the only thing left from the Mad Mouse Roller Coaster. It used to take up this whole park area.'

'I don't remember it,' Rick said.

'It got pulled down in '63 or '64, before your time, I guess. Just about right for my early days though. It's funny what you remember from your childhood. You and I could have been standing next to each other back in the day. You remember some happenings one way and I remember them another. They call that perspective.'

'Are you trying to tell me that what I remember might not have happened?' Rick said with a twinge of sarcasm.

Murphy whistled and exhaled. 'Wouldn't dream of it. I'm just saying that there are a lot more things to discover out there. Things about this case perhaps.'

Rick walked to the edge of the rotunda. He pointed back to the road.

'This is where I saw them that day, right here. I was over there and Whitey and the car were over there,' Rick said, pointing to the edge of the reserve.

The road was now off-limits to cars. It was a walking path and a bike track.

He'd had time to think about what Murphy said about remembering things. Did he know more than he'd thought? It was so long ago. He remembered some things clearly. Some not so clearly. Had Caruso kept anything back? Maybe. He'd kept

Jody's purse all this time. What made him suddenly change his mind and make sure that Rick found it?

Time to play fact or fiction.

Fact. He had seen the children several times the day they went missing.

Fact. He had seen the car. The blue and white Holden, several times.

Fact. He had seen Whitey and an older man together with the children.

No doubt about it. It now seemed to him like a waking dream, all so very vivid. He could close his eyes and see Jody's green eyes even after all this time. Nothing had diminished. How could that be?

'The brain is a mighty powerful thing,' his old man had continuously told him.

'Listen to your heart, give it a chance but always make your decision with your brain. It's the tops, kiddo.'

'You seem preoccupied,' Murphy said as he watched Rick pace the rotunda.

'Thinking. That's all.'

'Good, keep thinking. I like that.'

Rick stopped pacing. Something was bothering him. It kept coming right back to one thing, or possibly two things. Why had Caruso left him the purse and why had he killed himself? It made no sense.

'Devil's advocate,' he said finally.

Murphy nodded. 'Go ahead.'

'Why did Caruso kill himself?'

'I don't know. Because he was going mad? Seeing things? He did tell me that he had seen Whitey in a supermarket,' Murphy said.

'And why would he leave me the purse? The only piece of evidence that has ever shown up.'

'Maybe it got too hard for him to live with it. Left you the purse and then killed himself. Maybe he was absolving himself by giving the evidence to someone else and then killing himself. It could make sense.'

'No, you're wrong. It doesn't make sense. Don't you see? Look at it this way, devil's advocate again. What if he did see Whitey? If Whitey was dead then what would be the point of dragging out the purse? Nothing could be proved against a dead man. If he was alive then he needed to do something. He went to see you and when that didn't work, he made sure that I got the purse.' Rick was clutching at straws.

Murphy stroked his chin. 'Devil's advocate. So why suicide?'

Rick stared at the ground. He couldn't bring himself to actually say what he was thinking.

Murphy started laughing. 'Oh, I know where you're going with this. You are saying that Whitey's alive and Caruso did see him. And by your tone, I think you are saying that Caruso didn't kill himself and that somehow Whitey got to him. That is some story.' Murphy laughed again.

Rick said nothing.

'Ah, shit, you don't really believe that?' Murphy said, suddenly aware that Rick was serious.

'Devil's advocate.'

'Okay, I'll bite,' Murphy said after another moment of dead silence. 'You're saying what if Whitey didn't die in that fiery car crash? What if Caruso did see him? What then? Why kill himself after all these years? Are you sure he just wasn't off his face?'

Rick hunched over the railings as if he was eyeing something in the dirt just below the rotunda.

'Look, I'm not saying that Whitey is still alive but what if he saw someone that reminded him of Whitey? That could have triggered him to leave me the purse.'

'And then he killed himself?' Murphy said.

'I do have another theory,' Rick said.

'You seem to be full of them.'

'There was the other guy.'

'The guy you saw with Whitey. The older guy?'

Rick nodded.

'There were only rumours of another guy. We never seriously considered anyone,' Murphy said.

'Maybe you should have. Maybe if you'd found this guy it would have led to the children. Just being devil's advocate,' Rick added.

Rick remembered her eyes. As green as the lawn on the reserve. The first time he'd met her she saved his skin. The second time she stole his heart.

6

The Carousel of Life

Eric and Ian stood watching the carousel as it completed its umpteenth rotation. Kids squealing with delight gathered under the shade of the giant tarpaulin that covered the ancient toy. The older boys stood further back, some smoking, some showing off in front of the teenage girls. Cigarettes! The cool kids did them. Ian couldn't see the point and Eric had seen how they affected his father. Caruso, on the other hand, was ready for anything. He had stolen a pack from his older brothers and had been secretly smoking them ever since.

'Hey, kid, wot you up to?' boomed a voice from the other side of the dodgem car tracks.

One of Caruso's older brothers sauntered over. Eric wasn't sure which one he was.

'Little bastard stole my fags. You ain't seen him, 'ave ya?' he said with a growl.

They shook their heads. No point in getting him in any deeper.

'He's doing something for Spike,' Ian said who could not lie.

Caruso's brother gave a little grin.

'Bout time he was inducted,' he said.

'What does that mean? Inducted into what?' Ian said.

Eric looked at his friend. Ian certainly had guts.

Caruso's brother didn't bat an eyelid. He bit down on his cigarette, looked cautiously behind him then winked at the two boys and pulled a battered-looking wallet from his back pocket. Again, he looked behind him as if worried that he would be seen. When he thrust the tickets into his hand, Eric had no idea what they were. Ian, ever the eagle-eyed lad, knew what they were.

'What do you want us to do for them? These are fake,' Ian said, eyeing the tickets closely.

'Shut up, kid. Just take them. Use 'em on the carousel,' said Caruso's brother.

At that age, it was better to shut up and go along. When Ian and Eric fronted up to the ticket box, they both knew that they were guinea pigs. Spike's gang were notorious for ticket scams. They could feel the stares from the gang as they handed the fake tickets over to the ticket collector. The grizzled old codger barely glanced at the tickets, waving them through with a gruff harrumph. The gang would on sell them at a bargain basement price to any schmuck who fell for it.

Eric was not good on carousels. His head spun seriously out of whack. He leaned sideways on the pony, hanging on by the skin of his teeth. He was going to be sick. He looked across at Ian who seemed to be enjoying the ride. Barely making it back off the saddle, Eric ran to the corner of the marquee and threw up violently.

'Are you alright?' A female voice.

He didn't need this right now. He always wondered why he couldn't talk to girls as he wasn't overly shy. He just had nothing to say.

'I'm fine, just ate something I shouldn't have,' Eric said, not recognising Jody at first.

'Rick, you came back?' This was the second time today he had seen her.

'Er, yeah,' Eric said. Almost forgetting he had told her his name was Rick.

'Gotta watch out what you eat around here. So, you know Gino.'
It confused him momentarily. Gino? Then his brain clicked.
'You mean Caruso?'

'He's sweet.'

'We're talking about Caruso, right?'

A whistle blew and the carousel started back up again. The noise in the marquee leapt up several notches. He saw Ian waving madly on the far side of the tent. He was standing with Caruso's brother. Now he knew the tickets worked, he wanted them back.

'You here alone?' he asked almost as an afterthought.

'No,' she said softly.

She sounded like she didn't want to say anything further. Her upper lip formed a straight line. It seemed she was a little upset.

'Wanna go on a ride?' he asked.

The tickets worked so why not use them? He was doing his best to ignore Ian who was waving at him madly.

'Sure you're not rich, are you?' She smiled and her green eyes sparkled.

'No, just got a few tickets, and besides, you saw me throw up. I figure I owe you something for seeing that.'.

'That would be sweet.'

The ticket collector didn't even grunt this time. He sat in solitary silence, wishing the time to move more quickly. Sucks to be him, time moves as it wants.

The carousel moved slowly at first, gathering pace as it chuffed up to speed. People stood around its perimeter, watching it gather momentum. It appeared to be going slower than it really was. High up on his steed, Eric was under no illusions; it was fast. He gripped the horse's mane tightly. Jody seemed to be enjoying the ride. He watched her hair straighten as they were flung around and around. The air hazed over and for a moment, he thought he was going to pass out or at least fall off the ceramic horse. He did neither and as it slowed, he gained his composure. Why the hell he'd gotten back on after throwing up his lunch, he had no idea. But done is done!

'How do you know Caruso? I mean, Gino,' he said as they got off the horses and slid down the running board to the ground. Eric directed Jody to the entrance away from Caruso's brother who was looking to cut him off at the pass.

'Oh, some friends of mine know him.'

He found it difficult to call Caruso by his first name. When you only knew someone by a certain name, calling them by another is hard. Your brain isn't wired that way.

They reached the entrance of the carousel.

In the distance, Eric could see Caruso standing with Whitey. The children stood behind them.

'There's Gino now, and my sister and brother,' said Jody.

He was about to ask her about Whitey, but something stopped him.

She paused and then whispered something that Eric could hardly make out.

Then Jody took her hand from his and started moving towards Caruso and Whitey. For a reason he couldn't explain, he felt the urge to stop her.

'Don't go,' he said. She stopped in her tracks. She turned and looked at Eric then back at Whitey.

Eric saw the look on Caruso's face. He was deathly white, as white as the man's hair.

Whitey was angry. His face was bright red. He folded his arms against his chest and waited as she walked up to him. He continued to stare at her until with one flick of his wrist, he took her by the hand and dragged her behind him like a wayward child.

Caruso was frozen in his spot.

*

What had she whispered in his ear? Murphy looked down at his brief notes. There was no mention of Rick telling his interviewer anything like this. Was it an oversight? Or had Rick failed to mention it when interviewed? All possible.

'She said she was scared,' Rick said simply.

'Did she say what she was scared of?' Murphy said.

Rick put his hands over his face. He could never forget that. She was telling him she was scared and what did he do? Nothing. Whitey had taken her back towards her brother and sister. The look on Caruso's face had scared Rick. He knew something was wrong. A growing look of terror.

'It doesn't matter what she was scared of. She was scared and I did fuck all. I should have stopped her right then. I should have pulled her back from him,' Rick said, wringing his hands together, another habit he had when stressed.

'And then what? You fight him? You beat the crap outta him? Maybe in your mind but you were only twelve, remember that.'

Rick screwed up his face.

'I should have tried. That's all I'm saying.'

Murphy was scribbling in his notepad again.

Rick's mind was wandering. Something the old lady who drew the crop circles said popped into his head.

'*The beach has a memory,*' she had told him that first day. '*Stay here long enough and it will reveal all its secrets.*'

Did he believe in hocus pocus? Being a devil's advocate sort of forced him into a corner.

Then something his father told him popped in there too.

'*Memory of life, son. The saddest thing is when people find old pictures and don't know the people in them. You see those photos in the paper, you know the ones that say, "Can anyone identify the people in this photo?" "Seeking information", they call them. So, son, I guess what I'm trying to say is that once the pictures fade and the people in them go. Have they lived? If nobody talks about you, have you been alive? I guess when you have kids and your mum and I are long gone, they won't know who the hell we are, and once you go, well, our memory goes too. That's sad but that's life.'*

It was one of the longest conversations he'd had with his father. It might have been the same one when he told him to look after Sally, his girlfriend. *'She's a keeper, that one.'* Just one more thing he'd stuffed up.

He missed his dad.

Murphy had taken enough notes. He shut his notepad and slipped it into his pocket. He held up the plastic bag.

'Hopefully, we'll get a hit from the purse. Can't promise anything, though. The stains are over forty years old. But first I'll try and get the family to ID it.'

Rick sighed. He could only hope. If not, they had nothing.

*

Most of Rick's old haunts had simply disappeared over the years. One that remained was the Silver Sands Hotel or as it used to be called, the Espy. It was situated on the Esplanade of the beach south of the reserve. The Espy was where he got his first break. His first gig. The Anchormen's first show in 1973.

As he sipped his soft drink, he watched the barman pour beers from a well-worn tap. Rick had given up drinking. He missed it at times like these. The man approached hesitantly. It was like he didn't want to disturb Rick's thinking. He did anyway.

'They told me I'd find you down here.'

The voice was familiar but the person standing before him was a stranger. Tallish and bald as a badger, he had the look of a lawyer, which, of course, he was.

'You're looking good, Rick. Move over, you great lug,' said the bald man.

Rick shuffled over. Why did he know that he would come? Everybody seemed to know where to find him.

He sighed.

'Hi, Ian.'

'Thanks for the invite. I was surprised when you rang,' Ian said.

'No, you weren't. I bet you were waiting by the phone, especially when I told you about the purse.'

He stuck out his hand. Ian took hold of it and squeezed hard. You did this in business, well, in the law business anyway.

'Ya can't bullshit a bullshitter.'

'Caruso!' Rick said.

'Caruso!' Ian said.

Ian sighed. Caruso had coined many a phrase. Most of their early days had been scripted by him. He was prolific if a little verbose.

'Okay, you look like shit, Ian. What have you done with your hair, man?'

'Thought about a wig for the longest time but I got married to a good woman and shit, what did I need hair for anyway.'

The barman was back. He took Ian's order and then went back to cleaning glasses. Ian turned to his old friend and grinned. Rick tried to remember the last time he'd spoken with Ian. He couldn't.

'I'm sorry. I tried to call when I ran out of options with Caruso. I was a little desperate, I guess.'

Rick grinned. 'No problem. You must have had a lot of shit to deal with. Especially when he, well, he died.'

'No more shit than you would think for a guy who died destitute and alone.'

'His family…?'

'All gone. Couldn't find one,' Ian said. 'A couple of his brother's kids were interstate but they didn't want to know about him. He didn't have anything to leave them so they didn't give a shit. That was hard. They were going to bury him in a pauper's grave.'

'A pauper's grave! They still have that?'

'Yup and it's pretty much as bad as it sounds. They put you in a paper bag and bury you in un-consecrated ground normally at the back of some prison. Thanks to you, we got a spot in St Julien's just near your folks.'

Rick had responded to Ian's desperate email with permission for Caruso to be buried in a plot he paid for near his parents many years before.

'The old man wouldn't have minded. Mum, on the other hand…' Rick said watching as two old men sitting on high stools at the bar cheered their horse on the big screen. They were on a winner it seemed.

'Thought he was a rogue.'

'She was right. He was.'

'I kept in touch with Vince and Molly,' Ian said. 'The last time I spoke with them, Vince told me about Caruso leaving a package for you but I would never have guessed it was the key to our old box. That came from nowhere.'

'Yeah, going back to my old home was a real trip. The shed was much the same and I reckon he used it when he didn't have a place to stay.'

'Are you sure the purse was hers? I mean, it was a long time ago.'

'It was hers, Ian. I'd bet my life on it.'

'And Murphy's going to run it past the family? Do you think that's a good idea?' Ian said, sinking the last of his schooner glass.

'Why do I get the impression that you don't believe any of this?'

'That's not true, Rick. I believe that you believe it was hers.'

'Said like a true lawyer.'

'Gotta keep some perspective. But I guess Murphy will be diplomatic.' Ian laughed as if he'd made a joke. 'Besides, Caruso never said a word. Even when I went to see him in gaol, he never mentioned anything about any of this.'

'I guess it's possible – he had a lot of secrets. I suppose we need to find out whether Caruso knew more than he told us at the time. Is that possible? I mean, you knew him better than I did.'

'It's possible. Maybe he got the guilts and wanted to come clean before he, well, before he killed himself,' Ian said. He gulped his new beer down in three shots then put down his glass and ordered another. 'Good beer, this. I don't get out much.'

'Wife keep you on a short rein?'

'With two kids and a law career, you don't get much chance to drink at a front bar with your mates,' he said, then added after Rick gave him a look, 'Okay, I don't have any mates.'

Rick stared ahead. 'I can't believe that he shot himself.'

Ian sighed then took a swig of his new beer. 'Sorry I didn't tell you much at the time but I didn't know much myself. Happened in a shitty room of a hovel he was staying at.'

'Murphy said he seemed preoccupied but not scared.'

'You knew him as well as I did. He was terrified of guns. You know, because of what happened to his brother.'

'His brother was a thug. He used to bash him until Caruso learned to fight back. Probably got the gun from him.'

'I got hold of the coroner's report. It was pretty conclusive. Suicide.'

Ian nodded at the barman carrying two large bowls of beer nuts. When he put one down in front of them Ian dove straight in.

'Maybe they made a mistake; cops can make mistakes,' said Rick.

'What does your mate think?'

'My mate? Murphy?'

'Yeah, I'm sure he's got an opinion on the matter.'

In the background two would be swimmers entered the bar and shivered their way over to the food bar dressed only in tee shirt and bathers. It was far too cold for the beach today.

'He thinks Caruso was a junkie and that he killed himself. Oh yeah, and he thinks the purse is bogus. I think he's only humouring me. He's only doing this because he just lost his wife and he's feeling guilty.'

Ian laughed, not like a lawyer this time. He laughed like a friend. 'Well, maybe it's as simple as this. Caruso sees a ghost or a ghost that looked like Whitey and it spooked him and then he found a gun, a homeless guy with a gun. You're asking for it.'

'Did you hear about the letter he left?'

'Yup, also in the coroner's report. A suicide letter.'

'Doesn't sound like any suicide letter that Caruso would write,' Rick said.

'No, I'll give you that. But he could have copied it from somewhere. Handwriting experts say he wrote it.'

'Doesn't mean he meant for it to be a suicide letter.'

'So, you're telling me he didn't kill himself?'

Rick shrugged and looked at the wall of rock and roll posters that hung from the side wall. You couldn't go wrong with The Stones and The Beatles.

'You've gone quite loopy, my old mate. If he didn't kill himself, and I guess you're ruling out an accident, you're saying that someone killed him,' Ian said, slurping on his beer. 'Murder, you're saying someone murdered him.'

'Well, it's possible, isn't it?'

Ian looked sideways at his friend. 'Barking up the wrong tree, my friend. Caruso killed himself. End of story.'

Rick drained his soft drink and then looked back down at the beach. He changed the subject. 'Do you remember seeing Caruso with Whitey and the kids that day we went on the carousel? You were standing with Caruso's brother. You know, the one who gave us the bogus tickets. Whitey was with Caruso on the far side of the reserve.'

Ian screwed up his face as if in thought. 'I remember you and Jody on the ride and then Whitey but I can't recall Caruso being there. Although I remember telling the cops that there were kids all over the reserve that day. Thousands of kids, so I guess just remembering three would be a stretch. I remember walking back home that night. It was just the two of us because Caruso had to stay and help Spike.'

'Yeah, you came to my place. That's when we heard that the cops were looking for three missing children.'

'That spooked the living daylights outta me. I was convinced that they wandered into those water pipes at the dam. I kept thinking they'd never find their way out. I never thought that creep would have taken them.' Ian slammed his beer down on the bar as if remembering his anxiety.

'And that's why we have to do something about it.'

'But what's the point? Whitey's dead and now so is Caruso. We have nothing, Rick.'

'We have the purse, that's a good start.'

'But you're the only one who saw Jody with it. What if they're right about Caruso? I saw him in gaol a few times and if he wasn't off his head on drugs he was withdrawn, almost like he was in another world. We have nothing to go on.'

In another bar, a band was sound checking. They sounded terrible.

'Don't you think that the parents deserve to know what happened to their children?' Rick asked.

'Of course.'

'You know what?'

'What?' said Ian.

'You and I. We never went over what we remember about that day. We told the cops but we never spoke about it, the three of us. Maybe we missed something.'

'I dunno, Rick. I've tried to block out all this for years and now you're asking me to remember.' He went quiet. 'Actually, I do remember something about that day. Something I don't think anybody has said since. The kid, the youngest, Peter. I saw him looking out at me from a car. I couldn't swear it but I woke up the other day and thought about it. It might have been a dream... I dunno.'

'The blue and white Holden. Can you remember the plates?'

Ian looked at his old friend curiously. He shook his head slowly. 'Nup, got nothing.'

The conversation drifted. Old friend conversation. Little things. Things that had once been important. Rick told Ian about the old woman drawing the circles and what she had told him about the beach having a memory.

'Your dad would have called it mumbo jumbo.' Ian laughed then he went quiet. 'Sorry, mate, didn't mean to... well, drag up old memories,' he said.

'That was a long time ago.'

'That beach has a lot to answer for. You met Sally down there. Remember that day? That kid had you in a headlock, beat the crap outta you, funny shit.'

'Glad you thought so.'

'Er, so, have you seen her since you've been back?' he asked delicately.

'Another thing the old man told me was "never go back". Well, he didn't mean it like that, I guess. He was saying that once you're gone, you're gone.'

'You should call her.'

'Can't.'

'Eric would have called her.'

'I'm not that kid anymore. I did meet her daughter. Vince and Molly are looking after her. Sweet kid.'

'Even more reason to call her. She's obviously split up with the father...' Ian raced on.

'Don't.'

'Oh, I forgot, you're Ricky Deal, the rock star. I think part of your problem is that you think you're all a bit above all us mundane people. If you sit on your ass feeling sorry for yourself...'

'I'm not.'

He said it too quickly. He was feeling a little morose and it hadn't worked out very well the last time he'd spoken with her. It seemed his public life mirrored his private life. The more successful he became, the less time he had for the ones he loved. He had long thought he would grow old alone. He wasn't that fussed about it or hadn't been until that time. Some things were fixed points in one's life. The bits that couldn't be changed.

'So, what do we do now?' asked Ian.

'We hope we get a hit on the purse.'

'Then what?'

'If I knew that, I wouldn't be sitting in an old bar shooting the breeze with my past,' Rick said.

He could be an arsehole sometimes.

Luckily, the pub had a bistro. The coffee was hot and the toasted ham sandwiches were world-renowned. Well, maybe not world-renowned but certainly eagerly sought after by the locals. Ian wasn't finished berating his old mate. He pushed the dagger in a little deeper.

'And then there was the accident. You never called me. I had no idea you were in the hospital for all those months.'

Rick was usually comfortable with silence. He sighed deeply, knowing that Ian wasn't going to let him off lightly. 'I guess I didn't want anyone to know. Didn't want to worry Mum.'

'You're crazy. She knew something was wrong. She called me in a panic. She hadn't heard from you in three months.'

'I wasn't in any condition to call anyone.'

'But you rang Sally,' Ian said glibly.

He grudgingly acknowledged it although it wasn't something he mulled over. He guessed he'd been looking for some sympathy or something. It had been by chance that he talked to her at all.

'I sent her a message, an email message. Her Facebook page had said she'd started a new business. I was just congratulating her, that's all.'

'Was she happy?' asked Ian, 'I mean, with her life.'

'She'd had her daughter, Sophia. I guess she was happy enough. Didn't really ask her.'

'You didn't tell her about what happened?'

'No,' Rick said, lowering his eyes to the table. He stared at his mug of coffee.

'I can understand you not telling her but for Christ's sake, Rick, you never even told your ex-wife. She rang me in a panic too.'

He shook his head. He was tired. Tired of remembering those painful years. Tired of having those nightmares all the time. By coming home he'd hoped he could do something but it looked like he was as impotent now as he was all those years ago. He sighed, wishing that Ian would back off.

'And you never told the rest of your family,' prodded Ian.

He didn't have to say no.

'Dumb schmuck.'

'Caruso,' they said together.

It was something he said all the time. It was like a third person was sitting in the pub's cafe with them. Rick missed those innocent years. He missed Caruso. No, that was wrong; he missed the person Caruso used to be. The fact that he had weighed deeply on him. Maybe he was to blame. Maybe if he stepped in when he went to work with Spike, it might have stopped him from going down that path.

'You didn't see him after leaving school. I did. He was as bad as they come. Bashed people, robbed them, sold drugs to kids. He was more than a petty criminal,' Ian said.

'Yeah, I guess people change.'

'We've all changed. I have, you have, even Murphy.'

'We've mellowed. Maybe that's the problem, we've gotten a bit soft. I came back here all gung-ho, thinking I could solve a mystery that's been haunting me all these years, on my own. Thinking I could finally give the family some closure. Who am I kidding?' Rick said, slamming his fist down on the bar.

'Maybe you still can. Murphy wouldn't have agreed to help if he didn't think there was hope. Hell, he knows more about the case than anyone.'

The barman changed the background music. A seventies song by Leo Sayer started up over the PA system. Rick scrunched up his nose. This wasn't his idea of rock and roll. Ian, on the other hand, gave the barman the thumbs up.

'He doesn't believe me. He thinks it's a waste of time. And besides, he was there when they whitewashed it all and let Whitey slip through their fingers,' Rick said.

'Yeah, but he was just a constable. He was only seven years

older than us at the time. If his superiors want to whitewash something, he couldn't have stopped it.'

Rick looked at his friend and then stared out of the bistro window. There were few people on the streets as the winds had turned cold. He watched as a mother clasped the hands of her two children as they stepped out onto the road to cross. They were wrapped up in scarves and coats. The mother stoically pulled her charges away from the curb.

They trusted her. Rick could see that. He thought of Jody and the way she had whispered in his ear that she was scared. He felt low.

He watched in silence as the mother and her two children crossed the road and disappeared into an alleyway.

Okay, this was it. He took a deep breath and dove in.

'What if Whitey is alive and Caruso did run into him? Would he kill himself because of that? I can't remember Caruso ever being a coward. I can't imagine him running scared.'

Ian raised his eyebrows. Over the years, it had turned into a monobrow. 'I'll bite. You're talking hypotheticals now. If he didn't kill himself and it wasn't an accident, then somebody killed him. And for what? Because he'd seen someone who looked like Whitey in a supermarket?'

'No, what if he was murdered because he'd seen Whitey alive?'

'You're forgetting that he was a junkie and that he was bad. And bad people get killed for all sorts of reasons.'

Rick stared into his coffee. He really felt like a beer. 'Maybe you're right.'

'Of course, I am. I've seen a few revenge killings in the underworld. It happens all the time.'

Leo Sayer's song ended. Bits of conversations and pokie alarms could be heard from the dark and dingy room next door.

Ian drank the dregs of his coffee and placed the mug down hard on the table. 'Let me go through this with you. You're assuming that Whitey is alive and that Caruso did see him. And I guess if we're assuming that, you're assuming that Whitey killed him, or had him killed because he'd blown his cover. That about covers it?'

Rick winced. 'Maybe.'

'Pretty flimsy case, my friend.'

Rick knew it. He had to change tact.

'Do you remember a couple of weeks after the kids went missing, we ended up with Caruso down at the old crash repair on the Main Road? He wanted to see what was inside so we broke in. I remember him trying to tell us something that day.'

'Can't remember anything – well, I remember breaking into that place but I don't remember Caruso saying anything.'

7

The Memory of Loss

'Come on, guys, it's just a bloody shed. I mean, if they didn't want us to go in, they'd put a lock on it,' said Caruso.

'You only swear when you want to convince us. I know you, Caruso. The cops might be watching us right now,' Ian said.

'Don't be a pussy, Ian. The cops have better things to do than to watch this bloody shed,' said Caruso.

Eric suspected Caruso was right. The cops had their work cut out. It had been two weeks and still no trace of Jody, Hilda and little Peter. The whole community was in the middle of a total freak out.

Caruso scowled. 'Cops are clueless. They won't find them children anyway,' he added knowingly.

It was that comment from Caruso, it came out of the blue. One tiny slip of the tongue from him. It was like he knew the cops weren't even close to finding the missing children. Normally Caruso didn't let anything slip. Eric stared at him.

'Whaddya mean, Caruso? Why won't the cops find them?' asked Eric.

Caruso tried to ignore the question. But Eric was adamant. He reached out to grab him by the shoulders but he gave him the slip. Caruso's face turned sour and for a moment the two stood silently staring at each other. In the end, Ian broke the silence.

'Ah Eric, Caruso is just shitting you. He doesn't know anything, do you?'

Ian and Eric looked at Caruso. For a moment, he just stared back. Then his face broke into a wide grin. 'Of course I was shitting you. We're the three amigos, remember. Curly Larry and Moe.'

'That's the Three Stooges, dumbass,' Ian said with a wild smile.

*

Ian recalled none of it. He quietly shook his head as if it was all too much.

Rick was thinking of something else. Like how had they come to the notice of the police in the first place. It was a question none of them could answer. Rick thought it might have been because they mentioned seeing Whitey with the children. At the time, they weren't sure of his real name. Others working at the carny had also identified him as someone who they worked for at times and paid rather well. Some of the workers even denied he existed. Mostly no one could be definite about seeing him with the children. Rick was different; he remembered it well. He knew it was Whitey. So when the police finally picked up Rutherglen for questioning, it was weeks later.

'I remember Caruso being agitated when he found out that the police had Whitey. He didn't look scared, he just seemed nervous and when he was nervous, he smoked. That day he smoked nearly a whole pack of Craven A's. Then he told me he had to do a job for Spike and he shot off. The day they went missing, he told me he had to pack a car with some towels and clothes. I remember him making a point that the car had a big boot,' Ian said.

'The blue and white Holden,' Rick said.

'I told the cops that.'

'So did I. I also told them about Whitey wanting Caruso to load some things into his car,' Rick said. 'I bloody told them that.'

Suddenly it hit him. Why hadn't he thought of it before?

'It was the children's things. Caruso loaded the children's things into his car.'

The familiar drum pattern of the Rolling Stones' *Honky Tonk Woman* started up over the sound system. Rick's concentration was disrupted for a moment.

Something, an idea, forced itself into the front of Rick's mind. It was on the tip of his tongue. A statement. He didn't want to say it until he'd thought it through. He tried to imagine what Caruso might tell him after all these years. Finally, the idea coalesced into words.

'Whitey murdered those kids and put them in the boot. That's what Caruso wanted to tell us. I'm sure of it. And that Whitey didn't do it by himself. He had help.'

There, he had said it.

'And Caruso had a fair idea about what happened,' added Rick. 'Remember what he told us that day? "They won't find them children anyway".'

'I think you're putting too much store in all this. If Caruso knew anything, he would have told us.'

'So how do you explain the purse?'

Ian sighed. 'Your hypothesis relies on faulty facts. Firstly, Whitey is dead. It says so on his tombstone and secondly, Caruso did kill himself. Ask the coroner. You're fishing here, Rick, and it won't end nicely. Give it up before you get caught up in all the bullshit.'

8

Missed Chances

RICK WOKE IN A sweat. The ancient air conditioner of this two-star hotel rumbled and spat out stale air and although he got up several times in the night, the dream always returned with regularity.

Jody with the green eyes stared back at him as she whispered those words.

'I'm scared.'

He lay flat on the hard bed. His arms and legs were frozen beneath the prickly hotel blankets. Locked in a dream or nightmare that he couldn't move on from. It repeated ad-nausea.

And then the nightmare suddenly stopped. He spent the rest of the night in relative calmness. The sweat dried from his brow and he could breathe.

Breakfast was a banana and a coffee. That would do him until lunch. He didn't eat much these days. He didn't quite know where he'd lost his taste for a good meal. Somewhere back in his rock and roll days, he assumed.

The double gates of the cemetery were opened for foot traffic. The small church, built in the 1800s where burials were held, dominated the area. The oldest graves of the community stood next to the ancient gates. He was meeting Ian. Inside these gates, his parents shared a common plot in the catholic section. Caruso was buried in the newly opened non-denominational section. Neither Anglican nor Catholic, something in-between. Although born a catholic, Caruso had not taken the sacraments that now precluded him from that part of the cemetery. The Anglicans were more open in their burials but still, he ended up in the non-Christian part.

He figured it was the least he could do. Bury his friend in a friendly space. If not, Caruso would have been buried in a pauper's grave on prison grounds. Not something he wished for an enemy, let alone a boyhood friend.

In the distance, he could see Ian standing staring down at a grave. Rick assumed it was Caruso's. When he got close, he saw it was a nice grave. Not flashy. A little grass and a simple cross made it look homely. Simple and respectful, just like all the others in the cemetery. He noticed something.

'It's funny, he's the odd one out. Most of these graves are people my parents knew. Mrs Vanderhall lived across the road,' Rick said.

Ian laughed. 'She still lives across the road, albeit on a small pathway.'

The sun had been threatening to emerge from its cloud cover but it could go either way. Rain threatened.

They stared at the lack of a headstone on Caruso's grave.

'Haven't got around to that just yet. Thought I would wait until you got back,' Ian said.

'I was surprised that the church let him be buried here even though the coroner said it was suicide. I thought the churches frowned on that type of thing?'

Ian shrugged. 'That's why they have a separate part of the cemetery, I guess. They used to be pretty hard-core about that but things have changed. The church doesn't want to be seen as quite so adamant these days.'

'Softened with age like us?'

'Naw, I think it's just they get accused of so much these days it was something they could back down on.'

Cemeteries were quieter than the beach. All they could hear was the squawking of a magpie.

'Rick, do you remember Caruso saying that he wanted us all to be buried together?'

'It was definitely something Caruso would say. My old man used to say just put me in a cardboard box.'

'Listen, son. All those headstones are for blaggards and blowhards. Not for me. When I kick it, don't go to any trouble, you hear me?'

Of course, it was out of the question when his father did die. Rick's mother would never consider anything but a proper burial. And of course, his dad knew that.

'Your old man was a softy. I can remember playing around at your place and watching TV with you and your mum. Your old man would waltz in with a tray, tea, coffee and those horrible pasties he used to make, God awful they were,' Ian said.

'I think he knew they were horrible. Made me eat them every Friday night.'

'I used to have nightmares staying at your place. I don't remember Caruso staying much.'

'He wasn't allowed. His old man used to beat the crap outta him. Wouldn't let him go anywhere, do anything.'

'With the family he had, no wonder he turned out the way he did.'

'He was never cruel like some of his brothers. They treated him like shit.'

'No excuse on how he turned out though,' Ian said.

The noisy magpie had found a friend to play its song too. They squawked back and forth, ignoring the men below.

A figure appeared at the far end of the cemetery. The familiar gait of Joe Murphy walked the narrow path towards them. Ian turned towards Rick.

'When I spoke with him on the phone last night, I sorta invited him,' Ian said.

'You rang him?'

'Wanted to tell him how much of an arse you'd turned into. I wanted to know if he'd managed to get that purse to the family or his contact.'

'You don't believe it was hers.'

'I know, I know. Yesterday I was being an arse too. You don't have dibs on being an arse, you know,' Ian said, looking a little uncomfortable.

They watched as Murphy took his time ambling over to them. He would stop and read a tombstone then move on to the next one in his own time.

Murphy finally made it to Caruso's grave.

'Have I missed anything, boys?'

'We haven't been boys for a long time, Detective,' Ian said.

Murphy paused as if thinking about something else. Rick remembered that he'd lost his wife recently. He started to think it was a bad place to meet.

'Good that you got him buried here. Nice thing to do for a friend no matter how he turned out,' Murphy said.

'I think he would have preferred to be alive,' Rick said sarcastically.

'That is if he didn't kill himself,' Ian said.

'Ah, the theory rears its ugly head. Tell me you aren't a believer,' Murphy said, his thick greying eyebrows raised alarmingly.

Ian rubbed his bald head as if he had a head full of hair. Something he'd done as a child when he had plenty. 'Let's just say that I'm agnostic at this point.'

The three stood staring at the grave. In the end, Murphy gave a little shrug and then moved to sit down at a nearby wooden bench. He took out his notepad from his coat pocket and flipped it open. It was a ragged well-used blue-and-white policeman's pad.

'I did some tracking of the burnt-out Holden they found at the bikies' place,' began Murphy, thumbing through the pages. 'Yeah, here it is. Plates were gone and engine number scrubbed off but they say it could have been a 1958 Holden sedan.'

'That's pretty vague although I'm pretty sure the car Whitey tried to pick me up in was a Holden, a blue and white one. Possibly a '58 model.'

'Lots of blue and white Holdens around in those days. You sure you aren't just saying that because he was driving one on the reserve that day? That wouldn't stack up in court,' Ian said.

'Ah, the lawyer makes a point,' Murphy said. 'The wreck was found in a hill's farmyard owned by the Blackjack's bikie club. There were always rumours that the club did favours for the criminal community for a price.'

Rick sighed deeply and exhaled. 'So, if you heard the rumours, why didn't you dig it up years ago?'

'Not as simple as that.'

'The cops couldn't get a warrant to dig. It was in the courts for years. I remember even when I was a junior barrister, they tried to get a judge to grant them access. Something always cropped up and it was knocked back. At the time, it was notoriously hard to get the courts to do anything provocative. It was like the bikies' lawyers always had something up their sleeve,' Ian said.

'The courts were crooked?' Rick said.

'Not necessarily,' Murphy added, 'although it seemed like it at the time. We needed actual proof and that was hard to get. The bikies kept their traps shut. But when we finally got permission to excavate, the relevant tests came up inconclusive. They could only be sure that the car had been painted white. And there was a shit load of white Holdens made that year.'

'What about the blue paint? The car I saw Caruso loading that day was definitely a white car with a blue top and blue side panel.'

'No flecks of blue paint were detected in the wreck. But that's quite normal. They burnt the car out before burying it. In a fire, all the paint would have burnt first. The bits of white paint were found under the chassis. So, no match according to police.'

'So, how do we prove that was the car that he took the children in?'

Murphy glanced at Ian. Both men were silent.

'We can't,' Murphy said. 'You remember anything else?'

Rick and Ian sat down next to Murphy on the dilapidated bench.

Ian lent over to Murphy.

'Caruso did tell us a couple of weeks later that the Holden had a big boot. Big enough to…' Ian paused and collected his breath. 'To put a lot of luggage in. And later on, he told us that nobody would ever find them – kids.'

'In what context did he say that?' Murphy asked.

'He just said it in passing. Don't think he meant anything by it,' Ian said.

'You don't think he meant anything by it?' Murphy said slowly. 'And you didn't do anything about it? Tell anyone?'

'Jesus, Joe, we were kids. How the hell would we know anything was wrong? He just said it. We didn't know what the hell he meant.'

For a moment, Rick thought the detective was going to say something. But he didn't. Murphy's hands were shaking again, just a little.

It was obvious to Rick that there was some loss of motor control. Was Murphy getting a bit vague? Was he losing his marbles as Caruso would have put it?

Murphy hesitated then put his wayward hand in his pocket and began to talk.

'Well, it does say in the report about the wreck that the model was an FB. They had extra-large boots. It might mean something.'

He sighed deeply. Rick wondered if the former detective was about to give up.

They looked like a strange version of grief sitting there on a cemetery wrought iron bench.

'Okay,' Murphy began in a low voice. 'I did some digging and I tracked down about fifty possible sales of Holden cars at that time. Some were out of town so I discounted them – that left thirty-five.'

'That's a lot of cars, Joe,' Ian said.

'Tell me about it. Luckily the rego department has digitised the old system and tracking a car has become a little easier.'

'Did you find anything?'

Murphy shuffled uncomfortably. 'Maybe. Listen, we went through all this at the time when we dug it up so it might be a red herring.'

He looked down at his notepad and flipped through a couple of pages. 'One owner was a registered company with its offices listed as being near the reserve.'

'Whitey's place?' said Rick, feeling a glimmer of hope.

'No. It was registered to a company. Don't have an actual owner's name yet but I'm working on it. I've got a couple of names of old owners of the company but no one in our age range group. We're looking for someone who would have been in his forties when the kids disappeared,' Murphy said.

'Shouldn't be too hard to find.'

'Don't get your hopes up. We knew all this back then. As I said, this guy might be a red herring. Nothing panned out back in the day. I've got the notes from the investigation. It turns out that

Whitey rented a flat a couple of streets away from the company address. But it's not like he was next door.'

'Pity we don't have a photo, then Ricky here might be able to ID him,' Ian said.

'Funny you should say that. There was a picture that was logged at the time. Somebody had IDed the guy as being seen with the children,' Murphy said. He fiddled about in his pocket before pulling out a crumpled piece of paper. He smoothed it out before handing it to Ian. He stared at it.

'It was so long ago. I've got a memory of the guy in my head but what if I'm wrong?'

'It's only a scan of a photo, a bit blurry but if you look closely. Back, middle.'

Ian handed Rick the copy of the photo.

He stared at the image, back row, middle.

*

The memories flooded back.

It was the very day the children went missing. He was standing at the entrance to the carousel. He looked down at his hand, which held a rose. Well, not a real rose, a paper one. It was his winnings. Winnings from the rack and stack 'em gunshot. He aimed and found a target. He had given her the bear and she had taken its rose from around its neck and handed it to him. It was after their ride on the carousel.

'Jody... Jody,' yelled Peter.

The little boy came running up to where they were standing.

'Come on.' He was annoyed. 'We have to go; all our things are in the car. He's going to show us a castle. Come on, sis.' He grabbed her around the waist and pulled.

'Okay, Peter, I'm coming.'

She turned to face Eric and shrugged her shoulders. She had short blondish hair that touched her collar and gave her a tomboyish look that he thought was different. He didn't know why he was attracted to her. He barely understood girls – they were certainly a different breed. He had been attracted to one the previous year but that hadn't gone well. He recalled fighting a boy on the beach – well, fighting was hardly the word, no, and that boy had finished him off in a matter of seconds. He'd never been so embarrassed.

'Who is this, Jody?'

He looked at the man standing behind her. It was Whitey. It was the man in the car. It looked like Whitey hadn't recognised him.

'Just a boy I met on the carousel,' she said casually.

He went red again. He was just a boy. Hell, in the moments he had met her, he'd hoped he was a little more than that to her.

'Come on, Jody, we're all waiting for you,' said Whitey.

His creepy smile did it for him. The way his lips curled into more of a snarl than a smile. He hadn't liked him before but now he hated him. He was taking her away. He watched as Whitey took her hand and pulled her along the path. In the distance, he could see Peter and his sister standing by a blue and white car. Peter was jumping up and down in anticipation of seeing a castle.

'Eric's got a girlfriend, Eric's got a girlfriend,' Ian said with a laugh when Eric could finally move his legs.

He was filling his face with an ice cream cone. 'Got one for you and Caruso but I couldn't find you so I ate them.'

'Where's Caruso?' asked Eric, looking around for his friend.

'He's still doin' stuff for Spike, I guess. Hey, there he is, over there.'

In the distance, Caruso was standing at the edge of the roadway with a couple of Spike's henchmen. He ambled over to them.

'Gotta stay, guys, sorry,' said Caruso.

They watched as he walked back to the group of thugs and without a glance got in the back of a car. The blue and white Holden.

Whitey and an older man got in the front seat. Eric stared after them.

*

'I'm not sure. I didn't get a good look at the older guy but he seemed to know everyone. It could be him,' Rick said, handing the photocopy back to Murphy. He was disappointed.

Murphy pocketed the grainy copy and went back to staring at his feet.

'We always thought that the perp had an accomplice. For one man to take three children on his own would have been problematic,' Murphy said. 'Are you sure about the age?' He flipped his notepad over a few pages. Something was not quite right. 'Maybe he was younger?'

'Shit, I was a kid. How the hell could I tell how old he was? Could have been seventy for all I knew. Besides, the guy I saw acted like a dad. He fussed over them. He looked rich,' Rick said.

'He looked rich?' Murphy said.

'Yeah, you know, he wore shorts and a proper shirt, not Speedos like Whitey,' Rick said. 'Oh yeah, and long white socks and sandals.'

Information was tumbling out of his mouth. Was it right? The picture had opened up the flood gates in his mind.

Murphy flipped to a new page and started taking notes. 'Shorts! Did you see if he was carrying a bag or anything?'

Rick cocked his head and thought for a moment. 'Nup, no bag, no nothing.'

'No jewellery, no watch?' Murphy said with particular emphasis on 'watch'.

Rick shook his head.

It suddenly dawned on Rick that even though the police had suspected there were two people involved, no proof had emerged. This might be the evidence that Whitey had help.

'Maybe that's why no one could pin it on Whitey. He had help from the very start,' Murphy said. He carefully put the notepad back in his pocket.

'So, you don't have a name?'

'No, one of the people interviewed in the weeks that followed was shown a lot of photos and he picked this one out. Not sure how reliable he was. As I said before, he thought he'd seen this guy with the children the day they went missing.'

'He could be the guy I saw that day. I'm not sure,' Rick said more hopeful than sure.

'Anyway, he'd be dead by now. Christ, you're talking more than forty years ago. He looks about forty or fifty in the photo and that looks like it was taken in the sixties or even earlier,' Ian said.

'Is there anything else you can tell me about the guy you saw?'

Rick shook his head.

'What about what you said about the little one?' Murphy was clutching at straws.

'I dunno. He said something strange. He wanted Jody to hurry because the man with the fancy car was going to take them all to a castle. But I told the police at the time and they, well, I don't think the guy even wrote it down.'

'A castle,' Ian said. 'How many castles are there around the place?'

'Funny you should say that. Whitey's family owned a place in the hills. They named it Hilltop Retreat. It was also known as "Castle Hill" but before you say anything, yes, it was checked out at the time and nothing was ever proven for it to be a serious consideration,' Murphy said.

'But he lived in a flat near the reserve,' Ian said.

'That's right,' Murphy said.

'So, if police have always assumed there were two people involved then maybe if we can find the link between the two men, then maybe...' Rick said.

'It's a long shot. Trouble is we have nothing new.'

'We have the purse,' Rick said, 'Any results yet?'

Murphy shook his head. If anything, he looked a little ambivalent.

Ian looked at the former cop who had dropped his eyes to the ground.

'Maybe we shouldn't put all our eggs in one basket just yet,' Ian said.

'It's the only basket we've got. It has to be the one.' Rick was desperate.

'Won't find out for a few days yet. Hopefully, by the weekend we might have something. I can't push my contact. He's the only one I've got left who owes me something. And I need to be sure with the family. I just can't go bowling in unannounced.'

'You've been warned off from talking with them, haven't you?' Ian said, reading between the lines.

Murphy cocked his head and grinned. 'It's not something I'm proud of but my old boss would turn in his grave if I bothered the family with, what he called, trivial matters. Sad but true.'

9

Old Times and Places

THE DISTRICT LIBRARY WAS not somewhere Rick generally sought refuge but Murphy had been insistent. He had something to show him.

Around the corner, Rick saw the former policeman coming towards him wearing his black trench coat and carrying two white containers of coffee.

'Cappo extra strong with one sugar?' Murphy said knowingly.

He sat next to Rick on a low-lying brick wall separating the library from the Town Hall.

'Is this an old police trick?' asked Rick. 'You know, different setting, same old questions?'

'No trick, Rick. Had a shit day. Anniversary of Sarah's passing. Couldn't sit still, all these thoughts going through my mind at a million clicks an hour. Had to get out. So, I thought, hey, why not go down and see my favourite rock star.'

Rick grimaced and took the coffee.

'I'm sorry about your wife. Must be hard… her being…,' Rick said, tapering off.

'Dead? Yeah. But still, I was lucky enough to have the love of my life be with me for a very long time. Not everyone can say that.'

Rick nodded. 'Sorry about yesterday, you know, meeting at the cemetery. I wasn't thinking. Do you go and see her regularly?'

'Yeah, can't keep away from the place. People must think I'm strange. Keep talking out loud to her. All these memories come back without me thinking.'

'I guess we're lucky that we have places we can go to see our loved ones. Some can't.'

The elephant in the room.

The children.

'Worst day was when I lost Sarah. But that one with the children that came a close second.'

'I sometimes forget that you were there too. I guess I had you pegged as just another cop back then.'

'One of the enemies, eh?'

'No, not really. At first, I thought you guys were just doing your job. It was much later when I had my doubts.'

They sat on the wall drinking their takeaway coffees next to the bushes that separated the Town Hall from the Library. They would need to finish them before going in. The sign told them that there was no eating drinking or talking in the library. There was also a sign that prohibited canine's unless they were assistant dogs. That had amused Rick greatly.

'Yeah, I think we let a lot of people down. Not only those kids and their parents but you guys too. Nobody seemed to take any notice.'

'You tried.'

'Not hard enough. Still don't know if this will do any good. I'm still on the fence about that. But we struggle on.' He stood up with his empty coffee cup and shook his leg. 'Arthritis, I'm afraid. Trouble when you get to be an old fart like me. Things start not working properly. You, on the other hand, have quite a way to go,' Murphy said.

The wind suddenly picked up, sending a flurry of brown leaves down the street disappearing into the distance. It felt like rain was on its way.

'I'm not that far behind you, Detective.'

'You've got to call me Joe. I left all that stuff behind me a long time ago.'

'It seems you haven't quite left it all behind. You're still here listening to my rantings.'

'Yeah, I guess so. I think I've got that tunnel vision your missus said you had.'

'Ian's been talking to you too. Nothing much gets past you, eh, Joe.'

'Strange…'

'What's strange?'

'That you should say that. It seems that now after all these years we're remembering things that may have made a difference back in the day, that is…' Murphy said, drifting off.

'That is, if the police had listened,' Rick said, finishing his sentence.

'Sometimes I think back to those days and wondered if I had just gone down to the reserve and saw things for myself, things would have been so much clearer today. I was there but I wasn't. I was in the police station while they were being taken… if…'

'If nothing. I was there on the reserve. I saw her and her siblings. If anyone should have done anything, it was me. I saw Whitey and the other guy. Shit, I even saw one of my best friends load their things into his car, for Christ's sake.' Rick paused for a second. 'You and I both know that it wouldn't have made a slight bit of difference. Shit happens every day.'

'Still, I should have done something.'

'You were a constable then. You were a newbie. You can't be expected to suddenly become this experienced copper.'

'That's kind of you to say. But I still felt I let them down that day. And I've always regretted not doing more. If I'd listened to the kid's dad who was worried and didn't waste time fiddle farting around, we may have been able to find them before it was too late. I may have cost them their lives.'

'That's a bit harsh. For the longest time, I stewed over the smallest thing. It might have been different. But now I know that it didn't matter what I said back then. Nobody listened. That's what I'm worried about now too.'

Murphy thought again. 'You could be right.'

More silence. More thinking.

'It's not that we're suddenly remembering things now. My nightmares have been coming back to me all these years. Little bits of my memory will come back when I least expect it. I don't know why,' Rick said finally.

'Who knows how the mind works? They say the brain is like a computer. Given a prompt, it can spew back the info into the mainframe ready for disgorgement.'

'And I've just been prompted.'

'It would seem that both of us have been.'

A hawk swept over them landing in the tallest tree around. It was from there it could spy its dinner.

'So why are we here? At the library, I mean. Why meet here?'

Murphy stood and nodded for Rick to follow him. Part of the library had been newly renovated but the newspaper section was in the old crusty part of the building. It smelled of stale air and polished wood.

'Just wanted to show you this.'

He went directly to the broadsheet section.

'I've been here all morning. I got the librarian to find these for me. They were in the archive room in the basement,' Murphy said. On a table, several broadsheet papers were laid out. On the first, a massive picture of a young Whitey being led into police CID back in the weeks after the children went missing. Rick saw the look on

Whitey's face as he was shuffled through the throng of press; he had a look of superiority. He was sneering as he entered the building for he knew that there was a rock-solid alibi waiting for him.

In the background, holding the press back, was a very young-looking Joseph Murphy in his constable uniform. He was struggling to manage several photographers from getting into the building.

'I was just cannon fodder for the department back then. I had no influence. I was elated because I thought we had the guy. When he was let go a couple of hours later, I was dumbstruck and so were Mr and Mrs Milburn. I had to take them home in the police car. It was the worst car ride I ever had. When I got home later that day, I was spent. Sarah was waiting for me. That was before we were married. It took me a while to get out of that funk.'

He then pulled out another paper.

The headline read.

'SUSPECT IN MISSING CHILDREN CASE DIES IN CAR ACCIDENT.'

'And there you have it. In black and white,' Murphy said.

'Why are you showing me this? I know he died,' Rick said petulantly.

'That's not why I'm showing you this. Have a closer look at this photo. It looks like one taken of Whitey around about the time when we initially picked him up.'

Rick squinted. The black and white newspaper was a bit grainy.

'See, in the back, just here.' Murphy pointed.

The photo showed a smiling Whitey leaving the police station. Three steps down to the footpath. Right behind him was an older man with curly hair wearing a pair of Bermuda shorts.

'That's the guy I saw with Whitey,' said a stunned Rick. He stared at the picture, trying to be one hundred per cent sure. 'That's him. We've got him.' Rick spun around to Murphy.

'Hold your horses. We still don't have a name,' Murphy said.

'But somebody must know. He's right there in black and white,' Rick said.

'Yeah, well, a name would be good but just in case you'd forgotten, Whitey's still dead. I mean, I went to the guy's funeral,' Murphy said, turning the page on the broadsheet.

A thousand thoughts went through Rick's mind and none of them were good. It was hard when facts got in the way. One step forward seemed to take them three steps back.

*

Walking. Normally a pleasant pastime. Rick hadn't done this for so long; he wondered if his legs could take the strain. He slipped off his runners, slung them over his shoulder and started walking. The weather had been heating a little, but still, it was cold. His toes sunk into the cool wet sand, leaving big imprints. He remembered a game the three of them used to play.

'Stand like this. The first one to move loses. The one who sinks the deepest wins. Simple!' said Caruso.

Of course, it was a game that Caruso came up with. They would stand at the edge of the water and let the waves wash over their feet. They would sink further and further into the wet sand, and soon it would be up to their ankles, then shins. One time, Caruso stood there till he was covered up to his knees. It took both of them half an hour to dig him out. He certainly went above and beyond sometimes.

He kept walking.

Two dogs were battling to beat each other as their master released a ball from a throwing stick. They watched and waited. Funnily enough, it was the same dog who won all of the battles but the younger smaller one didn't give up. Rick laughed at the dog's persistence. He had been like that as a young man. Like his old man once said:

'You're like a dog with a bone, son. You gotta watch that. Could come back to bite you.'

Right!

Before he knew it, he was at the reserve again. He needed to see something for himself. He couldn't rely on his memories this time. He stood in the dip of the grassy area and looked towards the sea. All he could see was the high-rise apartment block. In the number one dock stood a huge cruiser five stories tall, its sails carefully stowed as it only came out in the summer.

An image of Caruso looking vulnerable came back to him as he looked down the street opposite the reserve. Out of the corner of his eye, he imagined the older man handing Caruso some towels and clothes. He did not doubt that these were the children's. He saw him hand Caruso something small. Something like a purse.

But was it a memory or something he thought had happened?

He assumed it was real as he had also assumed that he would be young all his life. Now he wasn't so young he knew one thing. Growing old sucked the big one.

Another assumption.

His legs were cramping now.

He made his way back along the beach. He stopped halfway and lay down in the coolish white sands and closed his eyes.

10

Remembrance Day

Ian and Rick walked along the esplanade and up Jetty Road to Vince's café. It was Remembrance Day and the café was open only for takeaway. The early morning crowd had given way to the lunchtime beach walkers.

'It was the darnedest thing. I went for a walk right down to the reserve. I don't know whether it was because of me actually being there but I distinctly remembered seeing the older guy give Caruso some towels and…' Rick said, holding the door to Molly's cafe open for Ian.

'I can't remember a second guy. Whitey, yes,' Ian said.

'I saw the older guy give Caruso the purse.'

'Are you positive?'

'I think so, but I'm not sure whether I'm just remembering things I want to or it actually happened. It's driving me crazy. I think it was her purse.'

'I guess we'll know soon enough if the blood's hers.'

Rick rubbed his arms.

'Jesus, that made the hairs on my arms go crazy,' Rick said. He thought about that for a moment. 'If it is her blood then she must have got it back at some stage.'

'So then if that's the case how did Caruso get hold of it again?' Ian said, still not quite confident that it amounted to proof. Ever the lawyer.

Rick was baffled by that one. So many questions rose from that purse, not the least was, why leave it till now? Why hadn't he given it to the police? Was he scared of being implicated? And what happened to the long straps he remembered?

'He kept it a secret for a long time. It must have weighed pretty badly on him,' Rick said. 'The Caruso I remember wouldn't have kept it a secret for that long.'

'The Caruso you knew was dead a long time before he died. Trust me, I know. I saw him in and out of gaol. That spark that we saw when he was a kid wasn't there in later life. Believe me on that.'

The two sat and watched as the veterans marched down Jetty Road on their way to the Arch of Remembrance erected back in the First World War days. Rick had flashes of his father when he was a child. He would gather up the young Rick and sit him on his shoulders to watch as the soldiers marched in line. Sadness flooded over him.

Suddenly, the door flung open and Sophia ran to the counter, waved at Rick then disappeared behind Vince who had been stacking coffee bags on the shelves.

'Hey, hey, young missy. No running in the shop,' Vince yelled long after she had disappeared out the back door.

'Sally's kid,' Rick said to Ian.

'That's Sophia? She was only a babe in arms when I last saw her,' Ian said.

'Twelve now. And don't I know it,' Vince said.

'She's got her mother's eyes,' Rick said.

The last of the marchers moved past and, in the distance, they could hear the bugler playing the last post slightly off-key. Vince shook his head.

'Kid's a beginner, only been playing a few months now. The old bugler has given it away, his lips have gone south. The kid was the only one we could get. I'm on the RSL committee now,'

Vince said. 'Oh, I forgot to tell you, Murphy left a message. Said he missed you yesterday but he was busy. He's got news for you. He rang the landline.'

'Doesn't he know he can ring my mobile?' Rick said.

'He's old school, probably doesn't even own one,' Ian said.

'Not everyone needs to be accessible 24/7, you know, unless you're a lawyer looking for a fee,' Vince said.

'Ya still got it, Vince. A little creepy but still got it.'

Ian and Vince could spend the whole day sniping at each other. On any other day, Rick would be glad for the banter but today he was feeling particularly low.

'It was the anniversary of his wife's death the other day. He wasn't in good shape,' Rick said.

'Anniversaries can be shit.'

Vince pushed two coffees over the counter.

'He said he missed you down on the beach this morning.'

'Slept in. It happens,' grizzled Rick, taking a sip at the coffee.

What he didn't tell Vince was the reason he'd slept in. He had spent the whole night thinking about Jody and her sister and brother. It was like the dreams were becoming living nightmares. The more they talked about them, the more he kept on thinking. His brain would not let go. What if he had done this and what if he had done that? It was relentless. It had made for a sleepless night.

Sudden laughter drew his attention to a pack of kids crossing the road with towels draped over their shoulders. They made their way past the Arch of Remembrance and onto the jetty, passing the sign that said officiously, 'JUMPING FROM JETTY PROHIBITED. FINES APPLY.' Was everything banned these days? It seemed to him that his generation had grown up and when in charge had set about banning everything that they had done as children as if to say, 'Hey, I did that when I was a child. Why should I let my kids have the same fun!'

Ian glanced at his friend watching the kids cross the road.

'You see something weird about that group of kids?' Rick said.

Ian looked again and ran his fingers through his absent hair. 'Mate, I'm a lawyer. I don't see anything, ever. That's how I can represent some disgusting people.'

'They had a dog with them. A dog without a lead.'

'An unfettered dog going onto the jetty. Sounds familiar.'

'Nero!' Rick said.

'Nero!' Ian said.

It had been a long time since they had thought of Nero. Rick's next-door neighbour's dog had adopted the three boys and went everywhere with them, including the jetty, where he would proceed to leap from the end and swim back to shore.

And then there was the legend of the Kombi-van. The one driven by a mad surfer right down the middle of the jetty and right off the end.

'You guys were imagining that. It never happened. I should know; I was always here, working in the old man's shop,' said Vince.

Ian's brow arched.

Vince disappeared into the kitchen.

'It happened, didn't it, Rick? I'm not dreaming, am I? My mind is kinda freaking out right now. Sometimes I remember something and I'm not sure it happened.' Ian's self-doubt was creeping in.

'Of course, it happened,' Rick said. 'If Caruso was here, he'd tell you it happened. Hell, he was so pumped. Do you remember what he did after that idiot crashed the Kombi through the railings and sank into the sea?'

'He dived in to see if there was anything in the front seat.'

'The driver was off his head. It sank slowly. He slipped out the window, took his surfboard from the top of the van and paddled out to sea.'

'Naked!'

'Caruso found the guys car keys. They were still in the ignition.'

'He reckoned he claimed the V-dub as pirate loot.'

They both laughed. It was exactly something Caruso would have done.

'Pity the cops took the keys back,' Rick said.

They drank their coffees in silence. That was the trouble about remembering things you had long forgotten. Maybe they were meant to be just that, forgotten memories. It was Rick who broke the quiet.

'It makes no sense.'

'What, the Kombi guy?' Ian said.

'No, I mean Caruso killing himself. It makes no sense.'

'You're not still going on about that, are you?' Ian had seen their friend on and off, mainly when he was incarcerated, but Rick hadn't.

'Let's just say for argument that Whitey was alive and that Caruso did see him? Why would that make him kill himself? Okay, I know he told the cops quite a few things that Whitey might not have liked but I don't think he came out and told them that Whitey had murdered the children or that there was someone else involved.'

'He sorta hinted at it though,' Ian said, looking thoughtfully at his coffee.

'But he never actually said it. All we got is a few bits and pieces of memory and what he told the cops. He never mentioned the other guy to me. Or not that I remember anyway,' Rick said.

'Maybe he didn't tell us on purpose. I know for a fact he didn't want us involved. Maybe that's why he didn't tell us about the other guy.'

Rick said thoughtfully. 'It just makes sense with two, doesn't it? I mean, the odds of one man getting away with it are huge. With two you could do it easily. Especially in full view of thousands of beachgoers?'

A pizza truck sped past the café and honked its horn annoyingly at people crossing the road in front of him.

'So, scenario time. What if Joe finds out who owned the blue and white Holden and where he lives? What do we do then?' Ian said.

'Maybe we should just ask him. He's over by the bench.'

Ian looked out the window to see the ex-detective in his black trench coat. It was still cold outside even though the kids were leaping from the end of the jetty.

'Rick, I'm not saying you're right about Caruso not killing himself but have you considered that if you are right, you might be in danger?'

Rick took a final slug of his coffee and gave a little chuckle. 'Danger's my middle name,' he joked, 'and besides, you would be too.'

Ian looked at Rick to see the corners of his mouth turn up into a half smile.

'You know, Rick, you are a shit. I do remember once when I went to see Caruso in gaol, he was so paranoid he told me he wanted to emigrate. You know, go overseas. He wanted to go to Italy, to his ancestors. I should have given him the money.'

'He wanted to escape. I can identify with that.'

*

The damn seagull was squawking again. Rick named it Gammy, because of its bung leg. Gammy had found a target, Murphy. He was standing right in Gammy's line of sight. As Rick and Ian crossed the road, they watched the detective doing the evasion dance. Murphy yelled his displeasure at the seagull as a stinging glob of seagull poo missed him by centimetres. The 'acid' landed on the ground in front of him and sprayed onto his scruffy black shoes. Not a good thing to happen when you're under a bit of stress. Murphy walked in circles to get away from the accurate seagull. He stopped when he saw Rick and Ian laughing at him from the opposite side of the street.

Murphy pointed to the hotel across the road. The Esquire.

'That damn bird will be the death of me,' Murphy said, rubbing his shoe against the pub wall.

'He's just protecting his patch, Detective,' Rick said.

'So, it's back to Detective, is it? Come on, Rick, we're workin' together here. Call me Joe or I'll have to start calling you Eric.'

'Well, I guess that's okay. It is my name.'

'Oh yeah, so it is.'

Rick could see Murphy's hand shaking slightly as he took a sip of his cold beer. It seemed to be getting worse. For a second, he felt sorry for the old man sitting alongside him on the tall bar stool. Was the slight tremor in his hands the start of something? Was Murphy aware of it? Two questions that wouldn't be answered in this sitting.

Murphy had some questions of his own.

'What was the last thing you remember when you saw Caruso putting things in the back of that Holden?' Murphy said. 'Apart from the purse, that is.'

Not even a 'hello', just straight into it. Rick stared into the cream of his coffee. He tried to remember looking at Caruso. Whitey had taken hold of Jody's hand and was leading her to the car. Something struck him as odd. If she had been comfortable with him taking her hand wouldn't that mean she trusted him?

That they'd known each other for a while? A family friend then? Or someone she'd met at the beach. A word came to his mind: 'grooming'. It had been a word he had heard many years later. Paedophiles did that sometimes, groomed kids, or prepared them in some ways. Hell, he'd gone to a catholic boy's school where grooming by priests was an art form.

'I think they must have known each other pretty well. She looked comfortable with him like he was a family member, but she was scared of someone or something. She whispered it to me.'

Murphy scribbled something down in his notebook. 'You said that Whitey handed him some towels then later, you said it was the older man.'

Rick thought about that. 'I'm pretty sure it was the older guy.'

'And then you said he picked up the purse and handed it to Caruso.'

Rick nodded.

'And what did Caruso do with it?'

Rick tried to recall. 'I think he put it in with the rest of the gear but I can't be sure. Why?'

'It's important. Then again, every little thing is important. I'm just not sure why yet. Did you see them get into the car?'

In his mind, he could see them all standing outside the car. The doors were open. They must have gotten in.

'Did you at least see who was driving?' Murphy asked.

'I assumed it was Whitey. He was driving when he tried to pick me up.'

'But it might have been the older guy?' Murphy persisted.

'It could have been, I guess.'

'Does it matter?' Ian said.

'Just trying to pin down the owner,' Murphy said.

'So, you think the older guy was the owner?' Ian said.

Murphy looked at them both sitting on the stools. They could see he was trying to hold back his enthusiasm.

'You know something,' Rick said, trying to read Murphy's face.

'Might be something,' Murphy said slowly. 'If you recall, I said that I spent some time looking at registrations of Holdens around that time and that I found one that was owned by a company with an office in the vicinity. I also found records of the same Holden being resprayed blue and white after it had been involved in a small bingle. It was registered to that business.'

'A name?' asked Ian.

'Working on it. Got addresses of a few directors of the company though.'

Suddenly, Murphy closed his notebook and slipped it into his pocket. 'One of them looks promising. It's just a hunch but it fits.'

Was this something? Was it a breakthrough?

The three sat quietly staring out of the hotel window. Murphy sipped a beer.

'Could it be the guy in the paper standing behind Whitey?' Rick asked.

'We still can't be sure,' Murphy said.

'It's a start,' Ian said.

'But we still need to tie these two guys together,' Rick said.

'So, it gets back to this. We need to know the rego number. Then we can tie this guy to the car and hopefully to the photo in the paper.'

'And to the car that was buried at the bikie property,' Ian said.

It was starting to hit home. Maybe they were getting somewhere.

'Should we tell the police? I mean, they just announced that they were opening the case again,' Ian said.

Rick looked at Murphy.

He coughed into his trembling hand. 'Not right now. We don't have enough evidence, they might...'

'Stuff it up just like they did before,' Rick said.

Murphy grimaced.

'I was going to say that we don't want to get our hopes up. I've been in this position before. Don't jump the gun,' Murphy said, draining his beer.

'But what you're saying is if we can find a name for the other guy and tie them both together, and the car, then we might have something,' Rick said.

'Just because he owned the car, that doesn't necessarily implicate him in a court of law, that is. He might be an innocent bystander,' Ian said.

'I doubt that,' Rick said.

'Innocent until proven guilty,' Murphy said.

'So how do we get the rego numbers?' Rick asked.

Murphy thought long and hard. 'I need you both to remember more about that day.'

'More?'

'Spit it out, what do you want us to do?' Ian said, ever the lawyer.

Murphy shifted nervously on his barstool.

'Well, there is something we can try to get the rego numbers.'

'What?' Ian knew something was up. He looked from Murphy to Rick then back again. That was his problem; he missed things. Something was going on here. He sprang to his feet and turned back to the bar. 'I'm gunna get a couple more beers, tell me or don't tell me when I get back. I don't care.'

*

'You're joking, aren't you?' Ian spat out his beer and sprayed the table.

'Hypnotherapy. You want to hypnotise us?'

'I've got an acquaintance,' Murphy began quietly. 'Look, it's not an exact science, that much I'll give you, but I'm trying to work through this positively. It might not be for everyone but all I need is proof of the two of them together and I can tie it all up. We might be on the verge of something here,' he added.

'You think that'll work? It's hocus pocus, Joe, and you know it. No court in the land will convict on that evidence.'

'We don't need to convict. We just need those plate numbers. The trouble with you lawyers is it has to bite you on the bum before you'll take it seriously. I'm sayin', let's not let it bite us on the bum. Let's do something upfront. The address down by the reserve is still in the name of the business who owned the Holden.'

Murphy stopped. Rick wasn't listening. He'd hardly said a word since he sat down. Other things crept into his mind.

'So why would they use the car? I mean, if they could walk there…' Rick said.

Murphy looked at him curiously.

'I think you were probably right when you said she knew him. I think Whitey groomed them, met them before and had given them money before. They were used to him, happy to be around him. He promised them a ride in the flashy new car. I mean, what kid wouldn't be impressed by that? He might have told 'em something like, "Kids you'll love it. It's a sports car." They'd have to be impressed. That's why the car was important. It got them all together and kept them together. After that, it was easy, and besides, he was taking them all to a castle. You said it yourself.' Murphy paused. He'd had a while to get into the mind of the crim.

'That's what Peter said. He was trying to get his sister to go quicker, I think.'

The Esquire hotel had a busy PA system. Food orders were

constantly being announced. *'Number sixty-nine, your chicken parmigiana is ready.'*

'The kids had to have known them both from before,' Murphy said. 'It's the only way they could get them in the car.'

'Classic paedophile modus operandi. Impress the youngest kid and the others will follow,' Ian said. 'Seen it in countless cases.'

Murphy nodded. 'Stands to reason. I interviewed the parents many times. The mother was especially forward in saying that she instilled in her kids the fear of strangers. She said they would never have gone with a stranger willingly. She was very strong about that. So, in my mind, they groomed them. Probably met them at least twice before. Maybe more. They may have been to his house before. And Jody told her friends that she had a boyfriend on the beach. Maybe it was Whitey.'

'No. I'm sure she told me that it was a boy. She said it was a boy like me. That much I remember.'

Both Murphy and Ian looked at him.

'She took my hand and looked in my eyes. Then she whispered in my ear. She said I was better looking than her boyfriend.'

'I thought she told you that she was scared. That's what you said before,' Ian said.

'No, that was later in the day. When we were riding the carousel, after the ride she took my hand.'

'So why didn't the boyfriend come forward? And how come the police never mentioned a boyfriend?' Ian said.

'I told the police that. I told them several times.'

Murphy cocked his head to the side, reading his notes. 'I can't find it in my notes but they interviewed hundreds of kids at the time,' Murphy said, 'probably got lost...'

'Just like all the other evidence.'

When Ian was on a roll, no one could stop him. He was a lawyer after all. He continued.

'What about the parents? Did they know their kids were spending time at the beach with a couple of older guys? I mean, are they supposed to be friends of the family?'

'Good question. As far as I remember, they knew nothing about them meeting anyone on the beach, although the mother did hear that Jody had a boyfriend. But no one could identify who it was,' Murphy said.

'So, are you saying the kids kept it secret from their parents?' Ian said. 'Even the young boy, Peter? It would be hard to do, wouldn't it?'

'That's the ultimate in grooming, isn't it? Don't tell anyone about our little secret?' Rick said.

Murphy sighed. The more he thought about it, the more disgusted he felt.

'Two guys and a car and a boyfriend? Getting a bit crowded, ain't it?' Murphy said.

Rick looked back up from his coffee.

'Okay. I'll do it. I'll do the hypnotherapy thing,' Rick said.

'Shit,' said Ian.

11

Getting into Rick's Head

THEY WERE IN A white room. Rick stared at the walls and wondered what little gems might come out. What if all his foibles came up when he was under? Anyway, he'd had doubts whether he could be hypnotised. Didn't it work on the weak-minded? He'd heard that somewhere.

'Listen, it won't take long and I promise you won't give up anything you don't want to. Hypnotherapy doesn't work like that,' Murphy said. He was in the business of making sure Rick was relaxed and that Ian didn't say anything stupid. He was much too late for that.

'Besides, I wanna hear you cluck like a chicken,' Ian said.

Ian made all the moves and noises. That got Rick going. The only thing he knew about hypnotherapy was what he'd seen on those TV shows where the presenter, usually with a goatee beard, made fools of a line of seated idiots. At that moment, he felt like a prime idiot.

'Don't listen to him,' Murphy said.

A man in a white coat entered the room.

'Hi, I'm Dr Phelps.'

Rick nearly bolted. He had a trim goatee, which made his smile look fake.

'So have you ever been hypnotised before?' Phelps asked.

He sat on a small stool opposite Rick who was ensconced on a rather uncomfortable metal chair. He shook his head and squirmed in the chair. He thought the idea was to get the patient to be at ease, but this chair made him uncomfortable.

'Normally we would do this one-on-one but the detective here–' said Phelps.

'It's just Joe,' he said with a twinge of tedium.

'Okay. Joe has given me a list of questions he wants you to answer if you can. Do you agree?' said Phelps. 'And this gentleman is?' He nodded in Ian's direction.

'His lawyer, just in case he says something stupid,' Ian said.

Murphy sighed.

Rick grimaced.

Ian sniggered.

'Is there a specific time and location you would like me to start with?' said Phelps.

Murphy looked at Rick then at Ian. He pointed to the first item on the list.

'This one will do nicely,' Murphy said confidently. They both knew that if he could somehow get back to the point where he saw the car, then maybe they would get lucky and see a plate. It was a long shot but that was why they were here.

Phelps nodded and told Rick to relax.

*

He was back at the reserve. The sun was brighter than he'd remembered. At first, all he could do was shield his eyes against the incessant light but when he took a breath, he noticed he wasn't alone. The reserve was teeming with kids. Hundreds of them. He looked behind him and he saw the carousel tent complete with a grubby tarpaulin for a roof. That was something he'd forgotten. And the smell. Oil and grease mixed with chips frying on the food counter. Also, the smell of the sea wafted into his nostrils. It was the smell of his youth. He looked towards the rotunda and saw several youths sitting on its steps smoking and sipping bottles of Coke.

Then he realised he was holding someone's hand. She beamed at him. Her green eyes fluttered as if he had said something smart, something funny. Then she was gone. She ran from him towards a group of people waiting for her. Two men and two children and Caruso. One of the men was Whitey. He couldn't forget that face.

The scene was very familiar. He remembered it clearly.

When Jody reached the group, Whitey took her hand. Eric watched as the older man handed Caruso some clothes, a towel and a colourful purse. Caruso moved to the back of the car and placed the clothes and towel into the boot. He handed the purse to Jody who took it carefully in both hands. Whitey turned and stared at Eric for a moment before turning his back on him. He watched as they all got into the car. He was supposed to do something.

'The number. What was the number?'

The car began to drive away. He glimpsed the black and white number plate on the rear of the car.

*

When Rick regained his senses, he felt calm. He couldn't remember much about what had happened. Had it worked?

Both he and Ian were quiet as they drove back to the beach. Rick needed a drink badly. Seeing as he had given up alcohol these past ten years or so it made little difference. His mouth was dry and his stomach rumbled like a bastard.

They both retreated into their thoughts. Returning to the beach was somewhere he could feel comfortable and he was glad that Ian had held off discussing what had happened. Rick sat on his bench and watched as Gammy, the seagull, selected another victim, this time a dog. The dog was waiting for his master to throw a well-mauled ball. The master strode down the beach, scooped up the ball and kept on striding. The dog sat back down on its hind legs and sprung into action when the master decided to fling it. He threw one right into the waves skipping it over the top like a pro. The dog leapt into the chilly waters uncaringly and paddled manically to the ball. He clamped it between his jaws and swam back to the land where he casually dropped it in front of the master only to get back down on his hind legs and wait for it to happen again, and again. Dogs were like that. They either had a very short memory or were persistent buggers. The dog even ignored Gammy who was swooping like a mad gull.

'So, I guess I spilt my guts,' Rick said.

'I was amazed at the detail. I mean, it was forty years ago. But like the quack said, the number plates might not be exactly right. Shit, I was there that day and I don't remember most of what came out,' Ian said.

'You weren't looking, Ian.'

'I guess you only remember what you can see. I remember seeing you with Jody but that's about it. I bet that Caruso could though. I reckon he remembered every detail. I think it drove him crazy. He used to tell me some other stuff he'd done, stuff you wouldn't believe,' Ian said.

'But not about the children?'

'Nup. Nothing about the children.'

'Maybe Caruso didn't know any more than we did. Maybe it's because Murphy's pushing us to remember.'

'Shit, I don't know, Rick. All I know is that everything has been a little strange since you came back, or since Caruso died. It makes no sense. And if he didn't kill himself, if somebody did him in, we could be in serious shit. So, anything we remember has to be a bonus, right?'

They were both thinking of Murphy.

'He's at the Department of Licence and Registration right now,' Ian said.

'What was it like when you had to get Caruso out of gaol?' Rick said, changing subjects.

'It was hard. I hate goddamn prisons, not because of the people – it's more like the smell of the place. It gets into every part of you, just like your soul is rotting away before your very eyes. I reckon I wouldn't last a night in that place. He was in and out all his life. How the hell he survived I have no idea. He was the loudest and hardest of us all. And the worst of it was, he deserved to be in there.'

'I don't think I could have coped.'

'I waited in the visitor's rooms next to the holding cells. This was for prisoners who were being transferred to other prisons. I hadn't seen him for some time so I didn't know how he'd be. At times in the past, he'd been in reasonable health for a junkie but this time, I hardly recognised him. What I saw was a stumbling middle-aged man with thinning hair and pale skin. I told him that I was here to bail him out and he just stood there as if he didn't understand. They gave him his bag of clothes and we were out. When we reached the main gate, he did something weird. He grabbed me around the neck and hugged me close. He whispered in my ear.

'He said, "Thanks, pally."

'Remember when he always called us pally? But the way he looked at me, I wasn't sure he knew my name, let alone his own. I said to him, "Caruso, it's Ian. Do you remember me?"

'He just looked at me curiously and then grinned. "Ian?"

'It was like a whisper from the past. Somewhere in the back corridors of his mind, he remembered something. He said to me, "We were at the beach."

'Then I said, "Yeah, Caruso. You remember when we were kids. Do you remember Eric?"

'"Eric?" It was like another glimmer of a memory. Then he said, "Where's Eric? Is he at the beach?"

'I said, "Yeah, Caruso, Eric's at the beach."'

The seagulls around them suddenly rose in a frantic panic attack. Someone had foolishly opened a fresh wrapping of hot chips. Gulls were mad for hot chips.

'It was really weird. He was like a kid. I took him to a halfway house and tried to settle him in. It housed former addicts and alcoholics with low incomes. I wasn't sure about the place but he seemed not to mind. I guess he'd lived in some pretty horrible places by then.'

The smell of hot chips was making Rick feel hungry.

'I checked his bags to make sure he didn't have anything he shouldn't have. But all he had was a mass of doctor's prescriptions. I guess those doctors either didn't talk to each other or he played one off against the other. I took the drugs he didn't have a prescription for. I tried talking to him but he was as high as a kite. They tend to keep them well medicated in prison.

'When I went to see him the next few days, he seemed a little better. I tried getting him to remember the old days – you know, the three of us together. The last time I saw him before he disappeared again, he asked after you. He said, "Tell Eric I know what happened."

'I asked him then. I said, "What happened, Caruso?" Then he clammed up as if he couldn't trust the walls. He would point at the ceiling then put his finger to his mouth.

'Then he put his finger back up to his lips. "Don't tell, don't tell."

'"I won't tell… I promise," I told him.

'This seemed to calm him a little. The doctor treating him told me that he would get better if he kept up with his meds and didn't succumb to the drug battle that was raging all around him. Apparently, he was good for a while but like so many, couldn't sustain it and fell back harder on the drugs. It was a battle Caruso had to face. I felt bad about that but there wasn't much I could do at the time. When I left him that night, I had a feeling that I might not ever see him again but then again, I'd had that feeling before. That was six months before he died.'

Another cloud rolled on over their heads making the chill bite. Rick flipped up his coat lapels to cover his ears. He hated his ears being cold. He gazed out over the ocean and watched as the waves pounded the beach.

'What do you think he meant by "Tell Eric I know what happened"?' Rick said.

'I'm not sure. I guess it could be about the children. He was pretty addled though. It could mean anything. I told Murphy about it.'

'What did he say?'

'Nothing, he just wrote…'

'It down in his notebook,' finished Rick. 'He writes a lot of stuff down. I guess he's done it all his working life, why stop now? Have you noticed the twitching?'

'Caruso had it at the end.'

More waves pounded. A dog ran from its master down along the jetty. It too had had enough of the cold.

Just like the old days when they could just sit and not speak. It was a gift. A gift of being total friends who could sit in each other's company and chill out. It was a gift Rick had forgotten he had.

He watched as a group of kids ran down the steps to the beach laughing madly. They had been like that once. Not a care in the world. Where had that boy gone? Was it possible to capture the innocence of youth?

12

I Remember Like It Was Yesterday

GAMMY'S GANG WAS CIRCLING a group of nippers on their boards. The gulls were out en masse looking for dinner and the nippers were getting in their way of a fish feed. They circled and squawked so loud they could be heard from the foreshore. Ian stood and looked at the jetty.

'Didn't realise that it was that long ago. You know, when the jetty went down,' Ian said. 'May '85.'

'Yeah, well, they tried patching it up but they put this one up about ten years later. It's not the same.' Rick gazed down the length of the jetty. Over the side, he saw the remnants of the circle woman's latest offering.

Ian walked over to the Arch of Remembrance and glanced at the plaque. 'It says here that it came down in '63 as well.'

'May '63. Another storm.'

'That's about the time the three of us met.'

'Yeah, my family moved here at the end of '62, I think. I vaguely remember the old man telling us one morning that the arch had come down. He was upset. I guess we don't remember the old one,' said Rick.

A thought took him back to when the jetty came down in a storm. He'd seen Caruso that day. He mentioned it to Ian.

'You never told me you saw him,' Ian said.

'I must have forgotten. I'd come back to see Mum. I was staying at a hotel just down the road. The band had a few months off. I ran into him just over there.'

'What did he say?'

Rick looked up at the gathering seagulls and thought back. 'Can't remember exactly, small talk mainly. I seem to recall him saying that he was getting off the junk and getting a job, seeing a girl. I think he was trying to get away from the gangs and stuff. I said for him to come on the road with me. Probably not the best suggestion for a junkie.'

'What did he say?' asked Ian.

Rick tugged at his shirt sleeves. 'I think he just laughed and said that I would cramp his style. I should have made him. I was going through some stuff at the time. I should have been more forceful. It might have made a difference.'

'Mate, don't beat yourself up about it. Shit happens.'

'Maybe if I had been more forceful, he'd still be here.'

Ian didn't disagree with him this time. Things were always different from how you remembered them.

Murphy arrived and brought coffee for the three of them. A tray of coffees from Vince's. He had done some digging and had news. He looked at them sitting morosely on the beach bench.

'Come on, guys. Life ain't that bad,' Murphy said, trying to lighten the mood.

He laughed as if he had cracked a joke. His hands shook and he was in danger of dropping the coffees. He paused to regain his balance. Rick pretended he didn't see.

'Shove over, boys. Let a man sit,' Murphy said.

It was tight on that bench. Rick felt a little uncomfortable. He wasn't used to this much closeness.

Murphy started writing on his pad furtively. Ian broke the silence.

'This reminds me of being in court. We had an absent-minded judge who kept forgetting that we were all there. He'd be scratching around on his notepad; head down, bum up. Then he'd look up at us and go… oh! That used to annoy the shit outta me.'

Murphy seemed worried and Rick noted that when he worried, his hands shook more. He stopped writing.

'Okay, this might be something, guys.'

'You got a hit on the purse?' Rick said hopefully.

'Not quite. Remember the shrink, the hypnotist?'

They nodded. How could they forget?

'Well, the numbers you saw when you were under proved quite illuminating. 464 707 or so you thought. It took me all day but I found one close enough. A plate with the prefix of 464 was allocated to a white Holden manufactured in June 1957. It's not conclusive but it gave me a good start.'

Rick looked slightly disappointed.

Ian elbowed him in the stomach. 'You didn't think it would be that easy, did you? This is good, Rick. This is a real break.'

'More than a break,' Murphy said.

'You found him?' Ian said.

Murphy grinned. 'The Holden was registered to a company but the actual owner was one Paul Stanley Elliott.'

'So, the older guy might be this Elliott,' Rick said.

'Could have been. It could also have been some other guy with a Holden. This guy Elliott has the right car and lives nearby. That's a bloody good start, but there's more.' Murphy looked at Rick and Ian then nodded slowly. 'Get this. It was only registered for that year. After that, it simply disappeared.'

'And ended up buried in a bikie's backyard,' Rick said.

'It's a long shot but it fits,' Murphy said.

'Is this guy alive though? Might not mean anything if he's dead?' Ian said.

There was that.

'Couldn't find a death certificate for Elliott. So…' Murphy said.

'He might be alive. And if he is, then we might have a way of finding the truth,' Rick said.

'Someone has to know something,' Ian added.

Murphy nodded. 'Our problem is the one of time. This happened so long ago and people's memories fade.'

'Mine don't. I see those kids every night when I close my eyes. Especially Jody's,' Rick said.

'So, what do we do now?' Ian said.

'Well, we know that Whitey or his family once owned the Hilltop Retreat,' Murphy said.

'What good would that do?' Ian said.

'According to the council, it is still owned by the Rutherglen family trust.'

'How does that help? Whitey's dead. He can't tell us anything.' Ian was getting edgy.

'On the contrary. We can still find out a lot especially if we can tie the two men together.'

'So how do we find a connection? We can't just stroll up to the Hilltop Retreat and knock on the front door,' said Rick.

'Who said anything about knocking on the front door? We could still go and have a covert look at the place.'

'You want to break in?' Ian said quietly.

'That would be against the law. But a stroll through the grounds might be just the thing.'

Ian looked at Murphy to see if he was serious. He was.

'I just need one of you bozos to go with me to keep an eye out.'

'I'll go,' Rick said.

Ian looked at him sideways. 'Are you sure? I can see it now. Aged rock star and ancient former detective sued for trespass on some wild goose chase.'

But all Rick could think of was what little Peter had said back on that fateful day.

'*He's going to show us a castle. Come on, sis.*'

'Could this Hilltop Retreat be the castle young Peter meant?'

'It's possible,' said Murphy.

'You don't think they might be up there still.'

Murphy didn't answer.

'I guess I'll have to come to make sure you both don't end up in the clink,' chimed in Ian.

'No, mate, just me and Rick this time. It's called plausible deniability. Just in case you have to bail us out,' Murphy said.

*

Rick drove a Jaguar. Didn't everyone? It was a far change up from the unreliable and sometimes crappy VF Valiant he'd had in his teens. In a way, he preferred the old Valiant. He had a lot of fond memories of that car. It was the car that he and Sally first went on dates together. Reliable and cheaper than a Jag to run!

Murphy smiled at Rick as he swung the Jag into the detective's driveway.

'Fancy,' Murphy said.

'It gets me to where I'm going, most of the time,' Rick said grudgingly.

'It might have been better to use a car that doesn't stand out so much. We might be spotted. But it'll do.'

Rick knew a typical copper's response when he heard one.

'I have a policy. Blend in. Look cheap, act rich,' said Murphy.

'Give me the address,' Rick said with a touch of impatience. It seemed Murphy had an answer for everything.

Murphy stared at the GPS unit on the fancy dashboard with scepticism. 'This thing work?' he asked.

'I punch in the coordinates and the GPS unit will tell us how to get there.'

Murphy flipped his pad open and showed Rick the address. He tapped at the GPS a few times.

'Take the next left and continue for the next five kilometres,' the female voice said confidently.

Murphy stared at the screen and grunted. 'I would've gone straight ahead. Shorter that way.'

Rick glanced across at his passenger.

'Just saying it'd be quicker, that's all.'

It was mid-afternoon and the sun was low on the horizon keeping the air brisk and cool. A coat would have been a good idea, thought Rick, as they drove up the steep hill.

'Turn left here,' Murphy said suddenly.

'It's not a good idea to ignore the GPS.'

'Just do it,' Murphy said gruffly.

Rick did as he was told.

'Pull over here, under that tree.'

Again, he did what he was told.

'Turn off the engine.'

Rick sat quietly. Waiting was not something he did easily.

Murphy stared out of the window at a bus stop across the road. In the distance, a yellow bus came rattling down the road and pulled over. A man disembarked. He looked both ways and crossed the road. He headed downwards away from the Jag, disappearing over the curve in the hill.

'The gardener going to work at the Hilltop Retreat,' said Murphy.

'How the hell did you know that?'

'He always catches the two-twenty from the train station in

the foothills. I knew it was him because of the logo he wears on the front of his overalls. Didn't you see it?'

'Of course,' Rick said sarcastically. 'What was I thinking?'

'You've gotta notice these things, Rick. If I hadn't, we could've just walked right in on him. Keep your peepers open.'

On Murphy's mark, they left the car and walked the long and winding way to the elegant country home of the Rutherglen's. Constructed in the late 1880s for a former governor, it spread from its original beginnings as a country home to a fully gated grand three-storey dwelling. At some stage in the past ten years, the back of the property had been restored. It looked empty now.

'It doesn't look like anybody lives here. What now?'

Murphy considered Rick's question. 'We get in somehow. Then we look for a spot.'

'A spot?'

'Yeah, a spot. Somewhere that makes sense,' Murphy said obscurely.

'You mean where the children might be buried?'

'Something like that.'

'So how do we get in?'

'We wait until three p.m. then you skip over the wall, open the gate and let me in,' said Murphy.

'What about the gardener?'

'He goes down to the hotel grounds at the back. We should have a good three hours before anyone else turns up.'

'And you know this how?'

'Trust me, Rick. Trust me.'

The front gardens of the Hilltop Retreat were manicured to an inch of their lives. A line of roses circled the lawn right up to the grand doorway. This was a place of style and money. The bay windows of the mansion consisted of rose-coloured glass which reflected the sun sending shards of light throughout the grounds. Rick pulled himself up and peered over the fence.

'I'll give you a leg up,' Murphy said, trying to be helpful.

'Not on your life. With my weight, I'd crush the life outta you.'

Murphy stepped back. 'I'll keep a lookout. I'll whistle if anyone comes along.'

It looked easier than it was. Rick pulled himself up on the lower fence and only had the spiked upper fence to deal with. This proved hard.

'Who puts up a fence this big?' he muttered to himself as he slung his body over the spikes. He looked behind as he straddled the fence. The sun was right in his eyes and he knew that if anyone was looking out those bay windows, they would see him as plain as day. Any moment he expected to hear shouting. He didn't. He dropped to the ground and swore as he landed slightly askew.

'Come on, we haven't got all day,' Murphy urged.

Nervously, Rick released the lock and pushed open the gate. Murphy waltzed in as if he didn't have a care in the world.

'About time.'

'Jesus,' said an out-of-breath Rick.

'Okay, you look this side of the house. I'll go to the other. We meet back here in thirty minutes, okay? No more than that.'

'Why?'

'Because that's when the gardener gets back.'

'I thought we had three hours? What am I looking for anyway?'

Murphy looked at him. 'You know. A spot. Use your imagination – anything that looks out of place. Take some pics with your go-go gadget phone.'

Around the side of the house, the grounds were a little more haphazard than the front. Lots of pine trees and little hedges adorned the windy paths. Rick found himself almost lost on one path. It took him down to a creek bed that made its way under a raised bridge and out into a forested area.

If he didn't know better, he could have sworn he was in the backwoods of a great forest, not the side yard of a house, no matter how grand. A kookaburra set off a group of birds nearby, which, in turn, set off magpies living in the trees. The creek meandered around the twisting path. He stopped. There was somebody up ahead staring at him through the thick woods. He looked again but the figure was gone. He stopped and checked his watch. He was late. Murphy would be waiting for him.

'Shit,' Rick said.

Suddenly, the sun disappeared and he was in darkness. Then he saw it. He'd walked onto the banks of a levee. Below him was a valley that seemed oddly out of place. It looked like it had originally been some sort of vegetable patch but now it was just overgrown with weeds. The hairs on his arm stood up. He took out his phone and shot off a couple of pics.

'Who the hell are you?' said a gruff voice.

A man came out of the wooded area. For a moment, Rick thought he was carrying a rifle but as he got closer, he realised it was a spade. It was the gardener!

For some unknown reason, he stifled the urge to laugh. This would have been a perfect scenario for a TV show his mum used to watch religiously. *Midsomer Murders*. But this was no laughing matter. There he was caught trespassing and when they found out who he was, he could see the headlines now. 'Rocker caught trespassing. MURDER involved.' Well, maybe not murder but he knew the tabloids well; anything for a good headline.

'Ah, he's with me,' Murphy said, appearing out of nowhere. He patted the gardener on the shoulder, made his way to a tree and looked it up and down. 'Yes, these are the ones. Do you know you have a rogue tree here? These are not natives,' Murphy added.

'What the hell are you on about?' asked the gardener.

'Ah, we're from the council,' said Murphy. 'We're checking all the non-natives in the area. Bad business, this, will have to prepare a report for the mayor. He'd be having kittens about all this. Rogue trees are his biggest bugbear. He hates them.'

The gardener looked confused.

'Of course, we'll have to tell him that the owners should have filed a release form. I'm sure they'll understand that a gardener with your experience could have missed it. It'll cost thousands to fix.'

The gardener gave him an angry look that soon changed to concern.

'Er... I haven't ever heard of this before,' said the gardener.

'I'm sure the council will take that into account when they speak with the owners,' Murphy went on.

It worked. The gardener turned on the spot and took off down the path.

Later in the car, Rick clutched at the steering wheel of the Jag. His heart was still pounding. It had been a close thing. He had a new respect for the detective seated next to him. He had also noticed that during the episode with the gardener he had remained resolute. No trembling hands; they were stock still. He looked across at him scribbling into his notepad. His hands were still steady. Maybe it was something that came and went.

'I think it's the agitation,' Murphy said finally.

'What agitation?'

'My hands. You were looking just before.'

'Sorry, man. Didn't mean to.'

'It's fine.' He held them up and folded his fingers up into fists then opened them up again. 'It's only when I'm conscious of them, that's when they shake. When I'm writing or doing something that takes my mind off, they're fine.' He stopped and scribbled something else into his notes. 'You saw something in there, didn't you?'

'I thought I did. I'm not sure,' Rick said, gripping the wheel even harder. 'Took some photos.'

'I'd like to see them. They might help.'

'Help? How?'

Murphy didn't answer. He stared out of the car window as Rick drove down the meandering road.

'I'm working on a theory,' Murphy said, writing furiously in his notebook. Suddenly he stopped, rubbed his hands together and blew gently over his knuckles.

'Sometimes it helps with the shaking.'

13

A Picture Paints a Thousand Memories

THE NEXT DAY WAS even colder than before. Rick arrived early. He should have known something was up. The beach was in an uproar. Gammy, the rogue seagull leader, stood guard on the jetty squawking at anyone who tried to pass. At first, Rick thought it was a food thing. But when he stood in front of the railings, he saw what they were making a noise about. The old lady had left another crop circle but this was nothing like anything he had seen before. Strange enough to send the gulls into a frenzy.

'Looks weird,' Ian said. He had crept up on him without making a sound.

'Christ… don't do that,' Rick said taken unawares.

'Why so early? What's Joe up to now?'

Ian had arrived at sparrow's fart (dawn). Rick knew that his old buddy would be worried that he and Murphy had been caught red handed breaking into the Hilltop Retreat. He was relieved when Rick called him late in the night and filled him in on the details of their escapade.

Rick said, 'Dunno, he told me he was working on a theory.'

Ian stood and looked to the beach. Several people had stopped to stare at the new drawing. Taking up a good part of the beach, everyone who walked by would be sure not to stand on it although there were a few who would leap from circle to circle, careful not to touch the markings. It was eerie to watch them pass.

Murphy was running late. When they saw him, he was on the

other side of the road, looking out of place. Instead of his trench coat, he had a long black dinner coat on, covering an old ratty suit. He looked like he was going to a funeral.

'Sorry, boys. Got side-tracked,' Murphy explained. Somehow, Rick knew this not to be true. The detective never got side-tracked unless, of course, he wanted to.

'Got some news,' he continued.

He sat down with a clunk. He had stuffed a newspaper inside his coat. He also had a yellow manila folder carefully tucked inside the paper. He exhaled for a moment, got his shaking hands into order then looked at Rick and Ian.

They let him settle. Whatever news he had for them could wait a few extra seconds. He took out the folder. There were several blown-up photos.

'These are the photos you took at the mansion. I transferred them from the phone and had them blown up. See, even old farts like me can work modern technology.'

He handed them to Ian who squinted as he tried to make out what they were. Murphy glanced at them then turned them the right way.

'Very artistic, Rick. You'd make a good photographer,' Ian said.

'You took about ten shots but these five I got blown up. Can you see something in them, something interesting?'

They both stared down at the photos. Ian scratched his head. 'What am I looking at?'

Rick pointed to the top of one photo. 'I just pointed my phone at the ground. I saw it in the distance, that's why I took the pic. It kinda looked out of place.'

'It does look odd, doesn't it?' Murphy was making them look hard. He gave a slight grin.

'Do you know something? Sorry, pal, you're the detective. Why don't you just spit it out?'

'But you're a lawyer,' Murphy said. 'If this was a court and you needed to know about this area, what questions would you ask?'

Rick stared at the photos he had taken. There was something surreal about them. He had not noticed it at the time but the colours were so vivid, it was almost like someone had spilt paint over a canvas. At that moment, he knew what an artist felt like.

'There's an indentation. See right there,' Rick said.

Ian looked closer. 'Looks natural to me.'

'You're looking through a lawyer's eyes. Look deeper,' Murphy said.

Then he saw it. A tuft of ground in the shape of a triangle. Made of sticks, grass and mud it lay on the ground right in the middle of the indentation.

'A triangle. It looks manmade but somehow natural. What does it mean?' Ian said.

'It's pointing down. Is it a sign of some sort?' Rick said.

Murphy smiled grimly and fiddled with the collar of his suit coat. 'Maybe. But we can't jump to conclusions here.'

'Ah shit, you're not saying that you think that's where the children are buried? Cause if you are, you're both fuckin' mad. No way, it can't be as simple as that,' Ian said.

'There's something else too,' Murphy said, ignoring Ian's barbs. 'Right there.' He pointed. 'In the background.'

Rick could barely make out the shape of a man standing in the shadows leaning on a spade.

'Is that the gardener?' Ian asked.

'Looks like he was watching all the time. He only came out when you started taking photos,' Murphy said.

'So, he didn't stumble on me?' asked Rick.

'No, not exactly.'

'You knew he was there?'

'Well, I guess I told you a little fib. He didn't go down to the back of the property – he only works the gardens. I suspected he might see you. I just wanted to see what he would do, you know, by following you.'

'Shit, Joe, Rick could have been hurt,' Ian said.

'It's all right, Ian, but I'm a little intrigued. You said for me to check that side of the house while you checked the other but you ended up following me. You never checked the other side because you already knew I would find this area.'

Murphy grinned. 'I told you I lied. I knew that area but I needed you to find it. I needed to see the reaction of the gardener this time.'

'You've been there before?' Ian said.

'I guess I should 'fess up. I came up here many years ago. I had a lead but my bosses cut me off. They said I was being a nuisance.'

'But why the subterfuge?' Ian asked. 'What the hell are you trying to do?'

'I came here long before Rutherglen, a.k.a. Whitey, supposedly died. I didn't have much of a chance to snoop around then. Sorry, but I had to be sure about the gardener.'

'And are you?'

He raised his eyebrows and pursed his lips.

'So how long have you suspected the gardener?' Rick was intrigued. He looked at the photos again.

'Do I think he had something to do with the children? No, he wasn't around then. I mean, he'd be in his thirties. Far too young. Do I think he's protecting someone? Yes, I do.'

'Who? If Rutherglen is dead, who then?' Ian said.

'That's the part I still have to work out,' Murphy said, scratching his head. 'But let me be devil's advocate for a second.' He paused as if to consider what he was going to say. 'If we believe that Caruso's death and the missing children are somehow connected then maybe we have to assume that someone is worried we know too much. Which means…'

'We could be in danger,' Rick said.

'So why the subterfuge with the gardener?' asked Ian.

Murphy looked down at his scruffy shoes and cocked his head as if considering the question but he kept quiet.

'I see! So, by being seen by the gardener you sent a message to whoever is doing all this. A bit dangerous, don't you think?' Ian surmised.

'Only way to flush him out,' Murphy said finally.

It was spreading out like a fantasy novel. Everything was linked to each other. The story just kept on getting bigger and bigger.

'Do you think he'll bite?'

'It's only a theory, Rick. He doesn't really believe all this. Do you?' Ian said.

Murphy screwed up his face. 'If there is someone out there trying to put us off the scent then maybe he'll do something to expose himself, or herself, especially if they think we're getting close.'

'But we're not close, are we?' Ian said.

'Well, he won't know that though.'

'So, what now?' Rick leant against the railing, watching as the children gathered around the crop circles. 'We wait?'

'We may not have to wait. There's something else I should tell you.'

Murphy never failed to astound both of them. Granted, he'd been at it a lot longer than they had. They were both relative novices at the crime game. He pulled out his newspaper and held up the cover.

'Today's paper,' he said, holding it up for them to see. *FACTORY YARD TO BE EXCAVATED* was written across the top, all in big bold letters. The next line said it all: *Police say they are looking at several areas of concern.*

'Why?'

'They've had a tip.'

'But they're not there. I mean, according to your theory, you think they're in the hills,' Ian said who wasn't quite sure what to believe.

'It's just a theory, Ian. And no, I don't think they'll find them in the factory, or the hills.'

'Not at the Hilltop retreat? I thought that's why we went up there.'

'I never said that.'

Somehow, Rick felt as if Murphy was not telling them the whole story.

'So, what do we do now?' Ian said, repeating himself.

'I'm goin' down for the dig. They might find something,' Murphy said.

'But you said they aren't there,' Ian said.

'They might just find something that will help us.'

'But no bodies?'

'No,' Murphy said. He grinned at Ian and Rick. 'It's just police stuff. They have to be seen to be doing something even after all these years. But it will be useful,' Murphy said.

'You know something else?' Rick asked.

'Two things. First, the factory they are going to dig up once belonged to Paul Stanley Elliott,' Murphy said.

'The guy who owned the Holden?'

Murphy nodded. 'They dug the grounds up years ago too. I was there. They found nothing.'

'Did they know that Elliott owned it then?' Ian asked.

'They did but his name never came up anywhere else.'

'So, we know something the cops never knew,' Rick said.

'Something like that. It's still a long shot; we haven't tied them both together yet.'

'And the other thing?' asked Rick.

'It was on a lead from your friend that we dug it up the last time.'

'Caruso?' Ian and Rick asked in unison.

'He was hanging about the station. The sarge told him to piss off… thought he was a vagrant. Caruso told me about the factory and a guy he knew, the foreman's son,' Murphy began.

'I remember that the station was particularly busy that day. I was on the counter doing mundane things. Old Sergeant Willow had me stacking forms and tidying the front office. As I said, boring stuff. Suddenly he yelled at me from his office.'

*

"Move that kid on, Murphy, before I chuck him in the slammer."

'I looked outside. A face was peering in at me. I went to the door and opened it. He was still there. It looked like he wanted to ask me something. Then I recognised his face. I said something like, *"It's Gino, isn't it?"*

'He peered at me as if I was a stranger.

'He said, *"Nobody calls me that."*

'He wouldn't look me in the eye. I could see him shaking a little. Just like withdrawal.

"Your friends called you Caruso, didn't they?" I said, trying to get him at ease. *"I've met some of your brothers too, I think."*

'He looked like he didn't trust me. I didn't think it was anything important, I just kinda felt sorry for him. He looked like he had been living on the streets. He just stood there.

'I asked him. *"Do you have something to tell me?"* I don't know why I asked him that. I mean, his face was quite blank. I remember he looked past me to Sergeant Willow in his office. He said, *"He wants to lock me away. He says I mess up his streets."*

'I said something flippant. *"Well, he likes to keep a tidy neighbourhood. You sure you haven't got anything to tell me?"*

'Then he just blurted out that he wanted to get a place and he needed money.

'I guess I wasn't surprised. I felt around in my pocket and pulled out some money; it wasn't much. I never had much in those days. He just stuffed it in his pocket quickly as if I was going to take it back from him. He started to say thanks then I could see he wanted to say something else. I just wanted to keep him talking.

'*"You don't see your friends anymore? Shame about that. I think you need them, Caruso, don't be too scared to go look for them."*

'I stuck out my hand to shake his. He took it and wouldn't let go.

'*"Naw they've got their own lives. Don't need a druggie as a mate."*

'I said again, *"You got something to tell me?"*

'He squeezed a bit harder like he was deciding whether to tell me. Then he whispered, *"You still on the case?"*

'Not for one moment did I not know what case he was talking about. The missing children. I think I said it far too quickly. *"Yup, still on it. It's sorta ongoing, if you know what I mean."*

'Then he told me, *"There's this guy you oughta speak with. He runs with us sometimes. His dad has this business, metal works, I think. Says that he might know sumthin' about the children who went missing. Name's Bill Santino."*

'I was a little shocked and surprised that he should tell me. It seemed to mean a lot to him that I should know.

'So, I told my bosses and after a while, they thought it important enough to prepare a raid. Left me right out of it though. They ended up bringing Bill Santino in. He told them where to dig.

Dug up some freshly laid concrete but found nothing. In the end, the report said that the kid just wanted to have a ping at getting some money. After that, he spent a lot of years in various mental institutions and workhouses. Now, he's out and about and making noises that the police got it all wrong back then. They should have been digging in another part of the factory. He reckons now he saw the children at this place and that when he was working one of the owners asked him and another guy to dig up a piece of ground in his factory. He reckons that's where they are. No one listened to him until now. And so...' Murphy paused.

'They're digging up the factory again,' Rick said.

'Why do you think Caruso told you about this guy? You think he believed the kid?' Ian was getting edgy. He stood and leant over the railings. The gulls were circling again, getting ready for any scraps thrown off the jetty by anglers. They squawked in their huddled masses.

'At the time, I didn't believe him. Still not sure I do now but hell, I'm being devil's advocate again.'

'So why not tell the police now that they're barking up the wrong tree? Why not tell them about Hilltop Retreat?' Ian said, 'Why not get them to dig there?'

'Because I don't think they're there either. It's too simple.'

'So why go to the trouble of going there in the first place?' Ian said, slightly confused.

'Had to rattle a few chains. The only way of doing it really. We're probably right off the mark on all accounts.'

'I'm going with you to the dig,' Rick said.

'Thought you might.'

'I don't understand. Why go if you don't think it'll do any good?' Ian said.

'Can you suggest any other options? I said I'd help you guys but if you've got any ideas, spit them out.'

Ian had none.

14

Survivor's Guilt

TODAY WAS THE DAY. Dig day at the factory. Rick managed to convince Ian that they would be fine and not get into any trouble.

'After all, we're not breaking the law,' Rick said.

'Maybe not this time,' Ian told him.

Rick saw the detective limping down the main road towards him. He wondered how long he'd had that limp. He had a new understanding of people who walked with a limp, a cane or a pusher. He knew exactly what they were going through. He thought back to the aftermath of his accident, the hours of re-learning how to walk. Rehab was a bitch.

'I like riding in your Jag,' Murphy said. 'It's roomy.'

He stretched his legs out and tried to lower the window. 'How in the hell do you open your goddamn window?'

Rick pressed the lowering button. 'Childproof locks.'

'Why the hell do you need childproof locks? The last I heard is that you don't have any kids.'

Good point, he thought. 'But I was in a band, they're all children.'

Rick was edgy. Murphy, on the other hand, had done this many times. The procedure, or 'dig', as it was known in the trade, was always the same whether they found anything or not. It was always full of nervous cops trying to keep the public at bay.

Even though Murphy told Rick he was sure they wouldn't find the children, he felt that they just might find something that would tell them they had once been there. That would do in his eyes. Whatever happened at least the police were keen to be seen doing something. No matter the outcome, Rick felt he had to be there. He kept on thinking about Jody and her siblings. Murphy gave a grunt and leaned back into the plush seat of the Jag.

He shifted around so he could see out the side window.

'Turn left here,' he said suddenly.

Rick looked across at Murphy who seemed keen for them not to be seen.

'Now, before we get there, just remember, we might not be welcome, private property and all that. Just follow my lead if we get caught.'

'I'm getting used to this,' said Rick.

Murphy smiled at him conspiratorially.

*

It looked like the set of some futuristic movie. Any moment a zombie would spring out of the dark and attack. It was a plain foundry where metals were cooked smelted and forged. Lots of chemicals and poisons, lots of places where you could hide things.

It was the metallic smell that caught Rick's attention first. That seemed odd for as Murphy said himself, the place hadn't been used for many years. Several outlying sheds surrounded the foundry. Between each building were tracts of land littered with rubbish and just the occasional bit of grass growing in patches. Everywhere you looked, rusted equipment and bits of metal made it hard to find a path through. The second thing he noticed was the police tape that sectioned off an area right alongside the largest building. This was where their focus would be today. People in uniform wandered around the site some taking photos, others staking out the land making it like a grid.

The main area they targeted was away from the public's eye. A man in an orange high-vis jumpsuit roamed the edges. It would be hard to remain unseen.

'You can't stay here. Oh, it's you, Murph. Thought you might turn up. If the boss sees you, I didn't let you in, okay? Sorry, can't let your friend in.'

'Come on, Tony, this is Rick. He was one of the kids there that day.'

Tony Streng looked at Rick. He squinted as if trying to picture him as a boy. Then he smiled.

'The Anchormen! I bought one of your records, *Planets Apart*. Good stuff.'

'You'd be only one of very few, Officer.'

Streng smiled.

'Don't get caught. But if you do, I didn't let you in, got it?' Tony Streng wagged a finger at Murphy and walked away.

Murphy's hand was as steady as it could be as he took hold of the tape and ducked under.

They watched as the grader took the first layer of topsoil and pushed it to one side. This was going to take a while. The problem nowadays was that most of the people who had been there all those years ago were either dead or had long forgotten any specific details. The son of an old foreman was considered close enough for the police to act. They had to be seen to be doing something. Rick watched intently.

Time went slowly. Rick thought about Jody. What would she be like today if she had lived? Murphy stood with his hands clenched behind his back. Rick wondered if that was to keep his twitching fingers out of plain view. A thin bead of sweat dripped from Murphy's pale forehead. He was looking old today. Rick was just about to comment on the lack of anything happening when all hell broke loose.

A scream to stop the digger came from the spotter. He stood in front of the machine and waved his arms excitedly. Two more spotters leapt into the hole, busily scooping back the mound of earth that threatened to topple over and fill the hole.

The distant sound of traffic became the only source of noise for a whole thirty seconds.

All motors were off and conversations ceased. Black clouds that had threatened to unload on them now did. It started bucketing down.

'Bones,' yelled one of the spotters.

The place erupted into chaos. Three things happened simultaneously. First, the yelling became more insistent; second, all radio communications to the waiting journalists were turned off; and third, several trucks full of black-suited Special Forces police cordoned off the area. It had become a military-like operation.

Murphy took hold of Rick's elbow and pulled him towards the street. 'We need to get out before these guys find us. Special Forces police are bad news. My mates at the CID are nothing compared to these guys. If we don't move, we'll be answering questions to God knows when. Let's go.'

He took Rick by the elbow and they ducked under the tape. When they were safely back at the Jag, Murphy spelt it out for him.

'This is how it goes. Nobody will say anything until they have analysed whatever it is they found to death. The guy who called out "bones" will be probably, at this very moment, getting briefed about what he had said and told never, ever, to say that word again. There won't be any bones until the police department or military want there to be bones. And TV presenters will be told en-masse that speculation on these matters doesn't help and that as soon as they had something concrete, they would announce it.

It's all a ruse to keep it all inhouse until they can work it out for themselves. I probably would have done the same thing.'

Rick gripped the steering wheel and then looked at Joe. His hands were shaking but Murphy's were still.

'They found them.'

Murphy slowly shook his head. 'No, no, my friend, I'm afraid not. They're long gone. They've dicked around for too long. Christ, they should have dug it up twenty years ago when they were there.'

'So, whose bones, are they?'

'Your guess is as good as any.'

*

The next day saw Rick back at Vince's. A double-strength mochaccino with skim milk went down too well. Vince poured Rick another. He was still jittery from his experience at the dig site.

'I'll just have a Nescafe extra hot, thanks, Vince.' Ian was going through the day's newspapers that Vince kept in the racks.

'Jesus, Ian, that ain't coffee. That's just muddy water heated up,' said Vince.

Vince was a coffee aficionado and slightly resented clients who had no taste.

Ian ignored him. He was reading the paper. 'Nothing in here. Arc you sure they found something? Pretty hard to keep that kind of thing outta the papers.'

It had been a hectic twenty-four hours since Rick and Murphy had snuck onto the dig site and still, there was nothing. It was strange. He put the newspaper down and slurped at his mug.

'Where is he anyway?' asked Ian. 'You'd think he'd be here.'

'He was checking in with some of his old colleagues to find

out what they'd found. I'm not so sure he's as welcome there as he might have told us,' Rick said.

Ian put down the paper. 'That day when you went off on that wild goose chase at the Hilltop Retreat, I was sure I'd get a call saying that you both were arrested. I was getting my bail speech ready.'

'What's your bail speech? Sounds ominous.'

'My argument would be based on your obvious mental disability and the lack of maturity for a man Murphy's age. You're lucky the gardener seems to have kept his mouth shut.'

'Maybe he kept his mouth shut because he has something to hide,' said Rick.

'Well, if there is someone out there who doesn't want us to dig any deeper, I'm just saying we have to be careful.'

'What if Caruso was right and he did see Whitey that day?'

'That's ridiculous. He's dead, pally.'

'Just for a moment use your imagination.'

'Hypothetically?' Ian sighed. He didn't want to get into this. 'I guess that could mean, and I say COULD, hypothetically mean that Caruso was killed and that we could be in real danger. But all that is just crazy talk. Whitey is dead and Caruso, whether we like it or not, killed himself.'

Rick glared at his friend.

'You can't argue with facts,' Ian said, draining the rest of his coffee.

Rick gazed at the window. He couldn't get Whitey's face off his mind.

'Do you remember that day at the cinema?' Rick said.

'How could I forget? It scared the shit outta me.'

'Caruso didn't seem scared.'

'He was a tough cookie,' said Ian. 'I guess he had his moments. He could be as soft as.'

'It was right before they went missing. I wonder if Whitey was planning it then?'

*

Caruso stood on the low brick fence and bellowed like Tarzan. He had got it down pretty well. It was an addiction really, the telly. Shows like the Samurai had them all leaping around with a carefully knotted school jumper wrapped around their heads. The latest craze was hard to define but it was pretending you were in a band like The Monkees. It was required viewing in most households and came on before parents came home from work.

'Cheer up, sleepy G. Oh what can it be… to a daydream believer and a homecoming queen,' bellowed Caruso.

'I think you'll find it's Jean, not G.' Ian prided himself on always being right.

'I think you'll find I'm right, pally,' said Caruso.

'Don't call me pally. Call me Davy. I can be Davy Jones – all the girls like him. Eric can be Micky, and you can be the tall, dorky one,' Ian said.

'The one with the beanie? No way. He's shit, man. I'll be Peter,' said Caruso.

'Yeah, the mad one,' Ian agreed.

Whenever Caruso disagreed, he'd swear. A habit that got him into a lot of trouble.

'There's a Jules Verne movie on at the flicks.' Ian loved anything verging on science-fiction. It was right up his alley.

'Yeah, Journey to the Centre of the Earth,' Eric said.

'You guys go. I think I'll just hang around here.'

This was not like Caruso at all. Eric had noticed a change in his friend. It had been subtle but all the same, he could see it.

'No way, man. You have to come. Besides, how are we gunna get in without your… er, particular skills?' Ian knew he would not have the guts to sneak into the cinema without Caruso's bravado. Caruso gave in.

How do you gain entry to a picture with absolutely no money? According to Caruso, it was easy, a matter of confidence and trickery. Two things he had in abundance. Armed with a pack of Vita Brits smothered with vegemite as lunch treats, they made their way quickly to the main street.

'Hey, hey, we're the Monkees,' echoed as they walked. One would start up the chant and eventually, they would all sing the refrain. People would look at them strangely. They reached the theatre halfway down Main Street.

'Okay, you guys know the drill. I go in and ask to go to the toilet. I slip out the back, you meet me down the side alley. I push open the door, then you've got ten seconds to get in or I let it go and you miss the movie. Got it?' said Caruso.

Simple.

They waited and waited. Something was up. The door did not open.

'Maybe he got caught,' Ian said, thinking the worst.

'Probably got watching the trailer. He'll be out soon.'

'We can't wait here. We'll be the ones getting caught.'

They moved back onto the main road where they could see the exit door.

Eric and Ian were about to give up. Both were annoyed that Caruso hadn't returned. Surely the movie must be started by now.

'Selfish bastard.' Ian was seething. 'I really wanted to see that movie.'

Suddenly the exit doors sprung open and Caruso stumbled out. A man was behind him. He reached down and pulled the boy to his feet. The man looked up at Ian and Eric. They froze. It was Whitey. He looked right past them as he pushed Caruso forward.

Tall, thin and white-haired, Eric recognised him straight away even though he was not in his customary Speedos. A tingle ran up Eric's arm. This was the man who had tried to pick him up. Jody's friend.

'Steal from me, will ya,' said Whitey.

Caruso was in trouble. Eric looked down the main street. If ever he needed a plan, it was now. They watched as Whitey pushed Caruso towards them. He twisted his arm behind his back and yanked. Caruso wouldn't cry out in pain. He was stoic like that.

'Whadda we do?' Ian was panicking more than usual. He started backing away, Eric grabbed his arm.

'Stay with me, Ian.'

Eric knew they would have one chance at this. People were walking innocently up and down the main drag. He could use that. 'You take that side. He can't get both of us at the same time. Okay? We run at him then he has to let go of Caruso.'

'Shit, shit, shit!' Ian was anything but eloquent. 'I... I can't.'

'Yes, you can.' With that, Eric pushed him out into the street. He faced Whitey and took a step forward.

'Hey, it's your little friends. They've come to help you. How nice of them.' With that, he pushed Caruso onto the pavement. A couple stared at them as they passed. Nothing odd in that. Just a parent disciplining his child. Probably a kid that deserved a good thrashing.

'I've got a mind to fix you all,' snarled Whitey.

A car swerved in front of Ian. He put his hands up in defence and waited for the collision. It didn't come only a verbal spray from the driver. He yelled at Ian to get out of the way. Eric saw an opportunity.

'Now!' Eric screamed at Ian. They both ran at Whitey, hitting him right in the midriff. He fell back onto the pavement screaming blue murder all the way. Eric took hold of Caruso's hand and yanked him to his feet.

'Hey, what's going on?' A woman, seeing the commotion, waved her hands in Eric's face. Eric lost balance and fell backwards with Caruso on top of him.

When he got to his feet, Whitey was gone and a young constable had appeared out of nowhere.

'What's going on here?' said the constable.

'Nuffin.' Caruso took charge.

'So, who were you running from?' said the constable.

Caruso glared at the others as if to say 'don't say a goddamned thing'.

'Sorry, Officer, we were tryin' to get into the flicks for free. The manager caught us and turfed us out,' said Caruso. He was good at stretching the truth. He looked innocently at the constable then grinned just a little.

Constable Murphy eyed them suspiciously.

*

'I remember that. I thought Whitey was going to kill Caruso. He had him by the arm, twisted it right back,' Rick said.

'At first, I thought it was the theatre manager who had him but when he started on him, I could hardly move, I was that scared,' Ian said.

'Me too. Good thing Murphy came past when he did. I don't know what would have happened.'

'I guess he didn't believe Caruso about Whitey being the theatre manager.'

'Would you?'

'Do you remember when he took us back to the police station?' Ian asked. 'He wanted to ring our parents. I was crapping my pants. They would have killed me. If they'd known half of what we got up to when we were out, they would have locked me up for my childhood. Believe me, if my kids had done anything like that, I would have hit the roof.'

'You think they didn't get up to mischief when they were young? If you think that, you're a bigger schmuck than I thought.'

'You're probably right but what I don't know can't hurt me, right?'

'If you say so.'

'I was scared of Murphy back then,' Ian said.

'So was I. We should have told him. Maybe he could have arrested Whitey or something,' Rick said.

'If he could find him. Whitey has been good at disappearing when he needed to. Murphy said that after they took him in the first time, they all got a kick up the arse by their bosses. He was dismissed as a suspect very early on. Lack of evidence, they said.'

'How the hell could that be true? Everyone must have seen him with those kids.'

'No one came forward. Or, let me rephrase that. No witnesses came forward that the police put any credence in. Most were kids like ourselves. Not one cop took any notice,' Ian said. 'Including Murphy.'

15

Old Rags and Horse Bones

THEY GOT THE CALL soon after. 'Pick me up,' followed by a gruff expletive. Murphy had yet to master the social graces of using a mobile phone. Rick and Ian drove to Murphy's tiny terraced house to pick him up. From the front gate, Rick could see the flower garden had grown a little wild. Murphy jumped in the back of the Jag and greeted them with the standard gidday then they were off.

The Stitch Road Pub was the only one that still served pony glasses of beer. Five fluid ounces. Possibly three big sips and it was gone. The three sat on high stools facing the bar.

'There was a hit on those bones found at the factory site,' Murphy said, right to the point.

'Did they tell you before the press, your friends?' asked Ian sarcastically.

'More like former colleagues. Friends is drawing a rather long bow. Especially now,' Murphy said. He did not elaborate. By the look on his face, it wasn't good news. 'Horse.'

'Horse what?' Ian said, gulping down his beer.

'Horse bones, that's what they found, and some old bits of hessian bags.'

'Horse bones? Who would bury a horse in that place?'

'Who indeed.'

Rick stared out the window of the bar solemnly. Things were getting stranger.

'There is something else,' Murphy said, putting his hand on the railing. 'Remember when Caruso told me about that foreman's son, Bill? It seems that there may have been someone else involved in digging those holes.'

'A third person? I thought it was just the two of them?' Ian said.

Murphy flipped through the pages of his notebook to find the entry. 'Seems that there was another. Caruso never mentioned him. But he knew him quite well. He's turned up. Well, that's not exactly true he's been here all the time. But there's a problem.'

'There's always a problem,' Ian said.

'One that you might be able to help me with, Rick,' Murphy said.

Ian swung around. 'No way, you're not going on another wild goose chase. Murphy, if you get caught that would be fair enough but if Rick here gets caught, the tabloids are gunna have a field day. Ex-rocker goes bonkers. Plate in his head detects aliens.'

Even Rick laughed at that one. He was intrigued. If truth be known, he'd enjoyed their last foray into danger. It reminded him so much of his childhood, he could almost see his old child-self getting excited.

'I'm in.' Rick smiled in anticipation.

'You see what you've done now. He's as bad as you are. I hope they catch the pair of you and throw away the key. Don't bother to call me when you need bailing out.'

'Ian, relax. I'm sure Murphy would not get us to do anything illegal.'

'Sure,' Murphy said, 'we just need to visit a prison. He's in there, been there for some time actually.'

'And why do you need Rick? I mean, can't you go on your own?'

'I could but I don't think I'd get much out of him. He won't speak to a cop or an ex-cop. And he was a friend of Caruso's. That's why it can't be you or I. Lawyers are even worse than cops to these guys. He'll speak to Rick, he's a rock and roller. Junkies and crims love rock and rollers.'

'He dug those holes with the foreman's son and Caruso. He might know more,' Rick said.

'But they were horse bones,' Ian said.

Murphy swivelled on his bar stool and smiled at the barmaid who was collecting glasses behind them. She smiled back.

'How did you find out about the third guy? How do we know it's just not another red herring?' Ian said.

'There's been talk around the prison that this guy's been saying that he and another guy were paid to dig those holes so we know we've got the right guy. He's been saying he saw some hessian bags in the back of a van near the site. He won't say anymore, he won't talk to the cops so we need to convince him to tell us or more to the point tell Rick here.'

'Now that you mention it, I do remember a guy Caruso knew in gaol. He used to abuse me all the time when I came in. He's a career crim, Murphy, probably not someone we should trust,' Ian said.

'Nonetheless, Rick might be able to get him to talk.'

'So why didn't the cops speak with him before?' Rick said.

'They did. They spoke with a lot of people including this guy. But as I said, he won't talk to cops. And you know how they treated evidence from kids.'

'That's your explanation on why they didn't do anything? Pretty piss-weak if you ask me,' Ian said.

'He's right. No one believed us as kids! Even young constables,' Rick said, looking at Murphy.

'Yeah, well, back in the day I had my own problems with being heard. One day, out of the blue, my boss Sergeant Willow told me to pack up my things and move them down to the basement and that I would be working for CID. At the time, I thought it was a promotion but when I got there all I did all day was cold case filing. Not even investigations, just bloody filing. I did this day in and day out. I got bloody sick of it. One day, the children's file landed on my pile. I mean, they'd only been missing for a year and now they were considered a cold case. That shocked me.'

'Looks like you're still on the case,' Ian said.

'Looks like we all are,' Rick said.

A familiar seventies song came on the P.A system. The Stitch Road was famous for its seventies theme, right down to the dated bar mats and old rock posters hanging on plasterboard panels. Rick's favourite poster was one of Alice Cooper. Not only was *School's Out* a master stroke of a song but it was also a part of his DNA growing up.

Murphy slurped down his beer and shook his head to clear it. 'Haven't really drunk beer since Sarah died. I sort of gave it up. Going to the local pub was our thing when we were young. It got difficult when the cancer came.'

Rick didn't know what to say. He waited for Murphy to continue.

'His name is Vic Tangini. He got put away five years ago for murder. He's doing twenty-five to life so he doesn't have a lot to look forward to. Can't promise him anything either. You just have to get him to open up, that's all.'

'Simple,' Ian said, 'easy job that.'

'Don't be sarcastic, it doesn't suit you. Actually, hang on, it does suit you,' Rick said.

Rick slapped him on the back and dodged Ian's stray elbow. Ian hated being touched.

*

Again, in the Jag. This time they would travel for two hours as the state prison was on the outer skirts of town.

'There used to be a prison closer to town but a couple of breakouts had prisoners roaming the city. That put the end to that one although they now use it for ghost hunts and high tea ceremonies,' Murphy said.

Impressive as it was, Rick felt a twinge of anxiety as he entered the restricted carpark area. This was an imposing place, especially the small but austere grave site they had to walk around on their way to the reception area. Rick couldn't help but think that Caruso might have ended up out here too. He shuddered as he walked with Murphy.

The air changed. It was thicker and tasted slightly tangy. He struggled to breathe. A sense of dread began to grow. It brought back a feeling he hadn't had for some years. Anxiety. The smell of hospital antiseptic hit him as they entered.

'He doesn't want to see you, Detective,' said the guard gruffly. He didn't know Murphy; it was just that he was bad-tempered. The job sucked the big one.

'Er, not Detective just, Joe. Retired!'

'Okay, Joe, he still doesn't want to see you. Can't force him either, unless you've got a warrant?' said the guard sarcastically.

Murphy looked at him then beckoned the guard with a wave of his hand. Reluctantly, the officer moved a few steps toward him. Murphy whispered into his ear. He looked at Murphy then at Rick. He shook his head from side to side.

'I'll go ask again,' he said.

'What did you say?' asked Rick, full of suspicion.

'Nothing really.'

The guard came back and motioned for them to enter.

'You've got thirty minutes.'

'Thanks, pal. I owe ya,' Murphy said with a smile.

The surly look he got from the guard told him he wouldn't want to be repaid anytime soon.

Inside the labyrinth-like inner sanctum, the air was even heavier. Murphy seemed used to it. He had spent many a long hour interrogating inmates and seemed hardened towards it.

'I don't want that a-hole near me,' said Vic, pointing to Murphy as soon as they entered.

A skinny dishevelled man sat at the table. He spat on the ground in front of Murphy who ignored it.

He spat again. 'Not talking to a cop bastard.'

Murphy waved Rick on to take a seat. Vic gave Rick a furtive look but said nothing. Murphy slapped his knees and stood.

'Well, I guess I'll just leave you two. I'll just be outside if you need me,' he said finally.

'Fuck off.' Vic was happy to see him leave the room. Rick didn't know what to say. He'd asked Murphy in the car what to ask but he just typically said, 'You'll know, just wing it. He'll tell you what we need to know.'

A small man, Vic looked even smaller scrunching up his arms and folding them to his chest. Tattoos crept out of his prison t-shirt. One arm tatt looked like a dagger of some sort; the other, a faded girl's name.

In the background, he heard a bell go off. He wondered whether that was the sign of something. Maybe visiting hours? He looked anywhere but at the man sitting in front of him. If he had nothing to say then Rick wouldn't force him. But Murphy had been sure that he would.

'Just listen to what he has to say. Don't force it.'

Well, that was something he could do. Just listen. He had trouble telling people what to do, his former band members being a point in question. And then there was this man sitting in front of him. In some small way, Vic reminded him of Caruso. And not because he was a convict. It was the same reluctance to talk. To say what happened. He even had the same vocabulary as Caruso!

Suddenly, Vic smiled a crooked smile.

'Liked your band, man. The Anchormen were brilliant. That other lot you had were shit. I liked your early stuff.'

For the first time, Rick nodded and smiled back.

'*Soldier Blue*, now that was sumthin'. *Screaming Fred*, too. Radical,' he said with a slight lisp that could have been because of the missing teeth.

'Glad you liked them.'

'Yeah, I was banged up then too. We smuggled your record in and played it in the cells. *Soldier Blue* went to number one in the big house.'

'Probably the only time it went to number one,' Rick said with a shrug.

The rumblings of the buildings air conditioner rattled the very bones in him. Because of the cold, it had been set on heat. The stale air blew right through them both.

'So, what are you doing here with that shit?' Vic said finally.

'I guess that shit is a friend. He's, er, helping me.'

'He's fucking with you, man, you know that. He ain't gunna tell you half of it. He's a scum bag. Like all cops, they're nice to you when they want sumthin'. I ain't giving him no favours,' said Vic, crossing his arms.

'I don't think he's asking for a favour. He just wants to know what you've been telling everyone about the time you helped dig those holes, that's all.'

Vic looked at him curiously. 'Don't know what you're talking about.'

Rick remembered what Murphy said: *'Just wait for him to talk.'* He waited.

Sometime later, Vic smiled again. 'You're Caruso's friend. You knew him in the old days,' he said, smiling at Rick.

For the first time since he arrived, he could feel himself relax. Rick nodded.

'We hung out a lot when we were young, that's all.'

'With that lawyer scumbag too. Jesus, man, for a cool dude you sure pick shithouse friends.'

'You've met Ian.'

'He used to come around when Caruso and I were banged up together. I used to tell Caruso to get rid of him. Sometimes he'd listen. He'd tell him to fuck right off but he always came back sniffing around.'

'He was trying to help.'

Uncomfortable silence.

'Anyway, I ain't got nuffin' to say. I only worked for them sometimes, nuffin' to worry about. Besides, no cop has ever helped me so why should I do anything for them? Got nuffin' to say,' said Vic, folding his arms again.

Rick suspected he was wasting his time. He didn't know what to do or say so he just told the truth.

'We were there that day,' began Rick. 'The day that those kids went missing. I knew Jody.' Rick paused then went on, 'I guess that's why I am like I am. Things like what happened to her change you. They haunt my dreams at night. And the parents! I think of them all the time. To lose one child is bad enough, but to lose them all? Well, I can't even imagine what they went through.'

Rick stopped again. He'd said too much. His head dropped down.

Vic just stared at him. Finally, he said, 'I got two kids myself.

They come and see me sometimes. I told 'em not to bother, don't like seeing them in here. Can I tell you a secret?'

Rick nodded.

'I liked Jimmy's voice better than yours. He rocked.'

For once, Rick had to agree.

He waited just like Murphy told him to. Vic started talking.

'I met Caruso through Spike. He'd been working with him for a couple of years. I kept bugging Spike for work. He got us to do things… things that I ain't too proud of. I seen things that, well, they broke my heart.'

Rick knew then he was about to hear about life at the absolute bottom.

'You know the only reason I'm talking to ya is that I liked your band,' said Vic at some stage.

Rick knew that. And of course, it was the reason why Murphy brought him here in the first place. Smart man, that detective.

'We was supposed to be workin' together. Caruso and I, that is.'

'What work did you do together?'

'We were Picciotto's together.'

'Picciotto's?'

Vic looked behind him towards the door as if it were all a big secret. 'Soldiers. It's Italian. We did things for Spike or whoever Spike worked for. Things you would never believe, man.'

Rick felt his heart beat hard now. He was too scared to ask what kind of things. But deep in his heart, he knew.

'We went to this house that Whitey had something to do with. He got us some shovels, then another kid came and Whitey dropped us down to this factory he also had something to do with. He told me and this other kid to get out. Caruso stayed in the car with Whitey. Whitey told us that someone would be by to tell us what to do. I remember looking back at Caruso as they drove off. He was scared, man. He didn't wanna go, I could tell that.'

'And what did you dig up that day?'

Vic grinned wildly. 'Lots of shit, man.'

And then he told him about the shit.

16

A Junkie's Lament

THEY SAT IN THE kitchen at Murphy's cottage. Vic Tangini was the topic.

'It's worse than we thought,' Rick said.

'Worse! Nothing could be worse than three murders?' said Ian.

'Maybe if you just tell us what he said. We can work it out together,' Murphy said.

Murphy was being a cop. Rick knew that. It was the way he did things, cop-wise.

'Remember that day we got caught at the flicks?' asked Rick. 'Whitey was waiting for us. Or more to the point, he was waiting for Caruso. I don't think he thought too much about us. We were just a couple of kids that got in the way. He wanted Caruso, he had something on him.'

'He can't have known he would be there, Rick. I mean, we didn't make up our minds until late,' Ian said.

'Yeah, that's what I thought too. Someone saw us walking to the flicks that day. They went and told him. That's why he was there.'

The kettle started whistling. Murphy stood to take it off the stove.

'Vic?' Ian said.

'Yup, that was his job, he told me. He kept an eye open for Whitey. He was grooming them both to do things for him.'

'Sexual?' Ian said as delicately as he could.

'Vic wouldn't say, although he did mention that he heard Whitey joke once about his brother liking boys. He told me that Whitey preferred to use kids from broken homes, single parents. Kids like Vic and Caruso that would do things for him without question. And to keep their mouth shut.'

'Whitey had a brother?'

'That's what Vic said. I asked him if he had ever seen him and he clammed up, said he shouldn't have said anything about him.'

Murphy scribbled it down in his notes. Rick continued.

'Whitey took Caruso, Vic Tangini and Bill Santino to the factory in the Holden. Then Whitey and Caruso left in his car. Vic didn't know where they went but when they came back to pick him up, he reckons Caruso looked like he'd seen a ghost. Vic asked him what was up but all Caruso would tell him was that he'd been to another house somewhere in the north. He couldn't tell Vic what he'd seen but whatever it was, shook the living daylights out of him. Meanwhile, Vic and the foreman's son had finished digging in the factory grounds. They were told to unearth some hessian bags and not to damage them. They dragged them out and onto the back of a truck that was parked on the side of the road. It took them several hours but the bags were buried exactly where they were told they would be. The only thing was that a couple of them had rotted badly.'

'They never looked inside?'

Murphy glared at Ian for interrupting but Rick ploughed on.

'No, they wrapped the hessian bags in some canvas sheets they were given and dragged them over to a truck parked on the opposite side of the parking lot. Two other guys were there to help them lift the bags into the truck,' Rick said in one long sentence. He hardly took a breath.

'Why them? I mean, they were only kids.' Ian ignored Murphy's glare.

'Because it was a kind of initiation. Gangs like that make

sure of their guys with things like that. Then they can't say they didn't know anything,' said Murphy. 'It's just a way of keeping everyone quiet and on the same page. They were testing Caruso and Vic.'

'They could only guess what was in those bags. Vic said that nobody talked about it then but he could only guess it was the children. He reckons that Whitey knew the cops were getting close,' said Rick. 'They knew that word was out that somebody was talking to the cops.'

'That's wrong, nobody was talking to us. That was the problem. We couldn't get any info from the ground. It was like the whole carny closed up shop. No one gave us anything. It was demoralising at the time.'

'Are you sure he said that they dug up the children? It makes absolutely no sense.' Ian looked quizzical.

'He wasn't sure. Of course, he bragged about it to other inmates but I'm not sure he saw anything but the hessian sacks.'

'Did Vic say any more about this house out north?' Murphy asked.

'He didn't seem to want to talk about it. I think he knew more than he was telling me but it was hard convincing him to say anything. Vic did mention that they were all shit scared of Whitey back then.'

'And what else?'

Rick went quiet.

'Tell me, Rick. What did Vic tell you?' asked Murphy.

Sometimes when people tell you horrific things, it takes you time to reflect. Your brain has a hard time translating a difficult conversation. And sometimes it takes you a moment to digest it and regurgitate it. This was one of those times for Rick.

'He told me that Whitey had taken other children since then,'

Rick said finally. 'He said he suspected he knew the place he'd taken them to.'

Murphy looked Rick right in the eye. 'Where? Did he say where?'

Rick shook his head. 'He clammed up. Wouldn't say anymore. He jumped up and got the guard. It was like he was freaked out that he'd said too much and that Whitey would find out.'

'But Whitey's dead,' Ian said. 'Why would that scare him now?'

'I think he knows a little more than he's saying,' said Murphy.

They sat in silence for a while. No one wanted to be the first to break it.

Red tea bags dangled in three mugs. Murphy poured hot water from the jug into them. 'You're not going to like this.'

Rick gave him a grim smile. He knew what Murphy was about to say.

'You need to go back and find out from Vic where he took them.' Murphy took a sip of his tea then gently blew over it to cool it. 'He might be the only witness left who knows where they are.'

Ian sighed. 'For once, I have to agree with Murphy. We have nothing but if we can find the place he took them, then maybe we can find something, a clue to where they are now.'

'You can do it, Rick. I know you can,' Murphy said.

'Jesus, guys. I don't know if I can do it. He looked real scared.'

'If I thought we had any other choice, I wouldn't ask you to go back. But we have nothing. Think about Jody. This might be our only chance,' Murphy said. 'You have to go back.'

Rick's face went red. Whatever option he had to say no had just disappeared.

*

This time Rick was on his own. Murphy had been summoned back to CID headquarters and Ian had his day job at chambers.

As he drove, he went through what he might say to Vic but as he steered the Jag into the carpark, he still had no idea how to approach the delicate subject. Hell, he didn't even know if Vic would see him. It would be easy for him to simply ignore the former rocker and leave him dangling, so to speak. He looked down at the passenger seat at the old vinyl record. He thought an old copy of the Anchormen's first single might come in handy. It wasn't signed as he'd only had time to scrounge around at a second-hand dealer to find it. He figured he could scrawl his signature on it if required. Out of his trunk at the hotel, he'd found an old photo of the band on tour in New York. He grabbed that as well. It might just get him inside. He sighed at the picture. He seemed contented then.

Vic didn't seem too happy to see him.

'You caused me a lot of grief, man,' he said as he slid into the seat.

This time they were meeting in the canteen. Rows and rows of trestle tables and yellow gaudy plastic chairs filled the bland space. There were few decorations. A large painting of the prison built one hundred years ago was the only show of ostentatiousness.

The canteen was empty. Nonetheless, Vic seemed preoccupied with the guards passing by in the corridor. He was on edge.

'I only agreed to meet you to set the record straight. All that stuff I told you the other day, you know I was just playing you. It never really happened,' he said nervously.

Rick noticed the dark lines over one of Vic's eyes. And the bruise on his arm.

'How did you get that bruise?' asked Rick quietly.

Vic twitched and wriggled. 'Fell in the shower,' he said. He picked up the vinyl record Rick had brought him and turned it over in his hand. 'Good days.'

'Thought you'd like it. You said you were a fan.'

'You only brought it because you want me to tell you more. Well, there ain't no more. I lied to you about doin' them things. I never met your man.'

'You can't tell me you never met Whitey. You told me you worked for him. With Caruso and Bill Santino.'

The prison walls were closing in. The shadows had started to creep along the canteen wall. It was grey and getting greyer. Soon it would be black. He needed to pull out all the stops.

'You said that you knew where he took them,' Rick said, bending in closer to Vic. 'I need you to tell me where that is.'

Suddenly, Vic's face went as white as a sheet.

'I…' He stopped as another prison guard slowly walked along the passageway, looking right at them both. It was like the guard knew what they were talking about. But of course, that was impossible. 'I can't.' He bent over so that his face was as close to Rick's as possible. Rick could see the tension in his neck. The next few words he whispered. 'He'll kill me.'

'He can't touch you in here, Vic. Besides, he's been dead for years. He can't harm you.'

Vic shook his head vehemently. 'You don't understand.'

Rick shifted back in his chair.

'Oh yeah, I understand that you would let the children's parents go to their graves without them ever knowing where their children are,' Rick said as cruelly as he could.

'No, you don't understand. Listen, if I tell you this, do you promise not to tell that cop, Murphy? If I tell you this and it gets out, I'm a dead man.'

'Joe Murphy's not a cop anymore. All he wants is to find those children.'

'No, you can't trust him. You can't trust any of them. He owns all of them, including your mate, the cop. Don't you see? How do you think he's been able to get away with it all these years?' said Vic. 'And there's more, he's looking to take another.'

Rick leaned back in. 'Who is planning to take another? Whitey is dead, Vic. Was it one of his gang? Is there a copycat out there? Who? Who, Vic? I promise, no one needs to know but me.'

'I just heard it. I don't know who it is, but I hear things.'

'Where, Vic? You know where he took them all those years ago,' Rick said urgently.

'To a cottage somewhere. I dunno, I've never been there,' said Vic in a whisper.

A cottage somewhere. Something triggered in Rick's mind.

'Whitey took the children there?' asked Rick calmly. 'Are you sure it was a cottage? Did you hear anything else?'

Vic slowly nodded. 'He's got other places too. But you don't understand,' Vic started to say.

'What don't I understand?'

The guard came in and stood behind them, his baton thumping in his left hand.

'Time,' he called.

'Just a few minutes more,' Rick said.

'I said time,' the surly guard said.

Vic stared at him and shrunk back into his chair.

'Can't say no more,' he said.

Rick had heard enough. It registered in his mind that he was under pressure now. Somebody was out there planning to do what Whitey did all those years ago. He could not let that happen.

*

He gripped the steering wheel as hard as he could. He had to think. He leapt out of the Jag. They were in here somewhere. He ferreted around in his boot. A yellow folder. He found the photos and spread them out on the passenger's seat of the Jag. Where was it? Had he seen it or was it part of his large imagination? The photos he'd taken were now laid out in front of him. He picked them up one after the other. It was there in the second photo. A dark outline just behind the trees. He stuffed the photo in his pocket.

'Shit,' he said as he gunned the Jag then stopped suddenly. He reached across the seat and pulled out his cell phone. He needed to hurry.

He paused before ringing Murphy's phone. Why didn't Vic trust Murphy? Was it only because he had been a cop? Or was it something else? Sure, Murphy could be secretive. There were several times Rick thought the old policeman was being less than open about what he knew but dismissed it as being a foible of his old cop days. Was it really because of that? Rick shrugged off his nagging doubt.

Anyway, Murphy was not answering. His phone didn't even go to the message bank.

He rang Ian's office.

'It's important,' he told the receptionist.

'I'm sorry but he's in court all day. Can I take a message?'

He thought for a moment.

'Just tell him that I've found the place,' Rick said before throwing down the phone and gunning the Jag again.

If Vic was right and someone was planning to take another victim, he had to go now. He hadn't a moment to waste.

*

It took him an hour of hard driving to reach the turnoff. He skidded around the last bend and there it was, the Hilltop Retreat, or as young Peter had called it, 'the castle'. He hid the Jag behind a neighbouring hedge and then charged up the hill. He had no plan. All he knew was that there was a possibility a child was in danger. All he could think of was Jody and her green eyes staring at him, whispering that she was 'scared'. He ran faster.

The afternoon sun was disappearing down the hill quickly. It concerned him that he would be going into these grounds again but this time with limited light. He hadn't liked it before when he had plenty of light. It gave him the creeps.

This time he didn't have to scale the fence. The main gate was ajar. He slipped in as the sun disappeared over the mansion. He was now in the slightly grey post-sunset gloom. A mist descended. He buttoned up his coat against the cold and found the path to the rear of the mansion. He glanced up at the bay windows as he walked the path. Was there someone up there watching his movements? He tried not to look. He couldn't do anything about that now.

He reached the part of the garden where he had taken the photos. He took out the crumpled photo and held it up. Yes, the mound was still there and the tiny turret made of mud and weeds still lay on the ground. He looked further into the woods. It was dark now and seeing was hard. He pocketed the photo and kept walking. Whatever was down this path, he was sure he would find the answer. It had to be here. If Whitey owned the Hillside Retreat, then it stood to reason that there might be a caretaker's cottage on these grounds. A piece of wood with a barely legible sign stood in the centre of the path. For a second, the breath he had been holding threatened to make him pass out. This is what he had captured on his phone camera. It read 'border private lane'. He had thought it looked like the outline of a cottage.

He stopped. A false lead. He exhaled heavily. The sign was on the borderline of the property. He looked behind the sign. The lane petered out. Nothing but shrubbery and thick dense trees.

He was disappointed. He turned to go back.

Something moved in the bushes to his left. An animal? He stood as still as he could. A large rat scampered away through the bush. He heard a splash then a gurgling sound.

Intrigued, he parted the bushes with his hand and saw a large pond full of reeds and swamp slime. To the right of the pond was a path along its edge. It seemingly followed the pond around to the far side. He stepped over the bushes and onto the pond's trail.

He was walking close to the edge of the pond. It was wet and slimy. He had to be careful he didn't slide right in. He stepped surely. On the far side of the pond, he noticed an old rowboat that had been pulled ashore and tied off at a tree. On board were two paddles and an old tarp. It looked like it had been there for years.

To his right, the last vestige of sunlight was beginning its final travels for the day. A red-orange glow made it hard to see. He shielded his eyes and for a brief second, he saw a building nestled in the corner of a field. As he got closer, he could see that it was made of stone. The roof was almost totally covered by Lucerne and moss. A narrow brick chimney stood out against the background. Rick thought he saw smoke but the longer he stood and watched, the surer he became that it was his vivid imagination.

The path he was on led to the front door.

He remembered an old childhood story that had scared him witless at the time. Hansel and Gretel had come across a cottage in the woods. The home of a wicked witch, she had them both in her cauldron before the children knew any better. He wondered whether this had been the cottage that Whitey had taken the children to. The thought sent a shiver right through him.

The windows and front door were boarded up and there was no sign that anyone had been here for a long time. He followed the path around the cottage to the rear but it was so overgrown that he couldn't make his way. He returned to the front and pulled at the boards covering the left-hand side window. One came loose.

His head began to spin just a little – a symptom of the head trauma he obtained in a car accident back when the band had stopped for a hiatus. He put his hand to his temple to stop the vertigo. In times of stress, it reared its ugly head. He paused to re-engage his damaged brain.

He picked up a stone lying near the front door and used it to smash a pane of glass in the left-hand corner of the window. He stood back to listen, then hearing nothing he smashed the right-hand pane. It broke inwards, the shattered glass tinkled onto the ground making little noise. Soon, he had a hole big enough to crawl through. This was it. He landed on the cold hard floor. Brick or stone, it was well-weathered.

Luckily, he had the torch on his phone. He took time to look around the front room he had entered. There was an old chair in the corner and a rickety table with a lamp on it. Apart from the few bits of furniture, the room was empty.

The door to the back of the cottage was jammed shut. He pushed it open and shone his torch in. To the right, a passageway led to several rooms. To the left, a kitchen and a side door. A basic standard pattern for a cottage made in the last century. Rick breathed in through his nose. A smell he couldn't quite identify flooded his nostrils. He felt growing nausea. The smell was overpowering. It seemed to be coming from the rooms on the right. He steeled himself and crept along slowly.

The first door was locked so he moved to the second. When he gave it a push, the handle broke off in his hand. Inside this room was a makeshift bed and mattress up against the far wall. Beside the bed were two iron hoops embedded in the wall. Another shiver went through his body. On the side was a small table. He shone his torch over the walls. Writing and initials were scratched into them. Nothing seemed legible. He found an old iron bar used to stoke fires and held it up to the light. He could use it to open the locked door.

A tapping noise sounded from the room he'd just come from. Poised with the iron stoker across his chest like a sword, he braced himself by the door. The noise stopped. He crept along the corridor to the locked door and paused. No further sounds.

The handle wouldn't budge. He jemmied the iron stoker into the architrave next to the lock and pushed it in as far as he could. He then levered it down. The wood split and the lock gave way in a cascade of splinters. He paused again but heard nothing. He levered the iron stoker one more time and the door jamb came apart and forced the door open.

He stood for a moment, catching his breath. He shone his torch into the room. At first, he couldn't see anything the light was too dim. Then slowly, he could see more. The room was packed with furniture and items. It was like an office. Computers and security screens all showing the outside of the cottage and another blank screen were positioned around the room. The computers were blinking in front of him. A giant battery UPS system lay under a table. His phone light flickered. His battery was giving out. He felt the walls for a light switch. He found one and turned it on. A bank of fluorescent lights flickered on. He stood in the middle of the room and stared.

The first thing he noticed was a red lamp that stood on a cabinet in the corner. It was blinking at him. He wondered whether it was connected to the security camera. If it was, someone would probably know he was standing there right now. He started to back out of the room but something caught his eye. A computer on the far right. On its opening screen was a picture of a girl.

'Jody,' Rick whispered. He went closer. No, it wasn't Jody. This girl had blue eyes. But it was close. Too close for Rick. He reached down and hit a few keys but the image suddenly disappeared and a password screen bobbed up. He hit it again but nothing happened. He needed to see her picture again but the computer had gone to another screen.

He heard another noise. But this time it seemed to be coming from down the passageway to the right not where he had entered. Was there another entry to the cottage? Was somebody coming for him right now?

He took a closer look at the security camera screen. It gave a long shot of a darkened room. He sat down in front of the screen. In the middle of the keyboard was a toggle switch. He moved it and the camera followed. He pushed it in and the camera zoomed in. He pulled back and the camera sprung back, ultimately showing the whole room. The picture was dark. There was little light in the room. Then he saw a bed with shackles at the head and foot. Another shiver went through his body.

Where was the room?

There was only one room left to check. His mind raced. This was it. This was where the monster kept his prize.

A voice swept through the room.

'Welcome, Eric. It has indeed been a long time,' a wheezy voice said.

Rick froze. A sudden feeling of familiarity made him tense. This was a voice that he'd not heard for so long. It was the voice of his nightmares.

'How do you know my name?' he asked, looking around to see where the voice emanated.

'Oh, I know all your names. It was such a long time ago but I remember, don't you?'

The voice was coming from the second computer with a blank screen. Sound but no pictures.

'Where are you?'

'You won't be able to see me. Oh, I could send you a picture alright. I've got all that set up but you know what I look like. I must admit, I have changed a little. Age gets to us all, doesn't it? I can see that you have changed too, Eric, or should I now call you Rick? No longer the innocent child. Quite the man. A rock and roll star, I'm told. Quite a legend. But I like the innocent days better. Back then, you all had an essence that I enjoyed,' said the voice.

'Whitey!' whispered Rick.

'I always hated that name. It was so uncouth. I am an educated man, Eric, but you children, well, like your friend, Gino, wasn't it? He helped me a great deal. Got a bit needy towards the end. I had to do something about that. But it all worked out well in the long run,' said Whitey.

Rick stood and looked to the door. He raised his stoker. He would be ready for an attack.

'Violence. I normally try to avoid it but on occasion, I have been known to use it. Eric, just give up and we'll come to some arrangement, I mean, before you die. As you are aware, I cannot let you leave. That wouldn't be nice. I've prepared a nice bed for you. Made it up, especially for you.'

'You want to murder me just like you murdered Caruso and the children.'

'Yes, yes, Gino was tedious and messy, not like the children. They were so sweet and innocent.'

'You won't get away with this. My friends are on their way. Probably be here in the next few minutes.'

The air inside the cottage became hard to breathe. Heat rose from the rows of screens and he started to sweat like a pig. If he didn't move, he feared he would pass out.

'Well, that's nice but I don't think they have any idea where you are. You see, I know for a fact that you couldn't contact them. How do I know that? Well, let me see, the old detective is currently unreachable and your friend Ian is in court, unable to receive any calls. Nobody is coming for you, Eric. All your friends are either dead or have better things to do. So, all in all, you haven't got a leg to stand on, so to speak.'

Rick could only grit his teeth. 'This is where you brought the children, isn't it? This is where you murdered them.'

He put a hand to his forehead and mopped away the sweat.

'Oh, my boy, you have a limited imagination. There have been many children. Yes, some of them were in that room but I have other places too. I don't limit my activities to one place.'

'You're sick.'

'And there's always room for one more.'

'Like the girl on the computer,' said Rick. 'Where have you got her?'

'A special place. Don't you think she looks familiar? I thought so myself. Except for the eyes though. This one has blue eyes but I prefer them with green eyes, don't you? Of course, you do.

I remember that day on the beach. It was a glorious day – sun, laughter, children. What fun we had.'

'You like them young, don't you? You pervert.'

'I do. Unlike some who liked the boys but I wasn't so choosy. I could take either.'

'I'm going to kill you when I get hold of you.'

He leapt to his feet and immediately went to his knees. The blood rushed to his damaged head too quickly.

'Such violence, Eric. But if it were only that simple then I wouldn't have had to kill Gino either. Alas, he made me. Just as you're leaving me no choice but to kill you.'

'You have to come in here first. Then we'll see who kills who. You're a sick old man.'

'Old, yes! But old has its ways. Oh, I won't be killing you myself. I have others to do that.'

Suddenly, the door sprang open and a man leapt at Rick. He turned before the man reached him. He jammed his stoker up and into the man's arms. It deflected off and Rick watched it as it sailed across the room.

'Goodbye, Eric,' said Whitey. 'It was good of you to drop by.'

The chair collapsed under the weight of the two men. Its wheels sent them crashing into the security camera, which made the lights blink even faster. Rick brought both of his arms up in a defensive move that caught the man off guard.

Then the power went out and they were grappling in the dark. Rick swung his fist around and caught the man in the face. He felt the bone crunch and blood ooze as the man fell back. Rick got to his feet and stumbled towards the door. Or where he thought the door was. He went face-first into the wall. The man took hold of the computer chair and swung it around his head. Rick found the door and crashed into the passageway wall. It shook him to his core. The man came after him without the chair this time and they bear-hugged each other to the ground. Rick took hold of his arm and pushed up. He felt a bone give way and the man's sudden exhaling of breath. He knew that he would have to act fast to get away. The back door was open. It was where the man had entered from. He ran to it with the man right behind him. He stopped just as he got to the door and forced back his elbow, which caught the man in the windpipe. He felt him go down in a heap. He made it out the door. He ran towards the pond but slipped and slid right into a giant elm tree. He slammed his head into it and slid to the ground. For a second, he thought he was back in the hospital. Back in neurosurgery. Instinctively, he put his hand to his head, then he blacked out.

*

He stared up at the night sky. Tiny dots were dancing before his eyes. The tree he had run into towered over him. He opened one eye then the other. His head hurt like a bastard and he knew that he was in big trouble. In the distance, he could see a torch. It was looking for him. He had fallen into a narrow ditch by the side of the elm. It must have been what saved him from being discovered when he was out like a light. He tried moving both his arms and legs one at a time. All seemed to be functioning, but still, he wasn't sure about standing just yet. The hit to the head not only knocked him out but caused blood flow of an undetermined amount. He could see, barely. That was a start.

He could hear no voices so he assumed it was still just his unknown assailant looking for him. He liked those odds better.

How long had he been knocked out? It couldn't have been for long or the man would have found him by now. He had not gone far from the cottage. He needed to get to his feet and get moving. Once he could feel the feet under him, he knew he could make it back out to the car. He felt for his phone. It was still in his pocket. Could he risk making a call for help? He decided not to.

The light was getting closer. He had to make a move. He pushed himself up to his knees and crawled behind the elm. At least that would give him some cover.

The overcast sky cleared and the moon appeared. This gave him the impetus to move quicker. It took him an hour but finally, he made it around the pond and down the trail past the mansion to the main gates. This time they were closed and he had to scale the fence like he had the first time. He flung himself over the fence and landed in a heap on the other side. He stayed down for a second to catch his breath and then he was off.

The Jag was a welcome sight.

He pulled his phone out but his battery had gone flat. He tossed it onto the passenger's seat, started the car and got out of there as fast as he dared.

'Damn phone.'

He gripped the wheel and then started to shiver.

17

Tales of Disbelief

RICK MADE A BEELINE to Murphy's place but when he got there and pounded on the door, he found no one home. He looked at his watch. It was three a.m. Where the hell was he? He thought about what to do next. He had no option. Ian answered the door on his third knock.

'What happened to you? You look like shit,' Ian said. He ushered Rick inside and quickly closed the door.

'Listen, Ian, we don't have much time. He's alive! I've found him.'

Ian looked at his friend. 'I got your message at work. I tried calling you, Rick, I tried calling about a hundred times. Sit down, right here.'

But Rick would not sit. He paced Ian's office like a panther.

'My phone's dead. There's no time,' he insisted. 'Ian, we have to go back. We have to go now! I tried raising Joe but he's not home. I don't know where an old fart like him could be at three in the goddamned morning but he's not at home.'

'Yeah, well, I know where Joe is so there's no help from him,' Ian said but Rick did not hear him.

Anxiety swept over him. He wrung his hands. Ian tried to calm him.

'Whitey's alive, Ian. I spoke with him. He tried to kill me. He's alive and he's got another child. We've got to go back. I saw the room he keeps them in.'

'Rick, please…'

Rick stopped and allowed Ian to steer him into a chair. He sat and put his hands on his head.

Anger and fear rose instantly but when he lifted his head and spoke it was vengeance that struck. 'I'm going to kill him.' This was serious big time. For the first time in his life, he knew he could commit murder.

'Why don't you start from the beginning and tell me exactly what happened.'

'There's no time, Ian. He's taken another kid.'

'Steady on. You're not making any sense, pally. Just take a deep breath.'

After Rick had told Ian as much of the story as he could, Ian woke his wife who tried valiantly to daub salve onto Rick's wounds. His face was a mess. His hands too. He realised that he had attempted to hit his assailant and, in the process, took off most of the skin on his knuckles. His clothes were torn and his knees were in not-so-good condition after smashing into the elm tree.

Ian finally got a message through to Murphy and they were on their way to the police station where he happened to be. Rick didn't ask Ian for an explanation. He was focused on getting back to the cottage as soon as possible.

The Franklin Street Police Station neon sign glowed brightly above the main entrance. Ian pulled up into an empty police car-only spot.

'Now listen, Rick, I have to tell you that Murphy may not be in a position to help us now. He's had a small problem,' Ian said, clambering out of his car.

It was six a.m. The main doors were not open but as Ian had called ahead, a uniformed constable was waiting for them. He let them in the side door.

Rick saw Murphy through the glass office window. He was slouched over, his black trench coat hanging on the back of a nearby chair. Close up, he wasn't much better. He hadn't shaved for a couple of days and there were bags under his eyes like he hadn't slept for even longer. As soon as he saw Rick, he leapt to his feet.

'Rick,' he said but stopped as Ian signalled him from behind.

'I haven't told him, Joe.'

'Haven't told me what?'

Ian shrugged and didn't answer.

A man dressed in a plain business suit swept into the office, holding a bulging file.

'He hasn't told you that he was arrested yesterday and has just spent the night courtesy of Her Majesty's Government. Detective John Hendriks,' he said, introducing himself as he walked past. He went straight to his office table and threw a file onto it. Pages slipped out and onto the floor. The man was mad.

'Sorry, arrested, for what?'

'Harassment, breaking and entering and general ignorance. Well, maybe not ignorance, but harassment and breaking and entering will do. Should be enough to at least put him away for a couple of months so we can get on and do our business,' said Hendriks.

'I can explain,' said Murphy. He got to his feet.

Rick interrupted him. 'Listen, I don't care what went on, Detective Hendriks, but we've got to move real fast. We've got to get back to the cottage,' Rick said, pounding the table with his fist. Soon, they were all standing in a group in front of Hendriks.

'Hang on, okay. Here it is.' He rummaged through the pile of papers. He picked up a sheet. 'Don't tell me, this is all to do with the Hilltop Retreat formerly owned by the Rutherglen family,' said Hendriks.

Ian sighed then looked at Rick. 'I knew where Joe was all along and when my wife was fixing you up, I rang and spoke with Detective Hendriks. I told him, in a nutshell, what happened to you, Rick. I knew you wouldn't mind but it was the only way we could get Joe out of the cell. I was going to tell you but, well, you had gone through a lot.'

'I should lock you all up,' said Hendriks. Ian looked shocked. 'Well, maybe not you.' He pointed at Ian.

Rick was about to ask a question but Murphy jumped in.

'Just tell us what happened.'

Hendriks glared at Murphy and was about to shut him down when Murphy said, 'You've got to at least listen to him, John,' he said as sweetly as he could. Hendriks gave a snort and spoke.

'This better be good,' said Hendriks.

To his credit, Hendriks didn't interrupt Rick anywhere during his story. He listened and then looked at Rick's injuries. There were times in a cop's life when you have to take evidence at face value. Was Rick a good witness? Did he have a drug habit?

'No, Detective, although I had my moments in a band. I wasn't a junkie and I'm telling you the truth.'

But Hendriks had done a little digging on the former rock and roller too. He wouldn't have been doing his job if he hadn't.

'It says here that you had a brain injury along the way,' he said.

'That's got nothing to do with what just happened. You've got to believe me. Whitey's alive and he's got another kid. If you don't do something now, it'll be on your head if he kills her.'

Ian took hold of Rick's elbow. 'Listen to me. You obviously went through something traumatic tonight, but Whitey is dead. Are you sure it wasn't someone just pretending to be him?'

'Jesus Christ, Ian, don't you think I'd remember Whitey's voice? It was him. You have to believe me.'

Ian lifted both of his hands and waved them like a preacher about to invoke the wrath of God. Murphy just stared at Hendriks.

'It's up to you, John. The kid doesn't lie, believe me,' Murphy said.

Hendriks swore loudly.

He picked up his phone. 'Get me the duty sergeant. I need a team for a search right now.'

He stared at Rick then slapped his thighs. 'Right, better get moving. I'll need you and you to come with me, but not you,' said Hendriks, pointing at Murphy. 'You're going back to the cells.'

Murphy put his hands together like he was pleading. He moved towards Hendriks. 'Come on, you know I can be of help. Who was the best guy you had at searches? It was me, wasn't it?'

Hendriks looked like he wasn't going to give in but in the end, he put his hands up in mock defence.

'Just promise me you'll do as you're told this time. Not like all the other times, hey, Murphy?' said Hendriks.

'You know me, John, of course. I promise.'

Somehow that didn't impress Hendriks.

*

The ride back to the Hilltop Retreat was a lot more crowded than before. Rick found himself sandwiched between Ian and Murphy in the back of a police cruiser. Rick looked across at Murphy. He was using his left hand to steady the trembling in his right. Murphy noticed him staring and smiled.

'It's not too bad today,' he said.

'You didn't tell me what happened?' Rick said.

'It was a case of mistaken information.'

'He was caught breaking into a private citizen's office, grand theft and harassment. He has an AVO out against him,' said Hendriks from the front seat.

'A simple mistake.'

'The mistake is you were caught, red-handed,' said Hendriks.

'Sorry, you've lost me. You were caught breaking and entering?' Rick said.

'The commander's office of all places,' said Hendriks.

'The commander. Who's he?'

When Murphy didn't answer, Rick knew it had to be someone of importance.

*

The Hilltop Retreat was just waking up when they arrived like a scene out of a TV cop show. Lights but no sirens. Hendriks didn't think it warranted an all-guns blazing arrival. The gardener stood in the main drive with his trusty wheelbarrow and shovel at the ready.

'You guys again,' he said to Murphy and Rick.

'And some friends. We knew you wouldn't mind. Is your boss around?' Murphy said, taking the lead. Hendriks pushed his way to the front.

'Detective Hendriks here, sir. We hope we haven't caught you at a bad time but we'd like to have a look around. There's been, well, a report about the cottage in the woods.'

'The caretaker's cottage?' he said. 'I'm afraid it's inaccessible at the moment. We're in the process of emptying the pond, which is nearby the cottage. The foundations are giving way and it's not safe.'

Rick stared at the man. Could it have been him who attacked him? He noticed the man was wearing a bushman's hat pulled down right over his ears, hiding something. Maybe.

'That's bollocks,' Rick said, 'he knows what's in there. He knows what Whitey's doing there.'

The gardener glared at him.

'Don't know what you're talking about. Detective, these were the men I reported who trespassed the other day. They impersonated councilmen. They should be arrested,' he said.

'I will look into that,' said Hendriks who looked annoyed that he had another complaint about Murphy.

'We want to see your boss. Where is he? Maybe he can explain why we can't have a look in the cottage?' Murphy said.

'I don't have a boss here. I work for the corporation that owns this building and many others. He lives in another state,' said the gardener.

'So, who lives here?'

'Murphy, let me ask the questions here. You have no authority,' said Hendriks.

Murphy swept his hand out. 'Be my guest.'

Hendriks looked at the gardener. 'So, who does live here?'

'Members of the family trust,' said the gardener.

Hendriks looked uncomfortable. He had a whole team of officers in the cars behind him. He didn't need problems with access.

'Ring your boss,' Murphy said, 'get him to give us the okay to "trespass" on your precious land.'

Hendriks glared at Murphy again.

The gardener stepped away, took out his mobile and put it to his ear. He walked and talked for a few moments before returning to Hendriks.

'Boss says it's fine to enter. Go ahead knock yourself out,' he said with a sweep of his hands.

The gardener led them down the path Rick had taken earlier. The first thing they saw was a huge flexible pipe attached to a pump stuck in the middle of the pond. The gardener had been right about draining the pond; the level had gone down by at least a metre.

Rick saw where he had smashed through the front window to gain access. The gardener took a key from his belt and opened the front door.

Hendriks motioned for three of his men to enter. Rick moved towards the door.

'You stay here. We don't want to contaminate whatever's inside,' said Hendriks.

The three uniforms disappeared inside.

Hendriks and two remaining officers proceeded to search the grounds. Rick showed them the tree he assumed was the one he'd collided with.

'Pretty sure it was this one. It was pitch black when it happened though. I knocked myself out but I don't know how long for. I was pretty woozy when I woke up. The guy who attacked me was searching over there,' Rick said, pointing to the far side of the cottage closer to the draining pond.

An officer took some photos of the indentations on the tree trunk. Rick looked to see if there were any other tell-tale signs of his being there but could only find some spots of blood about head high on the tree.

Murphy was being kept on a short leash. Rick knew it. He also knew that Murphy owed them an explanation about what happened.

'I got a lead,' Murphy explained. 'I needed to act quickly. Trouble is I wasn't quick enough.'

'Hendriks said that you've been harassing people, why?'

'It's a long story, Rick. You just have to trust me on this.'

'Which means you don't want to tell me.'

'Which means he can't tell you,' Ian said.

Murphy put his hands together and smiled. Suddenly, one of the officers came out of the cottage and waited for Hendriks to come to him. He had something in his hands but Rick couldn't see it. Instinctively, Rick moved towards the door. Ian and Joe followed.

The officer was shaking his head.

'Are you sure, Jacobs?' said Hendriks as Rick arrived.

'Checked every room. Had to force a lock on one but we gained access.'

'And all you found was this?' said Hendriks. He held up what looked like an empty watch case.

Murphy took the case from Hendriks and held it up to inspect it.

'The place is empty. Nothing,' said Jacobs.

'No computers or security camera?' said Hendriks.

'There's nothing. Only a couple of broken bits of furniture. No power or lights, windows have been smashed and it does look like the floors have been cleaned recently.'

Rick leapt forward. 'No, you're wrong.'

Before Hendriks could stop him, he ran through the door and into the main room. He stumbled over the broken glass and made his way to the back room. An officer was on his knees with a flashlight, peering into the corners of the room. Rick stopped at the door and stared.

It was all gone. Computers, screens, the beeping security cameras, everything. Even the banks of lights.

Rick went from room to room but found nothing. In the end, it was Murphy who stopped him.

'There's only one explanation. They came and took everything out. We have to find it, Joe, there's a girl. He's taken her. If we don't find her…' Rick began to taper off. Murphy took him by the arm and led him back out into the light. Hendriks was talking into his walkie-talkie. Rick stood in front of him.

'Okay,' he said finally. 'Finish what you're doing. We're out of here in ten minutes,' said Hendriks.

'No, they've stashed the gear somewhere. What about the house? We should search the house.'

'The house is empty,' said the gardener who had appeared out of the woods. He stood, leaning on his spade. 'But the boss says you're welcome to search it. He told me to tell you he doesn't want to be a hindrance. We get a lot of intruders here. As you can see, someone had smashed the windows to gain access. I dunno why. We never keep anything of value inside.'

For a moment Rick thought about causing a scene and forcing his way into the main house. He caught Murphy's eye who suspected Rick might act impulsively. He slowly shook his head from side to side. There was no need to make things worse than they were. Rick went silent. An hour later, they were back in Hendriks office.

Hendriks sighed deeply. 'So, the way things stand now is that the Hilltop Retreats owner has decided not to formally put in a complaint. But as for you, Murphy, bad news, I'm afraid. Judge Renly Shaw has activated the AVO against you and will bring charges for illegally breaking into his office. He accepts that nothing was stolen but he wishes to make an example of you.'

Rick glanced sideways at Murphy. 'A judge? You broke into a judge's office?'

Hendriks hadn't finished. 'And if it weren't for your friend here'—Hendriks nodded at Ian—'I would throw you both into gaol right now. He's agreed to go sponsor for you both, which means that if any of you put a step out of pace from now on, you'll go straight in the cells. Am I clear?'

'Detective, you're making a big mistake. I saw what I saw. Whitey's alive and he's got another child.'

Hendriks was quiet for a moment. Rick thought he might be reconsidering.

'Then why don't we have a report about a missing child? We'd have one, wouldn't we? I mean, if a child was missing, we'd fucking well know about it, wouldn't we?' said Hendriks, his face now as red as a council fire truck.

Rick went quiet.

18

Fire in the Hole!

BACK AT MURPHY'S COTTAGE, they sat in silence. Rick sat at the kitchen table opposite Murphy and Ian. Things were still uncomfortable.

'You guys believe me, don't you? I mean, that I spoke with Whitey and his henchman tried to kill me?' Rick said finally.

The distant sound of a blower used by Murphy's neighbour filled the gap in speech.

'Look, Rick, I know you've been through a lot, but you have to admit it's pretty far-fetched. I mean, a guy can't just come back from being dead,' Ian said.

'Hendriks thinks you fell and hit your head,' Murphy said carefully.

'Well, I did hit my head. I slammed into a tree. I was out like a light.'

'So, if the guy was trying to kill you, why didn't he do it then? I mean, when you were out?' Ian said.

'I told you this. It was dark and he couldn't find me. When I woke up, I saw his torch searching the grounds for me. You've gotta believe me. He's got another kid out there somewhere. I saw the room.'

'But the police looked in every room. They were empty. Why would they go to the bother of removing everything? Just so you could be proved wrong? That makes no sense.'

'What if that was just the monitoring room and the actual room was somewhere else? I mean, it would be easy to get the equipment out in a hurry.' Rick was desperate for them to believe him.

'Okay, agreed, the room under surveillance doesn't need to be there. It could be anywhere,' Ian surmised.

Murphy followed on. 'I guess the computers and security could all run from a backup UPS source or generator. It would be simple to set up. They could be monitoring a room on the other side of the world for all we know.'

Murphy and Ian glanced at each other.

'So, if the room was somewhere else, how the hell do we find it?' Ian said.

'Are you sure you saw a girl's picture?' Murphy said.

'As sure as I'm standing here,' Rick said.

'Are you sure it just wasn't a random photo?'

'It looked like Jody. At first, I thought it was but I only saw it for a second before it flashed off. It sure looked familiar.'

'And what about what Hendriks said about the child? Even if a kid goes missing for a few hours, the cops are told. Everyone is shit scared of a missing child and that's because of what happened to those three children all those years ago. It's because of them that parents are so paranoid all the time. People don't want to remember what happened,' Ian said.

'So, you're saying there can't be a child missing?'

'Hendriks is right. They would know about it,' Murphy said.

'Maybe he hasn't taken her yet,' Ian said.

'That's it. He hasn't taken her yet. So, there might be a chance to stop him.'

'We won't know until he takes her,' Murphy said.

'He's alive, believe me.'

But even as he said it, he felt the doubt in the room.

*

Murphy's little cottage house that he had shared with his wife had fallen into disrepair. He had done little to fix things since his wife died. Rick could see the small touches she had once done start to fade away. The yellow roses that had once grown so prominently in the front yard were only patches of their former selves. Weeds ran rampant. But Murphy didn't seem to notice. He sat on the porch with his feet dangling over the edge holding his cup of tea between his fingers. Rick watched as Joe tried to overcome the slight tremble of his hand.

'So, what do we do now?' Rick said, looking out onto the road.

Ian scratched his head. Murphy looked at the two then shook his head. 'Maybe I shouldn't be asking this but do you two still want to do something?'

'Are you saying that we should back off?' Ian said.

Murphy looked at them furtively. 'Maybe.'

'Sorry but I can't. I was there. Whitey's alive and out there. I need to do something, anything,' Rick said.

Ian looked at Murphy for back up but got none. It seemed that the former detective had something else on his mind.

'Maybe we missed something. Maybe if we go back to the cottage…' Rick was desperate.

'Listen, Rick, if we try and go back there now it'll just give Hendriks an excuse to lock you both up.'

Suddenly, Murphy sprang to his feet and disappeared inside. They could hear him swearing to himself. Then he reappeared on the patio with his long trench coat in his hand. From its pocket, he pulled out the empty watch box the police had found at the cottage. He sat back down.

'Shit, Joe, you stole evidence. Hendriks is going to freak out when he finds out. That means gaol time,' Ian said.

Murphy winked at him. 'Maybe! Maybe not. I wasn't going to tell you guys until I had it checked out but I think we need some good news, don't you think?'

'Okay, I'll bite,' Rick said, 'what's the significance of an empty watch box?'

'Well, for a start it's for a classic model Zenith El Primero, the first of its kind. Not your average watch. It was worth a fortune in its day and probably a lot more today. It's so rare they even have a unique serial number. Right here, see,' Murphy said. He pointed to a long number on the inner lid of the box.

'Okay, I'll bite again, what's the significance?'

'I've seen one before,' Murphy said.

'Yeah, so what?' Ian said.

'Firstly, I have to tell you what happened when Caruso came to see me that day. It was just after my Sarah died and I was pottering about in the garden, trying to get her roses to look, well, like they did when she was alive. I wasn't doing very well. Anyway, this scruffy middle-aged man is standing on the footpath staring at me. He was clutching a satchel to his chest like it was the only thing he owned in his life. Probably was too. His face seemed familiar. I asked him if he was looking for something and if he needed anything. I was just thinking he was lost. Then I recognised him. I asked him if he wanted to come inside.

'I've gotta say I just thought he was a junkie. I was determined not to believe anything he told me. I'd been down that road many times with unreliable witnesses. But when I looked at him, I could hear my wife saying "be kind". He came inside. We sat at my kitchen table. I made him a cup of tea, which he barely drank. He just kinda stared at it. He wouldn't let go of that satchel. He held it close to his chest. I asked him if he'd seen you guys lately but it seemed to bother him so I changed the subject. After a while and he hadn't said anything, I prompted him. I asked him why he had come to see me. He just said, "Are you still on the case?" I told him, "Always." That seemed to calm him just a little. He knew that neither of us could live without remembering, I guess. Then he told me he'd seen Whitey. I told him it was impossible as Whitey had died ten years ago. He was adamant. Said he'd seen him in a supermarket of all places. Said he looked right into his eyes and Whitey had smiled back at him and called him Gino,' Murphy said.

'What did he do?' asked Rick.

'Nothing. He said that Whitey simply walked past him and laughed. He swore to me that it was Whitey but of course, Caruso was pretty bad by then. He told me he was off the stuff but I dunno. I've seen a few junkies in my day and he looked like the classic case. I asked him if he was sure of what he'd seen. He said yes, positive. He said that it was time for him to come clean about what happened back then. Said he should have done more to help the children. I told him I don't know what he could have done but you know, when someone has it in their mind that they failed at something, it's hard to change their mind,' Murphy said.

'Did he say what Whitey looked like?'

'No. He just kept saying he'd seen him as if he knew I didn't believe him then he told me something I'd forgotten until the police found this.' He held up the box.

'An empty watch box?'

Murphy nodded. 'He told me that he stole something from Whitey.'

'What?' said both Ian and Rick simultaneously.

Murphy raised his eyebrows. 'He said he stole a few things but the most expensive was the watch. It seems that when Spike organised men for Whitey or the others in the hierarchy, they were meant to be paid by whoever they worked for. One of the jobs Whitey never paid him for made him so angry, he stole an item of value.'

Ian and Rick looked at each other and then at the empty watch box.

'He stole his watch?' Rick said.

'Yup, a Zenith El Primero,' Murphy said.

'Wait, how do you know it was the one in that box?' Ian said, still unconvinced.

'I don't know for sure.'

'How does that help us?' asked Ian.

'With its unique serial number.'

'Still don't know how that helps us? And he could have just been saying that. He wasn't very reliable.'

'Well, he showed me. He had it in his satchel. He took it out and showed me. It was wrapped in a white dust cloth. He'd looked after it very well. Normally, junkies don't have many possessions as they sell everything they have for drugs but there you are.'

'You saw it? You actually saw it?' Rick said.

'Silver and white, beautiful thing it was.'

'So, what you're saying is that the watch and this box might have the same serial number on it,' Ian said.

'Would it stand up in court?' Rick asked.

Ian scratched his chin. 'If we had the watch. And the box and watch match serial numbers then, yes, it would be circumstantial evidence linked to a prime suspect. I think it would work.' His face suddenly glowed like a man on the drink.

'I remember that day, when Whitey collared us at the flicks. He said that Caruso stole something from him. He was mad,' said Rick.

'I don't remember that as I was shitting my pants at the time,' said Ian.

They both looked at Murphy.

'Wait, wait, doesn't anybody see the elephant in the room? We don't have the watch. We only have the empty box,' Rick said.

Murphy smiled. 'But I might know where it is.'

More silence and more staring at the dead rose bush.

'Where?' Ian said.

'Well, the last I heard it was in the evidence room in the old Reserve Police Station,' Murphy said. 'The watch was found hidden away under floorboards when Caruso died.'

'I can just see another way you both can end up in the clink.'

Rick clapped his hands in anticipation. He was too far in to back out now.

'I'm just gunna say it again. Two old crocks in the clink. I can see that going down well. Is there no chance of asking your old detective friends for a look at the evidence? Legally, I mean?' Ian was covering all bases.

'Sorry, pal.' Murphy gritted his teeth.

Ian scoffed and gave a gruff laugh. 'It seems that Murphy here has run out of friends and chances. My mail from the office is that he's now known as a serial pest.'

Murphy did not try and rebuff Ian's accusation. 'You might be right. One of my last favours had been sending the purse to my ex-colleague for a quick DNA check. And Hendriks, well, he…' Murphy trailed off.

'He wants to lock you up,' Rick said. He was beginning to feel impotent. What they needed was a plan. He guessed breaking into Murphy's former office was at least something he could do.

'I'm in,' said Rick.

Ian sighed.

Three middle-aged men standing in the middle of Main Street at midnight sounded like a recipe for disaster. Rick got a flash of déjà vu as they stood waiting for clouds to cover the moon so they could gain access under darkness.

The plan was for Ian to stay up roadside to watch out for anyone approaching the old building. Murphy fished out a key ring with two keys. They looked rusty and ancient. One was for the front door the other for the evidence room.

Rick gave Ian the thumbs up as they entered the front door.

Murphy mumbled something under his breath.

'Did you say something?' Rick was full of nervous energy.

'Nah, just memories, that's all,' Murphy said as he passed Sergeant Willow's old office.

Rick followed him confidently. Murphy obviously knew the way. 'The door down to the basement is over here.'

Murphy stumbled as he reached for the doorknob. Rick figured it would be locked but Murphy shook his head. 'We never locked it.'

He twisted the knob and pulled it gently. It creaked and groaned as he dragged it open. He tried the light switch but there was nothing. He nodded back at Rick. From here, they would be able to use their torches as they were hidden from the street. The darkness was highlighted by two globes of light bobbing up and down as they descended the rickety stairs to the basement. Rick felt a chill crawl up his spine. He wondered if it felt weird for Joe. The tiny hairs on Rick's arms were pointing to the ceiling. No longer an office, it housed several old desks, cabinets and junk piled upon junk. The whole corner where Murphy's desk had once been was filled with cardboard boxes to the ceiling. A smell of dust mixed with sweat and old cigar smoke permeated every inch of the damp basement. This was where Murphy had his office for more than twenty years. You could hardly swing a cat in there now. Damp and dank was a good description.

'Here, help me move these boxes,' said Murphy.

The evidence room had been almost engulfed by a seemingly endless array of files. How many of these files had Murphy made? He'd had a long time to accumulate such crap.

People's lives. Crimes. Mistakes. Misunderstandings. Misdemeanours. Even murder. They were all here. What was to become of them? There was nobody left to read those files. Nobody had the time. This was the digital age. If it wasn't on a computer, it didn't get looked at. Murphy wondered how many cases could have been solved if somebody had the time to go through all this. These were Murphy's babies. Murphy's cold cases.

Rick lifted a couple of boxes and shuffled them over to make a space on the floor. Finally, the doorway was clear. Murphy stood in front of the evidence room and raised his key. Before, they hadn't broken too many laws but now this was serious stuff. Caught now they could spend time. That much he knew. They looked at each other and with a smug look, Murphy carefully put the key into the keyhole. It opened easily.

*

The evidence room was a mess. It was like a bomb hit it. Murphy knelt and tried to wedge open a cabinet. 'Ricky, give me some light over here,' he said.

Rick flashed his torch at the cabinet. Then his phone lit up with a message.

'Shit, it's Ian. Two guys are coming down. Quick, move it.'

Murphy scanned the office.

'Over here,' he said. An old office desk was upturned in the corner. Enough room for two to hide under. They made it just in time to see a wavering flashlight descending the stairs.

The two intruders stopped at the bottom of the stairs flashed their light around the room then proceeded to go into the evidence room. It had been a good thing that they hadn't tried to hide in there. They would have been caught red-handed.

A beam of light flashed on the intruder's face, then it was gone. It was at that moment that Rick realised that their two visitors were not friendlies. It was the beaten face of the man who had attacked him at the cottage.

The darkness was all-pervading. Rick couldn't see the end of his nose let alone Murphy, who was next to him. He could feel his presence so when the older man tensed Rick knew something was up.

'We've gotta get outta here,' whispered Murphy just loud enough for Rick to know that something was wrong. And not just the fact that they were hiding in a disused police station after gaining illegal entry hoping to steal some evidence. Not a very compelling defence if it came to that.

Rick could smell the petrol before he heard the two intruders splash it around.

'They're gunna torch the place.'

A blast of flame burst out of the evidence room and lit up the whole room. They were caught at the other end with the flames blocking their way up the stairs.

The two intruders bolted up the stairs and were gone in a flash.

This is how you get yourself killed, thought Rick as smoke began to billow in his face. Then the sirens started. Chaos and mayhem. Good name for a band, Rick thought, as they madly tried to clamber up the blackened stairs. He pushed Murphy upwards and when he wouldn't go any further, he pushed again.

'Come on, Joe, just another couple of steps.'

Truth be known, Murphy was not doing well. He stood on the steps and wobbled, trying to keep his balance. Rick could see his hands start to shake almost violently. Suddenly, Murphy stopped on the stairs. 'The satchel. I gotta get it.'

'Don't be stupid. You'll die down there.'

Murphy knew that Rick was probably right. He took a lung full of smoke and almost collapsed on the stairs. Rick paused. Hell, he would probably regret this. He turned and skipped down the stairs. He yelled at Murphy as he descended. 'Get yourself outta here,' he screamed as loud as he could.

*

The wind had picked up again. The flames brought the upper part of the building down first. Murphy and Ian stood side by side as the fire took proper hold of the building. The glass shattered and sprayed out onto the street as the fire trucks moved in far too late.

'Hey, you two.'

Ian spun around. 'Rick, you shit. You scared the living daylights outta us. How'd you get out?'

'Don't worry about that. We've gotta get outta here.'

'Shouldn't we stay and put a report in?' Ian said.

'And tell them what? That we were in there when the holocaust started?' Murphy said. 'Not bloody likely.' He took hold of Ian and Rick and pulled them back to the street. 'Just keep walking and if they yell, run.'

They walked briskly down the middle of Main Street, oblivious to the stares of passing people. Their clothes reeked of smoke, faces blackened by flying ash and debris.

'Rick, why the hell did you go back down? You could've been

killed,' Murphy said. He looked at Rick curiously, a look of triumph on his face. When he opened up his coat and showed him the satchel, Murphy smiled.

Had something gone right for a change?

Rick's face paled as he opened the satchel.

A colt 45 pistol was wrapped in an oily cloth but the watch was gone. In its place was a docket.

19

It Was the Day

VINCE'S CAFÉ WAS A haven for Rick. But after getting no sleep for the past two nights, he was showing visible signs of mental tiredness. He was ready to collapse. All he could do was wait for the strong coffee to kick in. It tasted bitter. Rick put another sugar in to sweeten the acidity. Vince was hovering. He was having a bad day too. The morning rain was keeping the punters away. It was a particularly cold spring so he opened the café early when he could. But when three aged men were your best customers, things weren't good.

Murphy sat near the door. Ian paced up and down and Rick sat in his favourite spot by the window.

'Okay, what have we got?' Murphy said. Ian was oblivious to the splashing of his coffee as he paced back and forward.

'Hey, don't spill my coffee or I'll kill ya.' Vince almost always overdramatised.

Ian stopped and sat next to Rick.

'More to the point, what haven't we got? Quite a lot I'd say,' said Ian.

'Are you sure that you recognised one of those guys?' Murphy said.

'I'm sure. He had my fist all over his face,' Rick said.

'Maybe we should go back to Hendriks. Maybe he'll believe us now,' Ian said who always believed that the law could and should protect.

'If we do that, he'll definitely lock us up. That place lit up like a candle.'

'He can't blame us for that, can he?' Ian said, knowing the answer was a definite yes.

They both looked at Murphy. He was quiet, sitting near the door staring out at the café's covered outdoor seating. Because of the weather, it was empty. The rain swept down under the awnings, filling up the dog's water bowl. Nothing fit. The two intruders, the gun that Caruso may or may not have used on himself, and the missing watch. Rick wondered about the sense of it all.

Silently, they watched the rain through the café door. The weather was turning eerie. Rick couldn't see the horizon. The sky had morphed into the colour of the ocean. It was one seamless canvas. Bluey grey. Even Gammy, the gull's gang leader, had disappeared. They could tell the mood of the beach. Murphy was thoughtful. Rick could see that something was bothering him.

'There was something else that day when Caruso came to see me. I wasn't going to mention it before. I was so sure he was lying about the whole thing. But I guess now that we have it, I should tell you. I saw the gun in his bag,' Murphy said. He patted the inside pocket of his duffle coat.

'You brought it with you? Shit, Murphy, why the hell d'you do that?' Ian leapt to his feet.

Murphy gave a laugh. 'It's perfectly safe. I still have my gun licence so I'm not breaking the law, technically.'

'Shit, it's not loaded, is it? I mean, goddam it, Murphy, if Hendriks finds you with that, then he will throw the book at you.'

'Calm down, Ian. Murphy knows what he's doing. You do, don't you?' Rick asked.

'Just keep it quiet. Molly will have kittens if she knows you're packing heat in here,' Vince said melodramatically.

'Vince,' Rick said, 'keep it down. You were saying you saw it in his bag?'

Murphy twitched as he walked. Rick could see that he was trying to stay calm too.

'Well, he was pretty out of it and the way he was holding the bag, it sorta flopped open. He didn't bat an eyelid. He just gripped the bag again and walked out the door. So, when it turned up alongside his body, I didn't give it a thought. I didn't have any reason not to think he took his own life. Pretty straightforward.'

'So, anything else you haven't told us?' Ian was a little peeved. Information was sometimes lacking from Murphy.

Murphy looked coy. 'It's obvious that Caruso hid the satchel before he died. If he thought that Whitey was alive, maybe he was scared and hid the watch too.'

'So, when they found the satchel under the floorboards was the watch there too?' Rick said.

Murphy nodded vaguely. 'They didn't tell me, I just assumed it was.'

'So, all we have is the gun and a docket,' Ian said.

'A gun and a pawn broking docket,' Murphy said with a small grin. 'We might be okay. I know the shop very well.'

They sat in Rick's Jag out the front of the Daily Pawn Broking House on Main Street several doors down from the now burnt-out police station. Murphy was in a pensive mood. And when he felt like that, he started talking.

'See that shop over the road? That's where Jody was last seen. Apparently, she went into the deli to buy some pies and pasties. The old biddy who runs the shop remembers her because she paid with a twenty-dollar note. "Fancy a twelve-year-old girl having that amount of money," she told the detective when she was being interviewed. The detective did ask her whether she said anything to the girl about the money. She said she didn't.'

Murphy stared at his notebook then continued.

'And I was just across the road. Sometimes I think about her being so close. In my dreams sometimes, I cross that road to get to her but every time a car cuts me off before I can cross. I get to the door of the deli and she's disappeared into the back of a car. I can only watch as it speeds away down the road.'

'That's some dream,' Ian said.

'Frustrating. If only I'd done something then, you know, somehow stopped them from leaving, maybe…' Murphy paused.

'That maybe they'd be alive?' Rick looked at Murphy.

Murphy's hand was shaking wildly. Murphy saw Rick looking and forced it to stop. 'I can do that sometimes. I can stop it.'

Rick knew Murphy didn't like talking about it. Probably an age thing. Maybe he thought that if he ignored it long enough it'd go away, Rick surmised. No chance.

'I think the same thing. I saw her on that day a couple of times. We talked, and we shared a ride on the carousel. What if, I ask myself.'

'You were a kid. I was a police officer. It's different.'

'You were only a few years older than us. Still young, Joe. Everything looks straightforward in hindsight. The fact of the matter is that we couldn't have done much. If it weren't those kids he took, it would have been someone else's. They're monsters and monsters don't stop,' Ian said.

'You're right, that's why it's important we do something now,' said Murphy. It was not the first time he told himself that.

Rick looked at the ex-detective and his shaky hands.

'We can do anything,' Rick said with reservation. Could a semi-retired lawyer, an old crock of a muso and a fully retired policeman, do it?

'*The proof is in the pudding,*' his dad had once said.

'What the hell does that mean, Dad? It makes no sense,' Rick had responded.

'*You'll find out one day.*'

This had been his father's answer to pretty well everything.

*

The line at the pawn shop moved slowly. Rick sweated profusely. He did that when he was under stress. And he was now. He wasn't breaking the law? Technical point. Of course, he was in possession of a stolen item, albeit a small piece of paper, but Rick knew the law. Semantics, that's all it was. That made him sweat even more than usual.

'Next, come on. I ain't got all day,' said the pawnbroker.

The man looked at the receipt and then back at Rick.

'This ain't yours. Another fella came in with this. What are you doing with it? I 'member all my customers.' He said it with a smirk.

Rick hesitated; he was not expecting this.

'It's a friend's.'

'Gotta show some ID,' he said loudly.

He looked out the window. A man in a suit was standing, peering in at him through the window. Rick's phone chimed. He had a message. He looked down at it.

GET OUT NOW.

The hairs on the back of his neck stood up in defiance. Too late. He'd have to bluff his way out. He forced himself not to look out the window. The door creaked open. A little bell rang. This was old school. Who had a bell to announce customers anymore?

He flashed his driver's licence at the shopkeeper. He barely glanced at it before shrugging his shoulders and reaching down below the counter. Rick could sense the presence of the man right behind him. He dared not look.

'That'd be ten dollars,' said the pawnbroker.

'Ten dollars? But the thing's worth a lot more than that, surely.'

'Nup, pretty common watch. Besides, he only wanted ten dollars. So that's what I gave him,' said the pawnbroker with a slight menace.

Rick's hackles were rising.

'So, in case he didn't come back, you'd get the rest,' Rick said, sensing a stitch-up.

'Have'ta keep it for six months after the customer doesn't show. Runs out tomorrow, guess I missed out this time. Ah, well, that's the nature of this business. Ten bucks, thanks.'

Rick handed over a crisp ten-dollar bill. He didn't want to use his credit card. Leave no trace.

The man handed him a paper bag. He opened it and peered inside. An old watch wrapped in tissue paper.

He looked back at the pawnbroker. He was about to say something when the shopkeeper did an unusual thing. He winked at him.

It all happened suddenly after that. The man behind him stepped up to the counter.

'I'll take that. This was stolen from our evidence room a while back. The person we suspected was Gino Caruso.' He flashed a police ID at Rick who was speechless. He stood like the proverbial shag on a rock holding a brown paper bag that contained a crappy old watch that had nothing to do with anyone. He handed it over.

'He was a friend of mine, Officer. I was also his lawyer. His family entrusted me with his estate,' Rick said, thinking on his feet.

'Estate, eh? He was a junkie. He had no estate,' said the policeman.

'Nonetheless, they gave me this receipt, which I was duty-bound to redeem.'

'Funny about that. A receipt went missing from the evidence room. I don't suppose you know anything about that?' said the cop.

'Don't know what you're talking about. My client left it to me,' lied Rick.

'It's evidence.'

'Evidence in what?'

The cop sneered at him, took the bag and walked out. 'Thanks for your cooperation.'

*

'You could have given me more notice. I had to give it to him,' Rick said, opening the back door of his Jag. He slipped in.

'Good, it might keep him off our backs for a while,' Murphy said.

'You knew? You bloody well knew he was gunna come, didn't you?'

'I suspected. That's why I got you to go in. Besides, that guy ain't a cop.'

'How do you know?' Rick said. 'Tell me, do you know something?'

For a moment Rick thought Murphy was going to open up but, in the end, all he did was give a little fake cough and try to explain.

'Listen, it doesn't matter who the guy is. Somehow, whoever is behind all this found out about the watch. I guess he realises that they made a mistake leaving the box behind in the cottage. He would have been ropable about that. He won't like making a mistake like that,' Murphy said.

'But I had to give him the watch. Now he's got it,' Rick said, confused.

Murphy grinned. 'Does he? Come, both of you.' He arched a finger at them.

They re-entered the shop. This time, they were the only ones inside. The beaming face of the pawnbroker surprised them both.

'Joe, you old scum bag. See what I do for you?' said the pawnbroker.

'Stan, thanks a lot, pal. I owe you one.'

Stan held another brown paper bag in his hand.

The watch.

'He's my brother-in-law. Part of the family. Known him for thirty years. He married my sister,' Murphy said in explanation to the others. 'When I realised the docket name, I gave him a call and explained the situation.'

'So, you expected someone to be here. You know to get the watch?' Ian said.

'Well, not really. Sorry, Rick, but I still think that Whitey is dead and buried. But there is someone out there who doesn't want us to dig any deeper.'

'You mean the guy who attacked Rick in the cottage?'

Murphy nodded.

'He'll be pissed when he finds he's got the wrong watch,' Ian said with a grin. 'I'd like to see his face.'

Murphy smiled, looked in the bag then gave the thumbs up to Ian and Rick.

*

Back in the safety of Vince's café, Murphy took out the empty watch box and held it in his hands. This time, his hands were still. He handed it to Ian and pulled out his notebook. Rick held the watch.

'Okay,' he began, 'serial number on the box is EL 71377.'

They both looked at Rick.

'Here goes,' Rick said, unwrapping the watch. He carefully took it between his fingers and turned it over.

'You've got to take the back plate off and the serial number should be right by the maker's name, but be careful to hold it by the cloth,' said Murphy.

Rick was all thumbs as he tried to pry the cover off. Eventually, he succeeded.

'This is hard to read, my eyes aren't good. Let me see,' Rick said, squinting as he held the silver and white watch up to his eye. 'E… L… seven… one – I think it's a one – three… seven… seven.' He stopped and looked at Murphy.

'Shit, spot-on,' Ian said. 'Of all the luck that hasn't gone our way, this is the first goddamned thing that has.'

They stood and looked at the watch in awe. Murphy carefully took it, wrapped it back up in the cloth then wrapped its box in another piece of cloth.

'We need to keep them separate still because if this was Whitey's watch and Caruso did steal it from him then we may have some chance to recover DNA from it, also from the box.'

'So, it still doesn't prove I'm right about Whitey then.'

'Ricky, my friend. Every little piece of positive info we get is a blessing. It's something we didn't have all those years ago. We need to get this to my DNA guy.'

'The same guy who's got the purse?'

'The very same. And with a bit of luck, they'll both come back with some positive hits on them.'

In the background, Vince turned up the jukebox.

'You guys want another coffee? Who's paying? I'm trying to run a business here. I need some paying customers,' said Vince, picking up the three empty mugs.

'So, the question is. Do we go to Hendriks with this?' Ian yelled over the jukebox.

*

Rick struggled to sleep that night. With all the thoughts madly thrashing around in his brain, he thought he would never get to sleep. He kept thinking of Jody. When he managed to close his eyes, her green eyes would invade his mind. She wouldn't budge. She kept on saying over and over, 'I'm scared, Rick.' He wasn't sure whether she had ever called him by that name. Eric or Rick, it didn't matter. He knew hers. Then her face would morph into the girl he had seen on the computer screen in Whitey's cottage. Then it would shift back to the three children. Jody, Hilda and little Peter. Peter would always interject with, 'Come on, sis, hurry up. He's taking us to a castle.'

He got up and sat at the end of his bed. He had to do that sometimes. The neurologist told him that it was to do with the imbalance of brain fluid in his ventricles. 'The trickle-down effect,' he called it. 'Your brain fluid acts on gravity,' the neurologist had said. 'Lying flat for a length of time is not good for you.' The trouble was you needed to lie down flat to sleep. Not good for the equilibrium of his brain.

His phone began to rumble. He looked at the hotel clock by his bedside. It read, in bright LEDs, four a.m.

Who the hell was ringing him at four a.m.?

He was tempted to not answer but the lure of the ringtone had him reaching for his phone. The number did not show. Unlisted. Normally he didn't answer these as they were mainly scammers or bankers. Either one, he didn't particularly want to talk to. He answered it anyway.

'For a moment, I thought I would have to leave a message,' said the strangely familiar voice.

'How did you get my number?'

'Ah, my boy. Do you think that you're the only one in this world with friends? I too have my ways.'

Whitey. Rick froze. Then he remembered his dream. 'I'm going to find you and when I do...' He stopped. Murphy would have had good advice in a situation like this. He couldn't think of it at that moment. He could feel his rage grow. 'The girl on the screen. What have you done with her?'

'Who says I've done anything with her? But mind you, she does remind me of someone else, though. Do you remember, Eric? Do you remember her sister and little brother? I'd almost forgotten his name. Little Peter, wasn't it? I remember you and your little friends back then. You were all so small, so little, so... deliciously sweet.'

'You can't hide forever. I'll find you,' Rick said, his voice tensing up.

'What? You find me? You and that old detective. I've got to tell you, Eric, that I'm afraid he's not going to make it, with his wife dying and the fact that he's probably going to be a vegetable soon. Do you see how his hands shake? His mind is going too. Do you notice him making mistakes? His former colleagues now think he's a liability. Nobody trusts him anymore. And as for that lawyer friend of yours, he has a nice family, doesn't he? I mean, his children are older than I normally like but I could make an exception, don't you think? And the little trick you pulled this afternoon with the watch. Do you think it matters? No one will believe you that it was mine. They think, well, I guess they all think that I'm dead. Fancy that.'

'We can get it checked for DNA you scum bag. Once we prove

it's yours, you'll be toast.' As soon as Rick said it, he regretted it. Why did he give that information up?

Rick hung up.

He tried ringing Joe. It was strange the things you recalled when stressed.

Memories flooded back to him like it was yesterday.

20

Summer Madness
and the Basement

It was a stinker of a summer. It was the year after the children disappeared. If you stood and looked out at the ocean, you could see the heat waves. Bulging ripples of heat. The only way to survive was under the water.

Eric, Ian and Caruso were hanging on by a thread. Being thirteen was neither here nor there. Not quite children and not quite adults. There were times when all Eric wanted to do was to sit in his bedroom and play the guitar he got for his twelfth birthday. It was hot there too but still he needed to be pushed to leave his beloved guitar.

'Come on, Eric, you gotta get outa this place. It's stinkin' hot in here.' Ian flopped down on Eric's bed.

They were changing. Eric had noticed it first. Caruso was sullener. Ian more authoritative and he? Had he changed too? He thought of Sally, the girl he met on the beach. His face flushed. Yes, he was changing too.

'Come on, can't be playing with that all day. Get some sun, my boy.' Ian had always used voices to change it up. He was a good mimic. In his dreams, Ian had visions of being a comedian.

'You'd be shit at it.' Eric was adamant.

'Nah, I'd be a legend. I'd be on TV. You'll see, one day you'll be stinkin' it up and watching TV with your six kids and ugly wife. You'll see me on Laugh-In. I'll be the famous one and you and Caruso can all go to hell.'

'Where is Caruso anyway?' asked Eric. They were halfway to

217

the beach. Nero had run on ahead. His tongue nearly reached the ground, it was so hot.

'Meeting us down at the deli. Had to do something for Spike this morning. Told me not to wait he would catch up.'

The conversation of them not trusting Spike was an old one. For a second, Eric thought that Ian was going to bring it up again. He didn't. Maybe he knew that it was the surest thing to piss him off. The endless talk and babble of doing the right thing was starting to annoy him. He knew that Ian was one of those characters they would call a 'goody two shoes,' but that too was old news. Ian had long since learnt to keep his mouth shut.

If this was going to be their last summer together then he wanted it to be friendly. Yes, they had discussed it. On his fourteenth birthday, Ian's parents were sending him away to board with a school so exclusive that Prince Charles himself had gone to it. It meant that they would be separated. Sad but true.

'You're a pussy. No one goes to boarding school anymore,' had been Caruso's predictable response.

And so, this year was to be the last. For some reason, Rick knew that once Ian went off, both he and Caruso would do the same. It was the end for them all. Ian had his school, he had his guitar and Caruso? Well, he had his gang.

They walked to the reserve. There was no sign of Caruso at the deli or on the beach. You needed money down at the reserve. Ian almost always had money. He pulled out a dollar bill and waved it at Eric.

'I'll take that.' Caruso appeared out of nowhere and plucked the brand-new crisp bill out of Ian's hands.

'Where the hell did you come from and give me my damn money back, you cretin.'

'Ah, I'm a cretin, eh. Hey, Eric, what's a cretin? Someone smart?' said Caruso.

Eric looked at his friend to see if he was serious. He was.

'Yeah, Caruso, a cretin's a good thing. Someone smart.'

'I'm a cretin! You learn sumthin' new every day. I'M A CRETIN.' Loud and proud. That was Caruso.

Although they were only a short distance from their beach, Eric could tell the difference. The air somehow seemed heavier down here. Of course, that was nonsense. How could the air be different? And he sweated more here, always had. This jetty was different too. It was higher and better built than theirs. Made of concrete and cement instead of tarred timbers. Although kids still jumped from the end of the jetty into the cool waters it just wasn't the same.

'So, you brought your little friends today. Good. They'll be helpful,' said Spike.

Every time Spike smiled, it showed a line of crooked yellow teeth. He had been the butt of so many jokes about them, he was hesitant to smile, which made it look creepier when he did.

Caruso turned to his friends. He seemed reluctant to include them. He walked over to Spike and whispered into his ear. Eric and Ian could only look on as this exchange took place. Spike got angry and swiped Caruso across the face. He stumbled backwards, holding his now red cheek.

'You'll do as you're told.'

There was no getting away from it when Spike wanted something done. You'd better just do it.

'It's alright, Caruso, we'll go with you.' Ian put a hand on his friend's shoulder. Then Caruso did something he probably would regret later on. He punched Ian in the face.

Ian rocked backwards and landed on the ground. This made Spike laugh uproariously. Caruso stood over his friend and spat next to him.

'You'll do as you're told, scum bag,' Caruso yelled at Ian.

Eric couldn't move. This was so unlike Caruso. He was hesitant to do anything.

'Caruso, what the hell?'

'Keep outta this, Eric. This is between me and scum bag.'

This was the first time any of them had raised a fist in anger against each other. It seemed so alien.

Spike looked down at Ian who was squirming on the ground. He turned to speak with another of his punks. Ian made a move to get up.

'Stay down, ya idiot.' Caruso's face was red with shame. Eric could see that he was almost crying. 'Stay down...'

Suddenly, Eric got it. He was putting on a show for Spike. He didn't want either Ian or Eric to go with him on whatever chore he had designed for them all.

'What is it, Caruso?' Eric made sure that Spike couldn't hear their exchange.

'You don't wanna know,' whispered Caruso.

Eric looked up. Whitey was standing behind Spike with a smirk on his face.

*

'Every word! You need to tell me every word he said,' Murphy said in a flurry of questions. Rick had driven to Murphy's house in a state of near panic. Ian was going to meet them there as soon as he could get away. He held back on telling Murphy what Whitey had said about Ian's family. He now wondered whether he'd done the right thing.

Murphy looked kind of ridiculous in his striped pyjamas but Rick was in no mood to crack any type of joke. Sitting together in Murphy's snug kitchen, they waited for Ian to arrive. Murphy stood by the old blue-and-white wood fire stove that he and Sarah had loved so much during her life. He watched the teapot boil; it started to whistle.

'Listen, I didn't tell you before but he has threatened Ian and his family. I have to tell him.'

Rick's hands started to tremble with delayed panic. Murphy put a hand on his shoulder to steady him. 'Tell me from the start, everything.'

Rick tended to ramble on when he had no focus. Whitey had spooked him, again. Murphy made him go back every time he got lost in his story. Repeat, repeat, seemed to be Murphy's motto. If Rick had any doubts that Murphy believed him about Whitey, he certainly wasn't showing it.

Ian arrived. Angry about his lack of sleep but anxious for Rick. He listened as he told him the story of the phone call. When it got to the part about Whitey threatening Ian's family, they were all on tenterhooks. Rick didn't want to lessen the threat in any way but to scare his friend like that, well, he couldn't do it.

What Rick wanted to say was, 'What could he possibly do to them?' but he knew that was a stupid question. A threat was a threat, especially where his family was involved. Ian listened calmly.

When Rick was finally finished, Ian looked his friend in the eye.

'Are you sure it was Whitey? I mean, he could have been someone pretending to be him. You know, to scare the bejesus out of us.'

'Ian, trust me, it was him. He's alive and he's out there. He knows we're onto him. He knew we had his watch, for Christ's sake,' Rick said desperately. If these guys didn't believe him then who would?

'He knows about the watch? How is that possible?'

Murphy looked a little pensive. Rick's story was convincing but there was something wrong with it, something not quite right.

'The guy who came into the pawn shop. I think I know who he is,' Murphy said finally.

'Who is he?' Rick managed to get out before Ian exploded.

'You lied before. You goddamned lied when Rick asked you straight out if you knew the guy,' Ian roared.

'Had to be sure, no doubts.'

'And are you sure now?'

Murphy's face went pale. 'He looked like a guy we arrested in the eighties for laundering money. Back in his younger days, he worked with Spike.'

'So, there's your connection to Whitey. If you worked for Spike, you worked for Whitey.'

Ian sat down and contemplated all he had been told. He started slowly.

'When Caruso told Murphy that he'd seen Whitey, I didn't believe it. I also thought that you may have hit your head too, Rick, but if you tell me that he's alive then I have to believe you and if he is alive then we have to protect our families. We can't do it by ourselves. We are all in danger, even Murphy here. What I do know is that we are too old for this shit. We need to convince Hendriks that he's real. If we don't, well, I don't want to think what could happen.'

For a second, Rick thought that Murphy would talk them down even if he wasn't quite convinced of Whitey's sudden health.

'One more thing,' Rick said. He looked embarrassed now. He thought about how he would tell them both. In the end, he just blurted it out. 'When he said that he knew about the watch, I blurted out that we were getting it checked for DNA. I was just being a smart arse. I should have kept my mouth shut.'

He looked at Ian then at Murphy. They were silent. Then Ian came to his rescue.

'Listen, Rick, you haven't told him anything he doesn't already know. As soon as he saw the old watch in its place, he knew we had the original and that we would send it for testing.'

'So, he knows, big deal,' Murphy said.

'We go to Hendriks now! Agreed?' Ian said.

They both looked at Murphy.

'Agreed,' he said with a sigh.

*

Another early morning visit to CID had not been on their agenda but as they pulled up in the Jag, they could see Hendriks pulling into the carpark of HQ. Another early morning phone call piped through to him by the duty sergeant was not something he looked forward to. Especially from Joe Murphy. He reluctantly agreed to meet with them in his office.

Hendriks sat quietly while Rick went through the story for the third time. He drummed his fingers on his table occasionally but generally, he sat in silence. It was when Rick mentioned the threat to Ian's family that he leaned forward and started taking a few notes. He scratched something then put his hand up to stop Rick mid-sentence. He picked up his phone and waited until it was answered. He asked the person to come into his office immediately.

Murphy started to talk but Hendriks put his hand up to stop him.

They waited in silence. Two minutes later, a man dressed impeccably in a grey business suit entered carrying a briefcase. He sat down and flipped open his case. He pulled a file from it and then looked at Hendriks. He nodded and the man began to speak.

'Detective Graham Parsons,' he announced to the room. 'At four p.m. on the fifteenth of July, I attended the premises of 14

Glenroy Parade, Winston to interview the director of the family trust that owns, amongst many other residences, factories and buildings in the CBD, the residence known as the Hilltop Retreat. Once a private address of the Rutherglen family, it is now owned by a trust and has among its managers a residence manager and a grounds manager. The interview was agreed to by the managing director and has been made free of any liability that might arise from my investigation. The interview was brought about by the accusations of two individuals, one Eric Donahue and one Joseph P. Murphy, a one-time detective located at the Reserve Police Station CID department.'

Rick glanced at Murphy. He had a bad feeling in his gut about this.

'Due to the nature of this report, the name of the managing director has been redacted, meaning it is not for public consumption. In my capacity as senior investigations officer, I have to uphold the sworn testimony of interviewees. It was given on oath and sworn before a judge of the Supreme Court. It goes as follows.

'"The Hilltop Retreat was owned by the Rutherglen family but since the death ten years ago of its sole heir Mr Anthony Rutherglen, it was bequeathed to the state. With the death of Mr Rutherglen, all assets have been held in the family trust. This continued rumour and innuendo of Mr Rutherglen is neither warranted nor legal. He was not charged with any crime during his lifetime and now with his death, he is being smeared by these two individuals. It should stop now. We, therefore, ask the commissioner to place an AVO on the two mentioned individuals and ask that they should be arrested and charged with criminal trespass."'

When he finished, he put his file back in his briefcase locked it, stood and exited Hendriks office.

Hendriks sat, drumming his fingers on his desk.

'You don't believe that crap, do you, John?' Murphy said.

Hendriks sighed deeply. 'That's not all.' He opened another file on his desk. 'It seems that three men, one middle-aged'—he glared at Murphy—'were seen leaving the site of a fire that consumed most of the old Reserve Police Station. I assume that's your old office, Murphy. Care to enlighten me on that score? Any of you.'

Noise from the busy office behind Hendriks filtered through. The soft constant rattle of a computer keyboard and the occasional mobile ringtone made it abundantly clear there was a lot going on there. Hendriks finished drumming his fingers on the desk.

'Okay, this is what's going to happen. You and you.' Hendriks pointed to Rick and Ian. 'Will leave here together and have nothing to do with this person.' He pointed at Murphy. 'Or else I will activate the AVO against you and toss you in gaol. Do I have your full co-operation?'

'What about my family?'

Hendriks paused for a second then picked up his phone again. He asked for a car and two constables.

'If you believe a threat has been made against your family, I am duty-bound to make sure all is secure. I will despatch a car to your home. Two of my men will be outside your house for their shift,' said Hendriks.

'For how long?' Ian asked.

'Until I find out if the threat is legitimate.'

Hendriks drummed his fingers a bit longer.

'You can both go now.' Hendriks pointed at Rick and Ian. 'I haven't finished with you, Murphy. There are a few matters I need to speak with you before you can go anywhere,' he said.

'He's under arrest?' Rick said.

Hendriks paused as if considering the question.

'It's okay, Rick, the detective and I have a few matters to discuss. No need to worry,' Murphy said.

*

Rick kept glancing at Ian in the driver's seat of his Prius.

'After all, we've been through, Ian, I didn't think it would involve your family. I'm sorry, man,' Rick said, finally breaking the ice.

'I don't understand. If it is Whitey, how the hell does he pretend to die ten years ago and then suddenly bob up again? It doesn't make any sense.' Ian looked across at Rick. 'You know that *they* don't believe you about Whitey.'

'Who are *they*?'

'Well, Hendriks for starters, then there's Joe.' Ian glanced at his friend.

'And you. You still don't believe me either.'

Ian cleared his voice. 'Listen, there was a time when the three of us were inseparable. You, me and Caruso. I would have done anything for you guys. You were my friends. My only friends. I haven't had many since those days. I want to believe you, but it seems like a giant hoax. Somebody's out there playing us. You know I don't blame you, Rick. But if anyone lays a hand on one of my kids…'

Ian finished by going a shade of red.

'If you need me to come around and explain this to your wife then I will.'

'No need. I told her on the phone that this was a police matter and that they received a threat because of something that happened in the chambers. Hendriks backed me up. He told her it was just a precaution. Anyway, I'm more worried about you, Rick. This idiot now knows where you're staying and he's got your phone number. Maybe you should go and stay with your family on the coast. Get out of the way for a while.'

Rick shook his head. 'No way. I need to find him, Ian. If he's got a girl somewhere I'm her only hope.'

'Don't be going around playing hero, Rick. Heroes sometimes turn up dead. And I want you to promise that you'll do as Hendriks says and not contact Joe. I know he's your friend now but you have to admit he's done some stupid things. I mean, breaking into a federal court judge's office? What kinda stupid shit is that?'

The Prius came to a halt in the only parking bay they could find. Rick gazed out the window at the beach. He exhaled slowly. It wasn't that he couldn't make that promise, he just wanted to keep his options open.

'Can't stay, pally. Some of us have to work.'

Rick watched as Ian drove off. He sat in his favourite bench and tried to make sense of it all.

The sun was going down on another day. This one had been particularly difficult. He was no closer to finding Whitey than before. And even though they had retrieved the watch Caruso stole from Whitey, in the end, it would not prove that he had taken the children and murdered them. It was stretching the imagination to prove to the police he was still alive. All they had was his word. And the fact that he had only spoken with him over the computer and his phone and not in person made it all the more difficult to prove. It was like Whitey was taunting him. Rick knew that he had the trust of Joe and Ian but that wasn't enough for him; he had to find this guy. Then there was the girl. Who was she? Had he taken her yet? Something else was bothering him about that image. He knew it wasn't Jody but why was it so familiar to him? There was only one thing to do. Find him then find the girl.

Simple? Not so simple. He found himself on his favourite bench facing the sea.

'Can I sit?' The voice came from behind but Rick knew who it was.

'Shit, Joe, if Hendriks finds out he'll have kittens,' Rick said instinctively. Still, he was glad to see the former detective.

Murphy grinned.

'Ah, he'll be fine. Besides, we're on a roll. We're almost there. Another couple of breakthroughs and we'll find this son of a bitch.'

The way he said it gave Rick a little hope. He smiled back. 'Better move inside before the spies see us.'

They went to enter Vince's café. It was closed so Rick took out a key from his pocket and held it up.

'Courtesy of Molly and Vince. They said it was the least they could do for their best customers.'

They took a seat at the back of the café and Rick made them both cups of tea.

'So, what do we do now?'

'Got some news,' said Murphy.

'Hope it's good news. We could do with some.'

The look on Murphy's face told him it probably wasn't.

'Vic Tangini is dead,' Murphy said, taking a sip of his tea.

Rick looked at Joe stunned for a moment. 'Dead, how?'

'Killed last night. Someone made it look like suicide. Seem familiar to you?'

'Caruso.'

'It had all the hallmarks of your classic inside job. The warden is still calling it suicide but I think Hendriks thinks otherwise.'

'Hendriks told you?' Rick said, looking quite amazed.

Murphy nodded. 'That's why he kept me back after class, so to speak. He wanted to know what we had talked about or, more to the point, what you had discussed with Tangini,' Murphy said.

'And did you tell him?'

'I told him that Vic said the cottage was where Whitey took the children and that's why you went there.'

'Did he believe that?'

'Not sure. Probably not.'

'So, you think that someone got to him in gaol,' Rick said, whistling through his teeth.

'There are any number of men in gaol that would kill at the drop of a hat. It's not uncommon, but I would say, yes.'

'So why did Hendriks tell you? Does he believe us now?'

'I wouldn't say that for sure but he's playing both sides. He's got his bosses over him telling him to go hard on me but if we're useful to him, he'll want us to stay in the game.'

'So, are we still in the game?'

'You bet we are. But that's not the reason I'm here. Caruso said something else the day he came around to my place. At first, we just talked about you guys. I think it was the one thing that kept him going. You and Ian. He told me about the time when Spike was looking to recruit a few kids to do some work for Whitey. Caruso told me he pretended to beat up Ian just to show Spike that you guys weren't tough enough. He regretted beating up on Ian. He said that it sometimes came back to haunt him like all the other stuff he had to do for Spike and Whitey.

'He told me that he was driven by Whitey to a house somewhere in the north. He said it looked like a family home, but inside, it wasn't quite homely. There was some messed up stuff happening in there. Chains bolted to the wall in the main bedroom. And it stank. Like they butchered a whole herd of cattle in there. Most of the rooms in the back were lined with plastic, walls, floor and ceiling. It was a sweatbox. The cellar was small. Whitey told them to dig under the floorboards and make everything bigger. They spent days down there, digging out the basement. Caruso thought he was just using them as cheap labour and that it was just a money-saving thing. Get kids to provide labour but he changed his mind. He thought that Whitey wanted to involve them so they would shut up. Caruso did say something strange though. I was asking him about the layout of the house and he said that I should look for the extra room. That was the room that seemed strange to him. When I asked him where it was; he just shrugged and said, "Look where you least expect a room to be." I did ask Caruso whether he dug up anything. And he said back to me, as quick as you like, that he hadn't dug up any bodies if that's what I was asking. And so, I guess I dismissed it,' Murphy said. 'To be honest, I didn't believe anything about the story.'

'You think it was the room I saw on the security camera.'

'It crossed my mind. It makes sense he would have a remote viewing area he could use anytime he wanted.'

'He gave you the address?'

'He gave me a suburb. I handed all the information over to CID. I was doing things by the book. I asked Hendriks about it and he said that although they did send out a team, they didn't find the house.'

'It sounds to me they didn't try very hard.'

'I don't blame them though. They get inundated with jumbled bits of information, which generally never end up working out. They tried looking but when they didn't succeed, they gave up. Simple as that. I might have done the same thing, given the information. But now it's different. He told us he took them to other places. This house might be the break we're looking for.'

'But we have no idea where it is. Both Caruso and Vic are dead and I guess Bill Santino is in some mental institution somewhere,' said Rick.

'It might be easier to find than all that.'

'How?'

'Well, if we had someone who could find the address through some court documents, then maybe we would have a chance. It might be the thing a QC could find.'

'Ian?'

'Ian,' Murphy said.

'You think that he moved the bodies again, don't you?'

'Don't get me wrong. If it is Whitey, he'd have moved them on when there was a whiff of police action,' Murphy said, 'but these kinds of sick people need a trophy.'

It took a moment to sink in. Suddenly, Rick looked Joe in the eye. 'So, the bodies might still be at the house?'

Murphy grinned conspiratorially. 'That's why we need someone to look into the state privy council to sneak a look at the titles.'

'So, you believe me about Whitey. Ian said that you didn't. He said that everyone thinks it's a copycat.'

'I have to admit that I thought it was a long shot that Whitey was still alive. I mean, I went to the guy's funeral. But there's something else,' Murphy said quietly. 'My guy came back with the goods. It was Jody's blood on the purse. And, the real kicker, the DNA on the watch matched one Anthony Rutherglen, aka Whitey.'

'We've got proof?' Rick said as if not quite believing it.

Murphy nodded then grinned.

'We might just have.'

21

P. S. ELLIOTT

RICK TOSSED AND TURNED in his sleep. Again and again, the face of Jody kept coming at him. One moment they were riding the carousel, the next they were standing hand-in-hand on the rotunda, staring out into a blazing sun. Had it been that hot? It must have been. He tried to wipe the sweat from his eyes. They stung. A man approached. She began to pull away from him, crying as she went. Then the scene turned to the cottage. He was standing next to the huge elm tree. He saw them arrive. The boy was complaining about being hot. He wanted to jump in the pond but Jody was telling him that he would drown.

'You can't swim, Peter,' she said. She tried calming him but the wailing just got louder.

'Don't wanna go in that place,' the boy wailed.

'But I have chocolate inside,' said a voice that Eric recognised straight away.

'Don't want any chocolate. I don't like this place. It's dark.'

Rick saw Jody squat down and take her younger brother by the shoulders. He could hear everything she said.

'Peter, I promise you that later we will go back to the beach and have a swim. Can you be patient just for now?'

Rick wanted to yell out that it wasn't safe. He wanted to yell out that Peter was right. It was dark. He wanted to yell not to go into the Hansel and Gretel cottage.

That was the trouble with nightmares. They made you immobile and restricted. Suddenly, the scene shifted again and Rick could see inside the mansion. He saw a man. The man he had seen at the beach that day. Not Whitey, another man. He saw that Rick was staring at him and he slammed the side door shut.

Rick woke with a start.

His phone was ringing again. It was four a.m. He let it ring.

*

Rick's face was haggard due to the lack of sleep and the nightmares when he finally did get a little sleep.

'You look like shit, Rick.' Ian prided himself on being honest.

Rick ignored the barb. 'Thanks for coming today. I wasn't sure you'd come, your family…'

'Are well protected. Anyway, why wouldn't I come? You're my best mate. Or you were back then, anyway,' Ian said, juggling two containers of takeaway coffee from Vince's.

'You were mine too.'

'Are you sure? I always thought you and Caruso were pretty tight.'

'We were, but I always felt a kind of distance with him. I never really knew where I stood, I guess.'

Ian looked to the sea. He sat down next to Rick on the bench.

'Is your family okay?' asked Rick.

Ian sipped his coffee.

'Fine, the missus kicked me out this morning, she said I was being too morbid around the house. She told me to go and play with my friends. I guess she's surprised that I have any,' Ian said. He took a long sip of coffee and shuddered. 'I'm off sugar. This tastes like tar.' He screwed up his face.

'My phone rang again last night.'

'Shit, Rick, did you pick up?' Ian said, dribbling a pool of coffee over his nice white shirt. 'Shit,' he said again.

'Didn't pick up. It got me thinking though. He's worried. He's worried that we tricked him about the watch. He knows we're onto him. We're close and he doesn't like it. He's trying to bully me.'

'But we're not close, Rick. We know next to nothing.'

'Yes, but he doesn't know that. That's why he's calling me. He's panicking. I can feel it.'

'So, what did you do?'

'I called Murphy.'

'Shit, Rick, I thought Hendriks told you to keep away from him.'

'Nah, he doesn't mean that. Hendriks told Joe about Vic getting killed in gaol. He doesn't believe it as much as I don't believe Caruso killed himself.'

'But we don't know that was Whitey. It might have been suicide.'

Rick looked at him. 'You and I both know it wasn't suicide.'

'Maybe, but seriously do you think Hendriks has changed his mind about Joe? Are you sure Joe wasn't bullshitting you? He can do that, you know. Joe Murphy is the biggest bullshitter that I have ever had the misfortune to know.'

'Well, I guess you can ask him that yourself. He's over the road waiting for me to give him the all-clear.'

Rick stuck his hand up in the air. A figure in a long black trench coat waved back at him from the front bar of the Seaside Hotel. Again, all that Ian could say was, 'Shit!'

They watched as Murphy dodged a couple of cars crossing the road.

'Okay, I have news for the both of you,' was the first thing he said as he slid his body onto the remaining part of the bench chair. He took out his phone and glanced down at it. He looked up and grinned at them.

'They're brothers.' Murphy put his phone away and took out

his notebook. He leapt to his feet as if he had to move. He leaned on the railings, looking down onto the beach.

'Who are brothers?' Ian said, still a little stunned at Joe's presence. He stared at Rick who looked like he'd just had heart palpitations. He nearly spat out his coffee. 'Whitey and P S Elliott?'

'The other guy?' Ian said.

Murphy smiled as he nodded.

'But the other guy was much older and didn't look like him?' Ian said.

Murphy pulled out a crumpled piece of paper from the pocket of his long coat. 'DNA don't lie. Got this back from my friend.' From his other pocket, he pulled out a plastic bag with the watch inside. 'At first, my guy said it wasn't a match. It couldn't have been Whitey's. Not with the DNA they had on file. But they did match it to Elliott.'

'I thought it was too long ago to get DNA?' Rick took the offered watch and held the bag up in the light.

'They can if it's been well protected. Caruso always kept it wrapped in a piece of cloth. My guy said it had not been Whitey's DNA but a maternal match. Turns out they had the same mother but different fathers. Anthony Rutherglen, Whitey, was a good twelve years younger than his brother Paul Stanley Elliott. He was born sometime in the twenties, I reckon. He would have been in his forties when the children went missing. He owned the land the business was located near the reserve. His father was a police commissioner. It all ties in rather nicely – his DNA was already on file,' Murphy said.

'Shit,' Rick said.

'Okay. They were brothers. How does that help us now?' Ian said.

Murphy paused then looked at the watch in Rick's hand. 'Well, I thought that Elliott might be dead, seeing as he was born in the

1920s but I found no death certificate. It's all a bit murky in that family. And as we know, or knew, from the newspapers, Whitey was buried in the city cemetery some ten years ago. Again, no official death certificate survives, only the coroner's report into the accidental death.'

'So, what you're saying is that he might be alive?' Ian said.

'He'd have to be in his nineties now. I guess it's possible,' Murphy said.

'He might have given Whitey the watch at some stage.'

'But did you ever see him wear it?' asked Murphy.

Both Rick and Ian looked at each other.

'Only thing I can remember is those damn Speedo bathers. I guess he might have worn it but I don't remember.'

Rick shook his head. 'Neither do I.'

'So, at the moment we have DNA from Elliott. We need Whitey's to tie him to the watch. And if we tie him to the watch then we tie him to the watch's box, which was found–' began Murphy.

'At the cottage,' Rick said, finishing his sentence, 'where he took the children.'

'It's been far too long for us to find anything relating to the children in that cottage. He would have made sure of that, besides–'

'You're still pretty sure he's dead,' Ian finished Murphy's sentence.

Murphy raised his eyebrows as if reconsidering.

'What? You think he's alive too?'

Murphy flexed his arthritic fingers and made a fist to stop the slight shake starting. 'No, I still think he's dead but there must be a connection somehow. If this guy is a copycat, then he knows far too much about Whitey. No, this guy is as smart as Whitey was so we need to look elsewhere.'

'You have somewhere in mind?' Rick said.

'There's gotta be something under that patch. You know, the place you took the photos.'

'Well, if we're not looking for graves, what are we looking for?' Ian said.

Murphy shrugged. 'We could be barking up the wrong tree but I could swear that whole area has been dug up recently.'

'So, there might not be anything there?' Rick said.

'All I'm saying is that it's a good place to start and besides, we don't have too many options left.'

*

It was midnight. They figured the Jag would be a little too conspicuous so it was three grown men crammed into Ian's small Prius. The drive through the hills proved more difficult than they had expected. The persistent drizzle had become heavier with each passing kilometre. On a damp road in the middle of the night with little or no street lights, it made seeing harder. Ian lent over the small steering wheel of his wife's more than adequate and economical car and stared at the road ahead. Any closer and he would be eating the steering wheel itself. The rain came down harder.

They parked well away from the Hilltop retreat and proceeded on foot. Ian's hands were red-raw as he helped Rick and then Murphy over the fence.

He handed Rick a torch and two small sharp folded spades through the metal fence. Ian looked tentatively at the huge gate.

'Just treat it like the old days when we played like ninjas. Just flip yourself over,' Rick said.

'Do I have to remind you that I haven't done any flipping for forty years?' Ian said.

The big old house was silent. The bay windows were dark and imposing. It looked as if they hadn't been opened for a very long time. Was this the place Whitey was holing out in? For all he knew, Whitey could be standing staring at them through one of those windows right now. The thought sent shivers down Rick's spine.

'This way.' Murphy looked remarkably calm for an ex-cop breaking the trespass law without as much as a stutter. He would have made a good crim, thought Rick, as he stumbled in the dark.

Trees at night looked more sinister than in the daylight. During a summer's day, they could be light and breezy but at night they cast huge dark shadows and stood in the actual spots where you wanted to walk. The trees told the paths where to go. The dark sky was punctuated by a row of high-powered garden lights that lit up the sides of the building. The moon gave some light when not hiding behind dark clouds. And it was getting cold. They grouped by the west window. Crimson silk curtains billowed outwards in the wind. Someone had left the sliding French door open. Rick moved towards it. Murphy grabbed him by the arm and pulled him back.

'We stick to the plan,' he said in a low voice.

For a second, Rick considered entering. 'But what if he's got her in there?'

'We don't even know if there is a *her*. We need to stick to the plan.'

Rick glanced back at the open door and sighed. 'Okay.'

They walked on. The footpath had recently been levelled. Its edges were tidy and its gravel raked over. This was a path carefully tended to. When they came to the fork in the path, they stopped. The cottage path wound around to the right to the left was the mound Rick had photographed earlier. They were silent as Murphy pointed to the mound. He opened his coat and from his pocket, he took out the two folded spades.

Murphy handed one to Ian. 'We're looking for anything that shouldn't be here.'

They had to use moonlight. The torch was for emergencies only. Luckily it was a cloudless night. Suddenly a solitary light shone from an upstairs window of the mansion.

'Whadda we do?' whispered Ian.

Murphy raised his hand for silence. His hand started shaking. He motioned for Ian to keep digging.

'Rick, go down the path and keep a close eye on that light. Whistle if anyone comes,' Murphy said quietly.

Rick nodded and crept up to the start of the trail. The noise of Ian's spade faded as he crept closer to the mansion. A dim figure stood in the window. It had paused to draw back some curtains and for a moment, Rick thought he'd been seen. But as he watched, the figure turned from the window and disappeared. He took another breath. Then he heard a door opening. Was that the front door? From his spot, it was difficult to see. Was it the caretaker? No, he only worked the day shift. Was it Whitey? He clenched his hands into fists. What if he came down the path now? What would he do? Would he punch him? He hadn't punched anyone in a very long time.

There was Whale. The drummer of his band. He'd punched him and got punched back. He rubbed his chin in the recollection of that drunken fight. It hadn't lasted long as they were both as drunk as lords. And then there had been that guy back at school. It was funny what the brain dredged up in memory when you were under stress. He remembered the guy. A big hulking teenager of Italian background, man-mountain came to mind. He had been picking on someone smaller, he didn't even know who it was.

He bailed him up and a fight ensued. Who won was debatable. Certainly not the younger version of himself. He got several hits to the face in exchange for his thumps to the chest region. In the end, it just petered out when their train arrived. After that, every time he saw the man-mountain it had been amicable. A quick gidday and a nod of the head was what they had become. A reasonable outcome Rick had thought.

Steps on gravel.

Someone had come out the front door and was headed this way. He froze for a moment. What was it he had to do? Whistle, that was it. He stopped himself. How dumb was that? Whoever was coming would hear it too. He turned down the trail and whistled softly under his breath.

More footsteps and then silence. Had the walker heard? He whistled a little louder this time.

He edged his way back into the bushes and held his breath. A stooped figure walked towards him. As he reached the turn in the path, the figure paused as if considering which way to go. Rick watched as the shadow took the path towards Joe and Ian. Rick could only hope that they had heard his warning. He waited and waited. It was getting colder and the dampness of the night was making things uncomfortable. There was little he could do.

He sucked in the air. Someone was coming back along the path. He made himself as small as he could by leaning back into the thorny bush. He could see now. The moon had shone its silvery yellow beam right on the path. The figure loped slowly towards him. He half-closed his eyes, hoping the man wouldn't see him. The walking stopped. He opened his eyes. He stared right into the eyes of Whitey. He realised that Whitey couldn't see him. But still, he held his breath as he stared.

He had aged but Rick knew it was him. His eyes were what gave him away. The way the clouds parted so that moonlight could lighten the path and the figure, was mesmerising. Although there was something wrong about him, thought Rick. Apart from the age. Something was not quite right.

*

Rick held his breath for as long as he could. Whitey stood as still as the trees around him, staring at something in the bushes. For a desperate second, he thought Whitey was about to say something. He was an old man, must have been in his seventies or eighties. If Rick couldn't beat him in a fight, he should retire himself. But the fact of the matter was that the stooped man standing on the path scared the bejesus out of him. Rick's body was rigid with fear. He looked into the steely gaze of a man he suspected had killed many people. How many was the real question? He was convinced now. He had killed Caruso. Jody, Hilda and young Peter. He had killed them all. A million thoughts fluttered through his mind as he stared at the old man. How could he live with what he'd done?

Rick swallowed hard. Did Whitey have the girl here? He felt the sudden urge to leap up and confront the man. It was at that moment he noticed another man standing a few feet from him. A younger man. A younger man with a rifle resting over his arm. He should have known that Whitey would not be without protection. He leaned back in the bushes.

Suddenly, the stooped figure started walking back along the path to the front door. Rick waited until he heard the door slam shut. It was then he realised that he'd been holding his breath. How long had it been? One minute, two minutes? His pulse was racing as he gulped in the air. He felt faint and braced himself against a tree. If he were to pass out, he wanted a soft place to land. But the sensation passed and his heart settled. A hand tapped him on the back. He almost slithered to the ground at the touch. A hand pulled him back up.

'You okay, Rick? What are you doing, closing your eyes like that?' Ian said.

'Did you see him? Did you see Whitey?'

Ian shook his head. 'No, I saw a young guy. Not the gardener. It looked like one of the guys that burned down Joe's police station that night. He came right up to us. We were hiding in the trees. He turned around and then left.'

'He had a gun.'

'It looked like a shovel to me.'

'You didn't see the old man with him?' Rick said in disbelief.

'Sorry, pal. He might have caught us if you hadn't whistled. We hid just in time.'

'We have to get inside. He's here and he might have the girl,' Rick said urgently. He made to walk back down the path.

'Hey, wait on,' Ian said, grabbing hold of him. 'If that guy does have a gun…'

Murphy appeared from nowhere, holding what looked like a soddened and dirt-encrusted hanky. He held it carefully between two fingers. He took out a plastic bag from his pocket and placed it carefully inside then sealed it.

Rick was about to ask him about it but Murphy said 'Ian's right. It's too dangerous.'

'You guys don't believe me. I saw him. He's here, right now! We have to get him. We might only have one chance.'

Murphy looked at Ian.

'Shit, you want to go in, don't you? This is madness.'

Murphy raised his eyebrows. 'I guess a quick look around couldn't hurt.'

'Couldn't hurt? Could get us thrown in the slammer.'

'I can't leave. If I'd done something that day when the children went missing, maybe they'd be alive now. You guys should leave, but not me.' Rick stammered the last sentence and then looked at his two friends.

Murphy put up his hand. 'Count me in.'

Ian nodded. 'Me too. I guess someone needs to watch out for the both of you.'

22

Enemy by Nature

THE HILLTOP RETREAT WAS in darkness. Whatever light that had been switched on upstairs was now off. Rick paused at the open door. This seemed a little too easy. Who leaves a door open at night in a mansion that has expensive things inside? Rick paused to consider the question then led Ian and Murphy through the open French doors. In his mind, he was sure that it had been Whitey he'd seen on the path. The question was. Where was he now? He looked at Murphy.

'You okay?' whispered Murphy. Rick gave the thumbs up.

Murphy grabbed his arm. 'Slowly, okay?' he whispered. Rick nodded. The three stopped in the middle of the living room. Ian pointed to the far wall where a staircase climbed upwards. A shuffling noise got their attention. Someone or something was coming down the stairs very slowly. Murphy pulled Rick back. The three slid into a dark area. One footstep, then another, someone was taking the stairs one at a time. Slow and precise. A thud made them jump just a little.

Then an eerie pause as they listened intently.

A dark shadow emerged on the stairs. Murphy motioned for Ian and Rick to stay where they were. He edged towards the archway that led onto the stair landing. Then the image seemed to disappear.

Rick waited. Ian got fidgety. He started to move back to the French door.

'I need some air,' Ian said.

Now Rick was alone. He listened carefully for any noise from the stairs but there was none. He stepped onto the landing. Just beyond the stairwell, there was a door. A dim light shone from a gap near the floor. He reached the door and tried the handle. It was unlocked. He heard a cackling sound from inside. It sounded vaguely human. He pushed the door open and entered slowly. He turned and closed it.

He saw the source of the light, a lamp on a divan, near the wall. In the corner was a bed. The light was low so he could only make out a figure lying on it. He heard a low moan as if the person was in agony.

Suddenly, the door exploded open behind him. He heard a yell but as he turned, something hit him from behind.

Then it all went black.

He lay on the ground. A girl hovered over him. She smiled and shone her green eyes on him. The carousel whirled behind them. Her short hair bobbed as she helped him to his feet. He had slipped on the running board of the carousel and hit his head. His world spun round and round, like the carousel. As he stood, Jody got close to him and whispered in his ear. 'I'm scared.'

The image turned grey and he was on his back in the back seat of a large car. A large police car. A hand stopped him from getting up. Night had turned to morning. The sun was out and it blinded him.

'I'm fine,' Rick said, annoyed that someone was making him lie down. It was Ian. 'How long have I been out?'

'Hours, mate, you fell down the stairs and hit your head.'

Rick rubbed his head. 'Someone hit me from behind.'

'Hit you? Who?'

Rick slid out of the back seat of the car and got to his feet. He was still shaky.

'I dunno. I went into the room and I saw…' he said. He stopped. What had he seen? 'Someone was on the bed, a girl.' He became more animated. 'Ian, there was a girl in there. I saw her. What if it's the one he took?' Rick started moving towards the door of the mansion. Ian ran after him and grabbed his arm.

'Rick, no. I wouldn't go in there.'

'Why not?'

At that moment, Murphy came out of the door towards them. He was followed by a constable and a plainclothes detective.

'Hendriks is in there.'

'I have to talk to him, Joe. I have to tell him about the girl.'

'Not yet, Rick. Just relax and trust me.'

'I saw her, in the room next to the stairs.'

'This officer is going to take us back to the station,' Murphy said softly.

Rick was having none of it. The constable moved towards Rick.

'Sir, if you don't get back in the car, I'll have to arrest you for interfering with a police investigation.'

'No need for that, Carver. Rick has just had head trauma, he's not feeling well,' Murphy said.

Rick saw his chance. For a split second, he had a choice. The adage of what you would do, fight, flee or freeze entered his mind. He wanted to fight. He sprinted towards the front door of the mansion. This caught them all off guard, especially Carver who dropped precious file notes to the ground.

Rick took the steps two at a time. The front door was shut. He reached it and pulled with both hands. It opened. Without a glance, he ran inside. He was at the bottom of the staircase. He could hear murmurings coming from a room directly in front of him.

He reached the door as Carver reached the stairs.

'Stop,' yelled Carver. Rick ignored him. He pulled on the door handle, ran inside then slammed the door behind him.

The room was filled with the morning sun streaming in from a bay window at the back of the room. He stared into the light and was momentarily blinded. When his eyes cleared, he saw Hendriks seated in a large white-backed chair. A man stood between him and Hendriks. It was the gardener. The man's cheeks were pulsing in anger as if he was having a coronary. To Hendrik's right sat an old man in a wheelchair. Two other uniformed officers stood by an ancient fireplace. They moved to cut off Rick's approach. Hendriks stood and waved them away.

'Is this the man who broke into my house last night?' The man in the wheelchair glared at Rick.

Hendriks looked momentarily distracted by Rick's sudden appearance.

'To trespass like that and scare the living daylights out of us. I want this man put in gaol. Do you hear me?' said the man in the wheelchair.

'I'm sorry, sir, but this man thought that someone was being held without their consent in this house,' said Hendriks, rising to his feet.

'Being held? What sort of nonsense is that?'

Rick had to say something. He knew he was right.

'I saw a girl, in the room next door.'

'The man's insane. Arrest him. Take him away, get him checked out in a sanatorium.' The man in the wheelchair was yelling now. Visions of Scrooge from the Dickens novel with long crippled fingers and nose to match made Rick gag. The gardener tried to placate the man but he just pushed his arm away. He wheeled right up to Rick and proceeded to abuse him mercilessly. 'Damn hippies, think they can come into my gardens and do whatever it is they do. Probably drugs and alcohol involved.'

'I saw what you had in the cottage. I saw her picture. Just check the room, Detective, please.'

Hendriks stood.

'Aren't you going to arrest this man?' said the man in the wheelchair. Hendriks nodded to the two uniformed cops.

'Please, Detective, just check the room. I saw her.' Rick was desperate now. Hendriks hesitated. He turned to the man in the wheelchair.

'Mr Elliott, maybe if we just had a look it might help?'

'You're Elliott? You're Paul Elliott?' Rick said.

'Officer, I want you to remove this man. I don't care if you lock him up and throw away the goddamned key. I want him off my property now,' said Elliott.

'Detective, you have to believe me. I saw her. She's in there.'

Elliott's face turned purple. It was like the man was having a fit. Hendriks looked at Rick then at Elliott.

He nodded at the two officers.

'We'll just have a look, I think, Mr Elliott,' said Hendriks.

'You won't,' he said. 'You've caused enough disturbance for my household. I will not allow this to go on. Please leave, all of you.'

'You're Whitey's brother. You were with him when he took Jody and her sister and brother. You were driving the goddamned car. I remember you. Whitey told Caruso that his brother preferred boys – that was you. You helped him murder those children,' Rick said, his voice at an alarming level.

Elliott gripped the sides of his wheelchair and lifted himself as if he was going to attack. The gardener took his hands and pushed him gently back into the chair.

'You go too far. My brother has been dead for years. You accuse him of horrendous things. He never even met those children. He was a humanitarian.'

'That's enough,' said Hendriks. 'You men, escort Mr Donahue back to the station. I will see you there,' he said, looking at Rick.

'You have to believe me, she's here.'

Hendriks looked at Rick then at the door of the room in question.

'I object to this,' said Elliott with a maniacal grin on his face. 'I could sue the lot of you, even you, Detective.'

That was enough for Hendriks. He walked to the door. It was locked. He looked back at Elliott who was fuming. Elliott spat out something to the gardener who then walked over to the door, took out a set of keys, selected one then inserted it into the lock. Rick held his breath. This was it. He was sure of what he'd seen. The gardener unlocked the door and stepped back. Hendriks opened the door and walked in.

Then a wail.

Rick moved to the doorway and looked in. There was a figure in the single bed. It was writhing and calling out in pain. The gardener rushed past and moved to the edge of the bed. Elliott and his wheelchair were now in the room.

An old lady lay as stiff as a board, howling and turning from side to side.

'I hope you are pleased with yourself. My sister is not herself. She is sick and has dementia. She walks the halls sometimes at night. That is why we lock her in, but sometimes she gets out and goes up and down the stairs all night.'

Rick stared at her. Had he got it wrong?

The two officers escorted him out the front door. Rick bowed his head as he reached Joe and Ian.

'Are you okay, Rick?' asked Ian.

Rick said nothing. In his mind, he had been sure he'd seen a girl in that bed. He was wrong. Had he been wrong about seeing Whitey? Why was the door locked now? It hadn't been before. Starting to doubt everything, he remembered something his father once told him.

'*Son, trust your instinct. We Donahue's have good ones.*'

Of course, he didn't know if that was entirely true. Over the years he'd made plenty of bad decisions based on instinct. But this time, his gut was telling him that he was right.

*

The trip back to Hendriks' city police station office had been a quiet one. Both Murphy and Ian sat in the back of the squad car with Rick in the middle. His head, still aching, was soothed by a cold compress that one of Hendriks men had provided. He pressed it against his forehead and closed his eyes.

For the second time, Rick, Ian and Murphy found themselves back in Hendriks' office. This time there would be no reprieve and although Elliott had decided ultimately not to press charges, Rick feared that Hendriks would have no other option.

'This is where we stand,' began Hendriks. 'And I don't want to be interrupted,' he said, mainly looking at Murphy. 'You were found on private property not once, not twice, but three times. That includes the time when you impersonated council workers, another misdemeanour. Then you broke into the cottage, or more to the point, you did.' He nodded at Rick. 'Breaking and entering is classified as a major crime. Then you dared to break into the man's house. For some strange reason, he has decided not to lay charges although I don't know why. If it were up to me, I would have added some more charges on top of that.'

'But you know it's all bogus, John. That guy is hiding something. I believe Rick when he says he saw something in the cottage and even you have doubts about the way Vic Tangini died in gaol. And I'd reckon that if you think that then Gino Caruso didn't kill himself either. Both were murdered. Don't you think it's all a bit convenient?' Murphy said.

Hendriks paused. Rick interrupted.

'I know what I saw in that cottage, Detective. And if we don't act another girl will die.'

Hendriks looked at them all. He sighed deeply. 'The evidence doesn't stack up, I'm afraid. Yes, I agree Vic Tangini was murdered but that could have been anyone with a gripe in prison. He could have looked at a person the wrong way.'

'Right after he'd spoken with Rick,' Murphy said.

'And told me things we didn't know,' Rick said.

Hendriks looked peeved. 'Now you're saying that somehow, an old man in a wheelchair is masterminding all these things. It just doesn't stack up. He's just an old man with a sick sister,' said Hendriks.

'I might have been wrong about the old lady but I'm not wrong about the girl I saw on that computer.'

'We didn't find any computers or anything anywhere. We looked, believe me. There was nothing and the fact that no such child has been reported missing, well, that's all we can go on. We can't find a child that isn't missing.'

'That's what the police said all those years back about the three. It was a week later when they admitted that maybe they'd been taken,' Rick said, 'and it was too late by then.'

Hendriks looked at Rick. 'That's not what the files show. Anyway, we're not talking about a case that happened forty years ago. We're talking about today, right now.'

If looks could kill. And they can. Rick had a feeling of what was coming.

'Okay, this is what is going to happen. You will not contact each other until I say it's okay. That means all of you for if you are found in each other's company, we will invoke the anti-consorting law against you.'

'That's unlawful,' Ian said. 'That law is for bikies and criminals.'

Hendriks stared at Ian.

'What have I just said? You have broken criminal law and therefore, you pay the price.'

Murphy put up his hand to calm things. 'We'll do as you say,' he said.

*

After all that had happened that day, Rick was almost glad to be back in his hotel room. All was quiet. Murphy and Ian had been duly dropped off by two uniformed officers. They'd said nothing as they got dropped off with Rick's last cab off the rank. It had all gone pear-shaped. Rick thought about a walk on the beach. There was little else to do. He walked to the reserve and stood on the spot where the carousel once ran. He lifted his face to the wind and closed his eyes.

His phone rang. For a moment, he didn't want to answer it. It rang and rang. 'Let it ring,' he said as he let the cool wind slap against his face.

The phone was insistent. Finally, he answered it.

'You don't answer your phone,' said a woman's voice. He recognised it straight away.

'Sally,' Rick said softly. It had been some time since he'd heard her voice. Something was wrong though.

'I need to see you,' she said.

23

Never Go Back

RICK DROVE TOO FAST. That was something she always told him. And that he didn't laugh enough. Two small things but in her mind, big enough to have been a problem. Those and a myriad of other things were enough to drive her away. As he pulled the Jag out of the freeway traffic and onto the seaside slipway, he tried to remember the last time he had seen her. Ten years? Twelve? More like fifteen, he figured.

Memories were a strange part of the brain. He remembered small things that might sit on the periphery of his consciousness but the big things were often vague and foggy. He rubbed his brow and wondered whether it was the result of the brain trauma he had received in the crash. He looked in the rear-view mirror and checked his face. He hadn't shaved for a couple of days and looked tired. Bloated! There wasn't much he could do about his appearance. It had been a sleepless weekend, especially after the disaster at the Hilltop Retreat. Could he have been so wrong? He was sure he had seen a girl in that room. He was sure he had seen Whitey alive and well strutting about the grounds. Or was it all in his mind? He was starting to doubt everything. Was his brain even working properly?

'You're not concentrating on the road,' she said. He looked across at her and gave a little shrug. He knew this would irritate her greatly.

'Just admiring the scene. You don't have a problem with that?' he said a little snidely. He bulged his eyes at her.

'Stop that,' she said, slapping him on the arm. 'You know I don't like that. Why do you do it?'

'Because I am beguiled by your looks and I think I'm a vampire,'
he said, bulging again.

'Seriously, you still haven't answered my question.'

He thought for a moment. Had he missed something?

'Last night. You said that you wanted to try being a musician
for a while and I asked you...' She prompted him by dealing a
blow to his ribs.

'Careful, I'm driving,' he mumbled.

'Well?'

He knew what was coming. Trouble was, he had no answer. It
had been a dream, a hope and a long shot. Somehow, even though
he knew he wasn't a gifted muso, he had to try. This was hard.

He turned the Jag onto Beach Road. He remembered the
conversation as if it had happened yesterday. He sighed when
he realised it was more than thirty years ago.

Vince was waiting for him by the front door of the Molly Muggins
café. He looked grim. As Rick approached, Vince looked at him
then pulled off the apron from around his waist and threw out
his arms.

'Thanks for coming, Rick,' Vince said, opening the café door
to usher him inside. When in, Vince pushed the door shut and
latched it.

'Is she okay? It's just that I got this manic call that made no
sense. I told her to calm down but I think I just made it worse. I
have a habit of doing that with her, I'm afraid.'

'Molly managed to calm her down.'

'The only thing I could make out when she called was something
about her daughter, Sophia. Is she okay?'

Rick noticed Vince's demeanour when he mentioned his
granddaughter's name.

'Listen, Rick, it might have been my fault, all this,' Vince said, lowering his voice. He checked over his shoulder to see if anyone was listening.

Then Sally walked into the room and Rick stopped listening to Vince. She looked… well, Rick couldn't actually put it into words. Her short stylish blonde hair framed her face in a way that made her look a lot younger than her years. But it was her green eyes and smile that Rick focused on. He had forgotten how striking she was.

'You came,' Sally said, standing with hands on hips.

Rick shrugged and smiled at her.

'You look good, Sally,' he finally got out.

She crossed the floor and gave him a peck on the cheek. Then she held him by the shoulders and looked him in the eye.

'You've put on a bit of weight,' she said with a smirk. 'But still, you look pretty good yourself.'

A thousand images of her when she was young flashed through his mind. Her with long curly hair (as she was when he first met her). Her hair shorter and blonder. And then there was that smile. It was the thing that he missed the most when they broke up. That and the way she spoke. He loved that too.

'You seemed a little upset on the phone. I thought there was a crisis of some sort,' Rick said.

'My fault,' Vince said, wringing his hands, Italian style.

'Bloody oath, it's your fault. If you hadn't filled Sophia's head with all those stories, then maybe she wouldn't have reacted in the way she did.' Molly swept in and gave Vince the look of death.

'I only told her to look out for strangers. I mean, we all know there are some kooks out there. Rick will tell you.'

Sally glared at her father. 'I'm sorry, Rick, I panicked when she didn't come home. I only just got here from down the coast and she was meant to be here and then…'

'Well, I guess I told her about what you and the guys were doing here...' Vince said.

'No wonder the poor child didn't tell us where she was,' Molly said as she entered from the kitchen.

'I was just trying to get her to be a little more aware of her surroundings. I mean, the girl dashes about without a care in the world...'

'She's twelve years old, you old cretin. She doesn't need to know about men being creeps just yet, does she? Let her have her childhood, for Christ's sake.'

'Those kids who were taken were younger than Sophia. That didn't stop that creep from doing what he did with them.' Vince realised what he said the moment he said it.

The horrified look on Molly's face told Rick that Vince would not live this one down.

Everyone looked at everyone. No one wanted to say anything. Rick figured he might need to break the silence.

'She's okay then?'

'She got freaked out by a stranger. She ran and hid and didn't come out for hours,' said Sally.

'A stranger?'

'Just somebody who dressed a little differently. It was a homeless person. She got spooked, that's all. An old lady with a stick, no big deal.'

'The circle woman? I mean, the lady who draws circles in the sand on the beach?'

Sally nodded. 'She's not used to people like that. When her father and I were together, we lived a pretty secluded lifestyle.'

'There are a few strange characters around,' Rick admitted.

*

They walked the promenade in relative silence just like a normal family would. Sophia skipped ahead to startle the seagulls. Sally caught Rick's hand a couple of times and he felt good when she did. Not like old times, he thought. Old times were a distant memory. Something in the dim dark recesses of his mind. He tried to remember why his father had given him a piece of advice back in the day. What had he said? *'Never go back!'* What did he mean by that? He was sure that if his old man had still been around, he would not have objected to him returning to his once love. He liked Sally. That, he had mentioned many times to him. *'Don't let that one get away,'* he had said many times. Well, at least twice. Once at their engagement party and once when he had turned twenty-one and they were partying out in the backyard. But that had been a lifetime ago. He glanced at her walking beside him. She saw him looking and pushed back a strand of her hair behind her ear. Another endearing thing he had missed about her. He sighed when she sighed.

He looked at Sophia. From the back, she reminded him of Sally when he first met her, on the beach that day.

'Sophia's father? Does he have any contact?' Rick said, trying a bit of small talk.

Sally shook her head. 'No, all that went south after I found out he was fucking his assistant.'

'And the latest husband?'

She sighed. 'A perennial gambler. He took all the money he had made, mine as well and gave it away.'

'Gave it away?'

A faraway look came into her green eyes. A look of despondency? She gripped his hand a little harder.

'Yeah, you know, business deals that were too good to be true. I'd had enough when he lost our house,' she said a little too angrily.

The fiery sun was disappearing over the horizon. It turned from bright yellow to red then a shade of purple that was quite eye-droppingly gorgeous. They stood for a while as it faded.

'Is that why you left town and went down south?'

'I had to get away. I had a lot to deal with.'

'And you left Sophia with Molly and Vince. You're lucky to have such good parents.'

They were both lucky in the parents' department. Strong and gentle at the same time. Rick grieved for his at that moment. Sally still had hers.

She smiled at Rick. He grinned back. Not always did he have the knack of saying the right thing at the right time. This time he did.

'So why panic now? What else is going on?'

'Nothing. I know, I know, I freaked out when she didn't get home on time.'

'And I guess Vince didn't help by saying three of his mates were hunting down a paedophile.'

'Yeah, well, I'm pretty sure he meant well. It's just that I remember those kids too. I might not have actually been there when they went missing but I was at home with my parents. After what happened, they went a little crazy too like other parents, locking up their children, doing stupid stuff.'

'Can't blame them. It was strange times.'

'And you think the guy is still out there?'

Rick went silent; he wasn't quite sure how to answer that. What good could it possibly do to tell her that Whitey was still out there abducting children and doing God knows what to them? He looked at Sophia who had stopped to admire a seaside sculpture erected for the annual competition. It was a girl dancer. A ballerina. Sophia smiled and looked back at her mum.

'Can I go and see if Claudia is home? She lives just over the park.'

'Didn't you just see her at school?' Sally said. Rick could see that Sally was slightly peeved that her daughter didn't want to spend every moment with her wayward mum. 'Go on, but be back by the time we get back from the sailing club.'

Every path along the beach led to the sailing club even the brand-new esplanade walkway.

Sophia groaned. 'Mum, I'm not a child anymore and besides, Vince and Molly let me do this whenever I want.'

She ran towards her friend's place.

'Since when have they become Vince and Molly and not Grandma and Grandpa?' Sally whined.

Rick looked at her and gave a sly grin. 'Don't look at me, never had kids, don't understand them.'

'She's starting to take liberties. A little late here, a little mouthy there...'

'Just like her mother,' Rick said with a grin. Sally smiled.

The sun was heading down and the tiny sailboats were being winched up the beach from the sea to hide under the double brick garage dug out under the clubrooms. You could fit fifty sailboats in the basement. Sally and Rick stood watching as the last of the boats were stashed away. The orange-red sunset was beginning to take place as they walked back along the boardwalk.

A shiver went up Rick's spine. He was remembering past deeds along this part of the beach. The ramp, now used as a sand dump, was once the place teenagers parked their cars hoping for a little privacy backed up against the greatest vision of a sunset gone rogue. Or colourful. One moment the sun was there, the next it was over the horizon.

Sally slipped her hand into his as they watched.

'Do you remember my old Valiant?' Rick said.

'I remember you taking liberties with a very young girl, right over there.'

'I remember that you never complained.'

She squeezed his hand even tighter.

'I remember the Silver Sands Hotel. That was where we broke up.' She pointed to the hotel. 'You told me that you and the band were going to move east. You broke my heart.'

Rick looked up at the sunset. 'The truth is I thought it would be easy to break up like that. I never thought I'd regret it the rest of my life.'

He looked at her. The years peeled away. She was the same. He, on the other hand, felt a little decrepit.

She laughed easily. 'I didn't realise until recently that I was choosing the wrong type of man. Two marriages and three engagements later, I guess it hits home.'

'I see you included me in that scenario. Probably fair enough.'

She shrugged her shoulders. 'You were my first mistake.'

This time, she didn't laugh.

'I know you, Rick, something is wrong. I can tell,' Sally said, leaning against the promenade wall. 'You could never hide things from me.'

He found himself telling her everything. From the purse that Caruso kept all these years to him seeing Whitey. The more he spouted, the more it sounded convincing to him. For a moment, he thought she would laugh at him. Instead, she put her arm on his shoulder.

'And you're upset that the others don't believe you?' she said softly.

He thought about that and sighed. 'I know it's hard to believe.'

'I believe you.'

If truth be known, it did make him feel just a little better. They stood watching the sunset from the promenade. The weather was trying to be better but the wind was beginning to pick up. In the distance, they could see Sophia and her friend Claudia at the ice cream stand. Even in cold weather, ice cream was the go-to food for kids. You could always rely on the flavour of a strawberry and vanilla cone.

*

He lay on his hotel bed fully clothed, staring at the ceiling. The day had started miserably with the disaster at the Hilltop Retreat but had finished on an unexpected high note. He couldn't get Sally out of his mind. Her eyes her mouth, the way she spoke. How he had missed all that. So, when his phone rang, he ignored it.

He drifted off into hybrid sleep. One dream had he and Sally together as they had been when teenagers. The next dream, slightly darker had them arguing about something or other. He could not quite pin it down in his mind. All he knew was someone was knocking urgently on his door.

'Don't you ever answer your goddamn phone,' said Carter, one of Hendriks detectives, when Rick finally gave in to the incessant pounding. He tried to explain that he rarely kept his phone on him but Carter waved his explanations away.

'A girl's been taken,' he said. 'We have to go, now!'

*

The station house was teeming with life. Every available man and woman seemed to be doing something. Rick barely got to the front counter before he was whisked away to a back office. He was left inside a darkened room and told to wait. He waited. He could see a flurry of activity through the meeting room window.

261

TV sets were on showing different news items. No picture of a missing child, yet.

Suddenly, the door flew open and Hendriks entered with Detective Parsons. The same one who had given the damning report on them. He didn't look at Rick before taking his chair.

'Thanks for coming, Rick,' said Hendriks. The lines under his eyes told him he'd had a bad morning.

Parsons opened the file, took out a glossy photo and placed it in front of Hendriks. He looked down and then slid the photo to Rick.

'Her name is Durra Hussain, born April twenty-first. Twelve years old. Last seen by her mother at six p.m. last night. She went missing from her dance lesson.'

'Her dance lesson started at four p.m. and her mother came to the centre at about six p.m. She saw her daughter finish her lesson. She waited with several other mothers for her to appear from the change rooms. She never came out. Other girls said they saw her talking to a man, who they thought might have been her father,' continued Parsons. 'Her father is currently serving our armed forces in the Solomon Islands, so it wasn't him.'

Hendriks took over. 'So, when she didn't emerge her mother entered the change rooms but there was no one there. A door leading outside was unlocked. She searched the grounds nearby and alerted the police no more than thirty minutes later. The media haven't been told yet. We have some matters to consider first before we tell them.'

Hendriks stopped and looked at Rick. He stared at the glossy picture. His heart dropped.

'It's her. It's the girl I saw on the computer,' whispered Rick.

Hendriks looked at Parsons who swooped on the photo and then gathered up his file. He was out of the door before

Hendriks said anything.

'And you're sure, are you, Rick?'

'Of course, I am. You have to search the mansion. You have to pick up Elliott. He knows where his brother is. I'm sure of that.'

Hendriks nodded slowly. 'Listen, Rick, although we understand you think it is this Whitey character. I have to tell you that we have proof that Anthony Rutherglen died ten years ago. It can't be him and it would be difficult for his brother to have had anything to do with it. He is wheelchair-bound, as you know. And we have searched the Hilltop Retreat from top to bottom and found nothing. We now think it might be a copycat. Someone who knew the story. Someone close to it.'

'I've spoken with him on two occasions and I've seen him once. You have to believe me. He wants to discredit me. He knows you don't believe me but you have to.'

Hendriks looked concerned. 'We are looking into all possibilities. We have an apprehension order out against the gardener amongst others.'

'What others?'

'Others who might have been around in those days.'

Was this going somewhere? It twigged something in Rick's mind.

'You think it might be one of us?' he said. 'Me or Ian?'

'No, we don't think it was you or the lawyer, Rick, maybe someone else close,' said Hendriks.

'Jesus Christ, you think it's Joe! You think that Joe Murphy abducted the girl?'

'You know that he's had some problems in his life? He lost his wife and well, he has a neurological condition.'

'You're fucking joking, aren't you?' Rick said. 'If you think Murphy's got anything to do with this, you are joking. He's the one who solved all this. You should be thanking him.'

'There's something else you should know. Earlier when we arrested Murphy for breaking into the judge's offices. I didn't tell you why he did it.'

'I know why he did it. He said that someone had protected Whitey all those years ago. Gave him an alibi and stuff like that.'

'It wasn't that, Rick. He was trying to find a file. A file that listed all the evidence found by police about the missing children. It listed secret evidence and people's identities. It also listed mistakes made by police at the time. It listed his very own mistakes. It would seem that he was trying to minimise his part in all this.'

Rick shook his head vehemently. 'You're fucking mad if you think that he's been doing anything but trying to find out what happened to those kids. And now there's another one missing. You're wasting your time with this shit.'

'That's where we differ, Rick. I have to find her. I can't do my job if you guys interfere with the case.'

'And so?'

'And so, I've put out a pick-up notice for Joseph Murphy,'

'You're arresting him?'

'I'm issuing a pick-up notice. I'm not arresting him. I just need him out of the way until we find the girl,' Hendriks said, scooping up the file from his desk.

'And I don't want you out harassing people about this too, Rick. Why don't you just stay in your hotel for a few days, okay?'

'I can help. You need me.'

'I need you to stay out of the way.'

'So, you only got me here to keep me out of the way.'

Hendriks laughed gruffly. 'We just needed you to ID the girl. You did that.'

Hendriks swept out of the room.

24

Endings at Number 63 Hindenburg Street

RICK SAT IN THE Jag and stared at the steering wheel. This was a mess. He thumped his hands down and swore loudly. At least they let him go. For a moment he thought they might put him in the lock-up to keep him out of the way. He picked up his phone and dialled the number. It went straight to message bank.

'Murphy, they're coming for you. Get out,' Rick said.

Then he drove and drove. He rang Ian. He found himself at the beach.

Vince stood by the door of his café. A young couple with their small child looked at him in anticipation of fine cake and coffee.

'Sorry I'm closed for… a stocktake,' he said, searching for a reason. Rick sat quietly in the back of the shop. He watched as Ian crossed the busy street and made for the door. When he got there Vince simply opened the door and nodded to the rear. He closed it and locked it behind him.

'Thanks for that, Vince, and you too, Molly. I know it's the start of your busy time.'

'No problems, my friend. Anything for the cause.'

'You can stay here as long as you like, Rick,' said Molly.

'I guess you're waiting for Murphy?' said Vince before going to the kitchen to make them a strong coffee.

'Are we?' Ian said, looking at Rick.

Rick peered through the windows behind him. He had told Ian on the phone what had transpired with Hendriks at the station

265

about the missing girl and the fact that Murphy might be on the wanted list.

'I left a message with him but for all we know, it may be too late. They might have already picked him up. I couldn't go around to his place; Hendriks' men might have been there. I figured that if they haven't got him yet they might be looking for us, hence hiding here,' Rick said.

'Thanks for the heads up. Oh, and I've got some info, Rick. The guy they called the commander. You know the office Joe broke into?'

'Renly Shaw?'

'Yup, the very person who gave an alibi to Whitey back during the original investigation,' Ian said, peering out of the window as if he was expecting to see a horde of cops surrounding the café. He flipped the venetians back to closed and continued. 'Yeah, sometimes people called him the commander. I guess it was just a nickname. Well, he's the former Chief Justice of the Supreme Court but like American presidents, they retain their title for the rest of their lives. At one stage, he was my boss when I worked for the DPP. I was just a junior and never met him. He was also the attorney general in a couple of governments twenty-odd years ago. But during the sixties and seventies, he was a lawyer employed by the Rutherglen family. It's his signature on the lease of the factory they just dug up and on the Hilltop Retreat.'

'Is his signature on any other properties for the family?'

Ian smiled. 'I have a list of properties right here.'

'I'll bet this was what Joe was trying to get his hands on when he broke into his office. Hendriks was trying to make out that Joe had bad intentions and that he was trying to squash evidence. This was what he was looking for. How did you get this, anyway?'

'The clerk of the court gave it to me. He has control over the archives. Now, this list might be a little out of date. It was made in the late seventies when the government nominated him as Chief Justice. It's straight from his files… not exactly public domain but… well, I didn't break any laws getting it.'

Suddenly, there was a knock on the door. They could see a figure peering into the café. A man in a black coat. Murphy. He sprang into the room, full of beans.

'Thanks for the heads up, Rick. When you rang, they were coming through the front gate. I got out over the back fence.'

'Hendriks gave me all this shit about you being involved.'

'I just think he wanted Joe out of the way,' Ian said.

'I guess he told you that I wanted to hide evidence.'

'He said that's why you broke into the commander's office,' Rick said.

'I don't think he believes that. He thinks it's a copycat – he's hoping like hell he's right. He doesn't want to believe Whitey's still alive, but I think I've got proof now.'

He took out Whitey's watch from his pocket. 'You remember when I said they found only one set of DNA on the watch? My contact now tells me that there were two sets of DNA recovered. Because they are brothers, it was a little messy. One belonged to P S Elliott and the other…' Murphy said, holding it up in its plastic bag to the light.

'Anthony Rutherglen,' Ian said.

'Whitey,' Rick said.

'But that still doesn't prove he's alive?' Ian said.

'No, but there is this,' added Murphy. He pulled a short whisky glass in a small plastic bag from his pocket. 'Rick, when you said you saw him that night, I figured that if he was here, he'd leave something for us. He did. I found this at the Hilltop Retreat. I went up the stairs and found a kitchen. It could have been anyone's but I took a chance. It came back positive for Rutherglen's DNA. It probably wouldn't stand up in court but what the heck.'

The three just stared at each other.

'Show him what you got, Ian.'

Ian held up the archive folder.

'You got it,' Murphy said. 'How?'

Ian looked chuffed. 'Well, basically through the clerk of the court. I told him I was looking into a matter and needed verification.'

'You bullshitted him. Jesus, this is what I was looking for when I broke in. I could have done time for this bit of paper. Shit, we've got it, the suburb, and the goddamned street address. It's all here,' Murphy said with a grin.

He pulled the document from Ian's hands and stared at it again just to make sure.

'Yup, this has to be it,' said Murphy, slapping Ian on the back. '63 Hindenburg Street, North End.'

Ian went pale. 'You think that's where he's moved the children to? It makes no sense. The guy owns a factory that has blast furnaces. I'd have thought he'd just burn them. Leave no trace.' Ian wasn't sure but it made sense to him.

'No, he wouldn't do that.' Murphy was just as adamant.

'I don't understand, Joe. Why go through all this? Why not get rid of the evidence for good? It's been forty years, for Christ's sake,' Ian said.

Rick looked at them both. He was going to say something but stopped. He needed to think this out. Then it came to him. 'He's a trophy hunter,' Rick said.

'He's a sick bastard,' said Ian.

'Sick bastard indeed.'

'You think he's got them under that house?'

'It's possible. I think that we'll find something there,' Murphy said.

'What about the girl? Do you think he's taken her there?' asked Rick.

'Might do. He doesn't know what we know. He thinks he's in the clear.'

'We've got to go now. He thinks he's still a step ahead of us.'

'It might be too late already,' Ian said.

'Don't say that,' said Rick.

'So, the question is. Do we trust Hendriks with this?'

Rick had asked the question quietly. In his mind, he knew what the answer would be.

'I don't think it's a matter of trust. I just don't think the guy's gunna believe us,' said Murphy. 'I mean, Rick here has cried wolf a couple of times and me, well, he doesn't trust me at all. The DNA stuff is not admissible, so, I say, we go ourselves.'

'Joe's right,' said Rick. 'If we show up at the station with this story, he'll just think it's another story we made up. Then he will lock us up and throw away the key.'

'Then it will be too late for the girl,' Murphy said.

'Shit.'

'I agree,' Murphy and Rick said simultaneously.

*

Rick stood still. There was something not quite right. Everything they were doing seemed to be too late. For whatever reason, Whitey was always one step ahead. Were they walking into a trap? What if he wanted them to go to this address? What was waiting for them there? Why was Whitey talking to him and him only? Everyone around him was sceptical of his existence so why him?

Why include him in all this lunacy? Rick's face went red, trying to think of a reason. He looked around him at the concerned faces. Ian, Murphy, Vince and Molly. Something was telling him that they were all being led up the garden path. And somehow, he was doing the leading. It struck him that Whitey was telling him things. Things that he was passing on to his friends. Why was that?

Suddenly, all hell broke loose. Sally thumped on the front door, screaming wildly. For a moment, Rick thought she was going to pass out. Vince opened the door and she fell into her father's arms.

'She's gone. Sophia's gone,' she sobbed.

'Are you sure?' Vince said. 'She might just be over at her friend's place.'

'Or hiding like the last time,' said Ian.

'Claudia rang me. She said that they were getting an ice cream when a man in a car pulled up alongside the van. A man in a dark coat took her. She rang the police,' Sally said.

A man in a dark coat. A dark trench coat. Ian and Rick looked at Murphy.

Then it struck him. Whitey had misled them all on purpose. It wasn't Durra Hussain who he wanted. It was Sophia. He had taken her. Durra Hussain was a decoy. She would probably turn up somewhere unharmed. What Whitey wanted was one of them. Or more to the point, someone who he felt a connection with. He wanted to prove that no one could stand against him. Rick had tried, they all had tried but Whitey wanted to vanquish them all.

Sally was inconsolable. For a moment, Rick thought about just taking her to Hendriks himself. If anything happened to Sophia, he would never be able to forgive himself. In the end, he knew he had to go with Ian and Murphy. Vince and Molly locked up shop and took Sally to the police station.

The car was quiet as they crossed town to the outer suburbs. Rick had convinced Sally that they needed to do this on their own.

Under stress, Ian always talked.

'So, tell me again. How are we going to get in? I mean, what if there's someone there?' Ian was in the back seat leaning forward as Rick drove and Murphy rode shotgun.

Murphy gave a little shake of his head. 'I don't expect anyone lives there.'

They all knew what that meant.

Murphy glanced at Rick who was beginning to tense up on the wheel.

'He'd keep it empty so he could "visit" whenever he wanted,' answered Rick.

Murphy nodded. 'He might have some of his guys keep an eye on it but he'll have it all locked up nice and tight. And because of that it's gunna be hard to get in. Good thing we've got the bolt cutters on board. And I've got this.'

Murphy pulled out the gun found in Caruso's bag. He hoisted it up by the handle.

'Shit, Joe, don't flash that thing around. It might be loaded,' Ian said.

'Of course it's loaded. I did it myself. I thought we might need some persuasion.'

'Just don't give it to me when we find Whitey or I might blow a hole in his head,' Rick said.

He kept on driving to North End.

The street lights were few and far between. Rick went slowly through the suburb, checking road signs as they drove by. The feeling that they were driving into a trap persisted. Whitey had always seemed a step ahead and if they were right about the house, it was inconceivable he would let them just stroll in.

Rick parked the Jag at the end of the street. It looked remarkably normal and suburban. He figured it was exactly the reason it was chosen. Whatever they thought of Whitey, he wasn't stupid. They seemed a little conspicuous carrying a tool bag, a small step ladder and a police-type torch with an elastic cord attached to a tool belt.

'We can't just roll up to the front door. It's not going to be as simple as that. Remember, if Sophia is there she'll be scared. We don't want to alert anyone. We've got to get in as quickly as we can,' said Murphy.

The moon played its part. It stayed hidden under a heavy dose of thick water-bearing clouds. Rain would not be a good outcome though. Rick looked up to the skies and grimaced. The house loomed up before them.

'It looks kinda normal.' Ian dropped the tool bag on the ground with a thud. 'Sorry,' he added. 'Bag's bloody heavy.'

'That's the point of it all. Normal on the outside. We'll see what he's hiding in there.' Murphy shook the gate as softly as he could. It was locked of course. Two industrial monster locks one on each side of the handle.

Rick looked across the street. A large block of industrial land stretched down the road. He had no neighbours. Although recently sold, the land had been unused for a very long time. He wondered who had bought it. Another question he filed in the back of his mind.

Rick took out the bolt cutters and clipped the first lock easily. The second proved problematic. He had to stand on the first rung and reach over the top of the fence. Ian held onto him as he attempted the difficult manoeuvre. He heard a clunk as he clipped the second lock.

Then an eerie silence.

The night had come in cold as if whatever was waiting for them inside decided to make it even more uncomfortable for them. Then the moon disappeared under a sky full of clouds. The old saying you could hear a pin drop crossed Rick's mind as they stood in front of the now unlocked gate. Of course, you couldn't hear a pin drop. But you could damn well hear a solid metal lock drop. It echoed throughout the dead of night like a hammer on an anvil. They waited for the shout. None came. Rick could hear Ian breathing hard.

'I've got a bad feeling about this,' Ian whispered.

Murphy lifted the handle of the gate. It creaked badly. If the clunking lock had been loud, the gate was worse. He pushed it open quickly. They were in.

Standing on the grounds of the typical suburban bluestone federation house felt creepy. The hairs on the back of Rick's arm stood to attention. Ian rubbed the back of his neck and Murphy, well, he just stood as still as a board, the trembling in his hands gone completely. Rick figured that he was in his element. The front door was curious. There were no obvious handles or keyholes, just a heavy wooden slab. Murphy felt around the door for any openings. It was completely sealed.

'No hinges,' he mumbled.

'Come on, guys, this bag ain't getting any lighter.' Ian shifted the bag from one hand to the other.

The only discernible path was down the side of the house. They couldn't use the torch just yet, at least, not until they were around the back and out of the way, even then it would be a risk. Suddenly a light went on in a window. They stopped. Ian touched Rick on the shoulder and pointed to the ground. He lay the tool bag down. If he had to run, he didn't want to have to lug the bag. Murphy hadn't moved. He was staring at the light.

The blinds had been pulled down on the bay window but with the light beaming onto it, he could see the rest of the room. No shadows. He bent down and peered closely. Then he stood and waved them on. He paused a second then quietly put his finger to his lips and pointed to the corner of the house.

'On a timer. The lights. They program them to come on randomly at night just to deter thieves and people breaking in.'

'You mean, like us?' Ian said.

'Yeah, but we're smarter than your average house breaker.'

The backyard was a mess of half-strangled trees, wild shrubs and overgrown buffalo grass. Rick suspected there was a method to this apparent wildness. With obstacles in their way, there was no obvious pathway to the house. The back door had been covered with mesh and boards and the windows facing the back were covered with steel bars. Not a good start.

'It's a bloody fortress.' Ian bent down and felt the ground. It was covered with a layer of concrete that ran up to the brickwork and up the walls to waist high. This was to stop anyone digging their way in.

'What about the windows back there?' Rick suggested.

'All alarmed and I saw some silicon residue on the window, could be explosives,' said Murphy.

'Explosives. Why blow the windows?' Ian was alarmed.

'If this place is what I think it is then I'd expect it. Could be a deterrent, dunno. We've gotta be careful.'

'Careful! Is that all you've gotta say?' With that, Ian plonked the bag of tools on the ground as if to say he'd had enough.

'Don't be silly, Ian, Joe's got a plan… don't you?' Rick looked at Murphy. He noticed just the tiniest quiver in his hands.

But Murphy was not listening. He was running his hands over the boards that covered the back door. He found a small box. 'Screwdriver!' he said, holding out his hand. 'Flathead!'

Ian mumbled then went to his toolbox.

Murphy had the lid off within minutes. A control panel with three switches, all blinking red.

'I've seen one of these before,' Murphy said, staring at the configuration.

'Is this safe?' asked Ian.

Murphy took some time to answer.

'Three outcomes. One, we get in. Two, the alarm goes off. Three, it blows us to smithereens. A one in three chance. I can live with that,' he said.

'Yeah, but will we?'

'Need the cutters,' mumbled Murphy, bent over the control panel. 'There's only one way into this place. It can't be the front. He wouldn't have wanted to be seen from the street. He would come from the back… down by that fence. Nobody can see.'

'But there's no keypad. How does he get in?' Rick looked into the small control box. All he could see were the three tiny LEDs.

'Infrared signal. A bit like…' began Murphy.

'A fob key on a car?' finished Rick.

'Exactly, it can be programmed to accept only one signal.'

'Okay, if it can only accept one signal how the hell do we open it?'

'We don't. We just disable the panel.'

'Which means?'

'Which means we'll probably only have ten to fifteen minutes inside before they get here.'

'If they're not here already,' Rick said under his breath.

'Isn't that cutting it a bit thin?' Ian said.

Murphy looked at them both. 'If this place is what we think it is then he'll be alone. If he's got the girl here, he won't trust any of his men to know. That's the nature of the beast. He's a loner.'

'What about his brother?' Ian said.

'Not sure where he fits in. I guess he's been the stooge all his life. He might not know what his little brother is up to. You can be sure that Whitey keeps this close to his chest. So, I guess it's the chance we take.'

The plan was that Ian remained outside as a lookout. If he saw anything, a quick text would alert them both. Rick looked at the panel. He watched as Murphy hesitated and then cut all three wires. The red lights blinked a few times and then went out. They breathed a collective sigh of relief. The moon decided to come out of its hiding and shine down on them. They scrambled to the back door. No alarms. So far.

Even the suburban dogs were quiet.

Rick figured that somewhere the alarm had probably already gone off. He just hoped they would have a few minutes. He placed a hand on the door and pushed. It creaked a couple of times then opened slowly.

Ian watched as Murphy and Rick disappeared into the dark house.

He cursed and made his way back out to the street.

25

Damnation

A RANCID SMELL MADE Rick retch as they made their way into the darkness.

'God damned stinks to high heaven,' he said.

'Another deterrent. Just a trick to make sure nobody goes any further.'

'Bloody good deterrent,' mumbled Rick as he pulled his jumper up to cover his nose.

Murphy swung his torch out and aimed it at the floor. The front part of the house was sparsely furnished. A couple of chairs and a small table in the corner. It looked like no one had been here for a very long time, a ruse if ever he saw it. Murphy held up his hand. Rick stopped. He could hear something. An undercurrent of noise was barely noticeable. Murphy motioned for Rick to open a door to his left. He shone his torch inside. A bedroom. They saw a bedframe with no mattress and a single globe on a long lead hung low over the bed. Rick checked his watch. They had only been inside for sixty seconds. He wondered how much time they had. They needed to pick up the pace. He ignored the other rooms. If Vic had been right, they needed to find the basement. 'At the end of a long corridor,' he'd said.

Vic was right.

Two locks hung from the door. Rick stepped in with the bolt cutters and without a word he snipped them both off.

'I'll go first,' Murphy said softly.

With his torch now free to light the stairwell, Murphy stepped

277

down carefully. Rick followed. As he took the first few steps down the stairs, a feeling of dread swept over him. He paused to get his nerve back. A little voice in his head told him to turn around and get the hell out of there. *'Rick, you don't belong down here. Get out.'* He didn't recognise the voice. He paused again then he thought of Jody, her sister and brother. He kept going. The metallic smell had morphed into a rotten egg gas smell, it was almost unbearable. What was sulphur used for again? He couldn't remember. Then he heard Caruso's voice.

'You guys aren't supposed to be here. It's bad, Eric… I'm sorry.'

Rick paused again. This time Murphy noticed. He stopped next to Rick. 'What's wrong?'

'Nothing,' lied Rick.

'We have to pick this up. We've only got a few more minutes.'

They reached the bottom of the stairs. It opened up into a large expanse. Murphy shone the torch around the walls of the basement. It was empty.

'There's nothing here.' Rick groaned with disappointment. 'There's gotta be something. Shine the light over here.'

Nothing.

Murphy moved back to the stairs and flipped on the lights. Bank after bank of fluorescent lights flickered on. 'No point doing this in the dark.'

It seemed unnaturally empty. There was not a shred of anything down here. You would expect a basement to have something.

'Notice something unusual?' Murphy said, staring at the far wall.

'Sure, there's nothing here, just dirt.' Rick always stated the bleeding obvious.

'See that there?' Murphy pointed to the wall nearest. Rick looked but shook his head. The detective strode over to the far wall. 'Normally I'd dicker around and lead you to the answer but we haven't got any time left. This wall here, it's new. Those walls back there are all part of the original basement. This is where he got them to dig. Here, give me the bolt cutters.'

Murphy took a swing at the wall with the bolt cutters. The plaster shattered and large pieces fell to the ground. 'There must be a door in here somewhere.' He moved down the wall a bit and smashed into the wall again. This time he struck metal. A door. 'There's gotta be another panel here too.'

Rick stood on something. 'Down here.' He went to his knees and flipped the lid of the panel. There they were, three more LED lights glowing red.

Murphy took the wire cutters out of his pocket. He hesitated. Rick grabbed them and sliced through them all. 'No time, Joe.' He grinned, stood and pushed on the metal door. It pushed back and opened. A dark coldness rushed at them. Rick shivered and it wasn't because of the cold air. All the hairs on his body stood on end. It was like entering the gates of hell, albeit a cold hell.

As Murphy stepped through the hidden door he felt a presence. It was all Rick could do to not turn and run. He turned towards Murphy.

'It's a trap,' echoed through Rick's mind but he couldn't stop his feet from edging forward. Murphy reached out and took hold of Rick, pulling him back.

'Be careful. Stay close.'

Rick didn't need to be told. He took a tiny step then another. Murphy flashed his torch just ahead but couldn't see much.

'Over there,' Murphy said quietly. He could see a largish object straight ahead, and another to the side. The closer they got the warmer it became. He was still a few metres away when he recognised what they were. He stopped. This was strange. Three large water tanks stood side by side.

'You okay, Joe?' Rick said under his breath.

For a moment, Murphy said nothing. His hand holding the torch began to shake just a little. He suppressed the shaking somehow.

'I'm fine. I guess I was expecting something like this.'

'Water tanks?' Rick said, a little confused.

'Not water tanks, acid tanks.' Murphy held up his hand. 'Hear that? That clicking sound.'

Rick listened intently.

'Not good,' added Murphy under his breath.

'It's coming from back here,' Rick said, edging his way around the third tank. The clicking became louder. He touched the corrugated tank and recoiled. It was hot.

'Give me your torch,' Rick said from behind. 'I can't see back here.'

Murphy had not moved.

'You okay, Joe?'

Rick began to worry. Whatever was happening down here seemed to have been affecting Murphy. He reached out and grabbed Rick's hand.

'Stop! We're outta time. I need you to go back right now.'

'Come on, Joe, we're here now. We've got a few minutes, haven't we?' Rick said. He wasn't so sure. Maybe Joe knew something he didn't. He edged his way forward.

'Don't go any further, Rick.'

Rick ignored the warning in Joe's voice. 'Just a quick sweep of the room, that's all, then we'll go, okay?'

What he wanted to say was that he had a feeling that Sophia was here somewhere. Rick moved on alone. It got even darker the more he moved beyond the tanks. The torch wasn't much help either. The space was cavernous. The further in, the warmer it got. The sulphuric odour was almost overwhelming. An occasional waft burnt his nostrils. He heard a noise behind him, he turned and flashed the torch back the way he came. The tanks looked like an octopus with cables snaking their way to the roof and the walls. Gangly arms extended from its head. An unnerving sight.

He reached a tunnel seemingly carved out of the rock. He ducked down and entered. He had to walk slightly stooped before he found himself in an opening. The walls were lined with a silvery substance, almost a light source in itself. He flashed the torch around the room. It had a symmetry that looked too perfect. Familiar, but strange at the same time.

He went closer to the wall and shone the torch on it. A flash here and a flash there. He felt a sharp pain travel down his torch-carrying hand and for a second, he thought he was having a stroke. His dad died of a massive stroke. The dying for him came before the drowning. No water in his lungs meant that he'd been dead before his body sank to the bottom and then washed up onto the shore just in time for his mother to walk up to a group of women.

'Don't look, my dear.' The crowd of onlookers told her.

Rick tried to get his breath back but found himself breathing in the fumes of the tanks. He bent down and put his hand on his heart. It was then he realised what he was seeing.

The walls were made of small bones, all neatly stacked and sorted against the far wall. Many piles of bones. What did that mean? Had he killed more than they'd thought? More than Jody, Hilda and Peter? He swayed but held his ground. He struggled against losing it completely and falling. He forced himself to take a breath.

He tried calling out to Murphy but his breath was ragged.

He knew they were human. Too short for adult bones. All children. But that was impossible. They lined the walls, end on end. There had to be hundreds. How many bones did a child have? He couldn't remember.

Suddenly, he was bathed in light. A bank of hidden lights came on. Rick blinked and shielded his eyes from the instant little suns that dotted the ceiling. A figure stood at the far end of the dugout.

At first, he thought he was imagining it all. The flash of light. The sulphuric smell. The haze that hung in the air. Someone was coming toward him.

It was an old woman. Her long-bedraggled hair hung down barely touching a shawl that covered her shoulders. Her long gown with frilly lace trailed on the ground behind her. Then Rick saw that she was wearing boots. Black army boots. That was odd.

She came closer. She was holding something.

'Are you okay?' asked Rick before he realised that he'd seen her before. Behind that door. The door at the Hilltop Retreat. She was lying on the bed.

The light was blinding him. He shielded his eyes again. 'Are you hurt?'

She cackled then let out a wail. He'd heard that wail before.

'I can help you. You're lost down here,' he said.

Then he saw what she was holding. A gun. Levelled at his chest. He recognised that gun. Rick looked behind. Where was Joe?

Another cackle. Then a realisation that all was not as it seemed.

The figure in front of him stepped a little closer. Rick saw the lines on the woman's face. Makeup was smeared, and eyes were darkened. Then a smile sent shivers down his spine and cracked the face of the woman.

It wasn't a woman at all. Made-up like a clown. Lipstick smeared and rouge hastily put on.

A clown with a gun? No. Then it hit him.

'Whitey!'

He couldn't believe what he was seeing.

'You hid like that. That's how you got away with it. You dressed like a woman and pretended to be sick.'

The laughter was maniacal. Then a high-pitched voice spoke. He recognised that voice.

'You noticed. I thought you wouldn't. Oh well, not to worry. I don't always dress like this.' Whitey's voice took on a deeper tone. 'No, sometimes I would go out and then don something chic. Your friend Gino was shocked when we met that day. I was dressed as myself. And you the other night. I let you see me.'

The gun cocked. Rick braced himself.

Whitey glared at him then continued to speak.

'It seemed the easiest way to avoid all the hoo-hah that was going on at the time. Besides, my poor brother didn't know if I was Arthur or Martha. A bit spent in the brain, he is. It was simple. Pretend that I was dead. Let him look after his sister. The sister that conveniently died ten years ago. I had my loyal friends to protect me. Money talks, you know.'

'Friends like the gardener,' Rick said. 'You're a sick bastard, you know.'

Rick took a step closer to Whitey. He could see that the gun he was holding was the one that killed Caruso and until just a few moments ago had been in Joe's pocket.

'What have you done with Murphy?'

'Kind of him to bring my gun back to me. I put him in the vat,' he said, stripping off the wig from his head. 'Only joking, he'll keep for now though. Keep your distance.'

'Where's Sophia?' Rick said anxiously.

Whitey's voice went up. He quivered with excitement. 'Ooh she is special, isn't she? Did it remind you of someone? But of course, you know who I'm talking about, don't you?'

Rick could see the gun shaking as Whitey got more and more excited. He was tempted to run at him.

'I wouldn't do that,' said Whitey, knowing exactly what Rick had in mind. 'I have to tell you that I am a very good shot. I've had years of practice.'

'You haven't answered my question. Where is she? Did you bring her here?'

'Now that would be a mistake, don't you think? I mean, I couldn't take her to those other places now, could I? You found my little hidey-hole in the cottage and of course, the mansion is out of the question. I used to have a nice place in my brother's factory but your little mate spoilt that.'

'Caruso.'

'Yes, I had to vacate that one pretty quickly.'

'You always seemed one step ahead of us. How did you do that?'

'Oh, I had many friends I could call on over the years. You know, they could tell me things, like when the police were going to look in certain areas. I always had plenty of time. And there was, of course, your friend, Murphy. He could always be a source of information when I needed it. I guess he just didn't know he was feeding me information.'

He had divested himself of his shawl and tatty gown by now. His blond hair now mainly grey was greased back into a ponytail.

Rick inched forward just a little. Whitey didn't seem to notice.

'You wouldn't have got any information from him. He was onto you. He had you pegged straight away.'

'That's where you are wrong, boy. Why do you think that I can get away with absolutely anything I want? It's because of people like him. Always predictable, always doing what cops do, everything by the book. Well, that's why I got away with all this.'

'You haven't got away with it. Look around you, all the evidence is here and when I find Sophia, you will be a dead man.'

Whitey sniggered. 'Anyway, I wouldn't worry about your friend, I would worry about you because in a few minutes, you'll all be dead.'

'We've got people coming for us.' Rick knew it was partially true if you counted Ian but he had to try.

'You mean that fool out the front? I wouldn't hope for anything there either. I remember you kids. Sticking your noses in where they were not wanted. Story of your life, I expect.'

'You murdered them. How many did you kill?'

'Oh, I lost count after Jody and her siblings. But they're all here. All friends of mine.'

'How many are down there?'

This made Whitey laugh. 'I know what you're doing. It won't do any good, trying to stall me so your friends can save you. They can't.'

'I think you know all their names and where you took them. You're a man who likes trophies.'

'Someone has to remember them. Don't you think it's a pretty shrine in there? I mean, in there they're glorified, remembered.'

'I bet you come here all the time to get that rush back. But like your brother, you're an old man now.'

'I still get the thrill of the young. Her hair is so soft and her skin is sublime,' said Whitey with a leer. 'And besides, I've still got a few more spots I've gotta fill. You'll do nicely. But alas, I think you'll be the last additions to my collection here. It seems that you've done some damage to the system. It's unstoppable now. I could just leave you here, knowing I added a few more bones to the pyre.'

It was now or never. He swallowed hard.

It was like Whitey could read his mind.

'You are thinking of rushing me. Makes no difference, you know. Hear that ticking sound? It started just after you got down to the basement, right? Well, it started when your detective friend cut the wires. Never cut the red wire. Surely you know that?' He laughed again. 'See those tanks there? All full of acid. I'd reckon we've got about two minutes before the first tank goes up, a further ten seconds for the second and… well, you know the rest. Won't be much left apart from a few shards. I'll miss it, of course, but hell… I'm still young. Maybe I'll just start again.'

Rick knew he wasn't lying this time. This was his end-game scenario. The trouble with end games is that someone has to lose. He was determined not to be a loser.

26

Damned if You Do, Damned if You Don't

HE LISTENED TO THE ticking. It was getting louder. He tried to think of what an acid explosion would be like. Would he have time to reach the stairs? Probably not. He was going to die down here. That much he could be sure of. But what about Sophia? Even though Whitey had said she wasn't there, she might be. Monsters lie, that much he knew about Whitey. And if she was, he needed to find her and get her out of here. He kept on thinking of Jody. She was driving him.

They were sitting on the back of the carousel horses. She on a white palomino, he on a black steed. She smiled at him as the ride began to slow down. Eric looked at the running board. He hated these things. It always made him sick. He could feel the swell of vomit resting in his stomach. He hoped he wouldn't bring it all up in front of her, again.

'You're better looking than my boyfriend,' Jody said.

He wanted to ask who her boyfriend was but the moment passed and he just smiled back at her. He tried to think of something cool to say but couldn't. Instead, he smiled at her and slid off the steed. He reached up and took her by the waist and pulled her to the ground gently.

Suddenly, her smile went sour. She turned to him. 'Find me,' she said. 'Come back and find me.'

Jody faded into darkness.

'Now if you would just move back from the door, I will leave you to my devices,' said Whitey, grinning like a maniac.

'No, you'll have to shoot me,' Rick said.

'I was hoping my tanks would take you out but no matter. A bullet should do the trick.'

'You killed Caruso. You shot him.'

'Shot him with this.' He nodded at the gun. 'Didn't see it coming. He was a fool, a doped-up fool. I knew he was stealing things from me. I made sure he found this, had to be sure he had his fingerprints all over it. And her little purse. That was a masterstroke. It got me close to you.'

'You made him a junkie.'

'At least he died easily, not like the one outside. He took a long time to die. Twisted his neck. Heard it snap. Don't like breaking too many bones, I like laying them out in my cave, nice and long and straight. His neck was brittle though.' He spat out the last sentence like a snake.

Rick's heart dropped. Ian! Had he murdered his friend? He wanted to rush the old man and drive him into the wall of bones. He gripped his hands tighter.

'Now move,' said Whitey, flicking his wrist.

Rick stayed put.

Whitey moved a couple of paces towards him. The clicking was now a rumble. Behind him, he could hear the acid bubbling away ready to be released. He stood his ground. If he was going to die here, he would take this miserable old man with him.

He stared across at Whitey. He wasn't scared. All that had gone since he knew the truth. Caruso had been right all along. He took a step towards him.

'Move back, boyo, or I'll fix that smile of yours,' he screamed and wobbled the gun in front of his face. Rick tensed, ready to pounce. The tank behind him bubbled over and he could hear the hissing of the acid as it hit the ground. A stream of it was heading his way.

'You took those children. You and your brother. You murdered them and when he was getting too close you murdered Caruso. You knew exactly what you were doing. Just like you knew we were coming here tonight. You waited for us. You wanted us to be a part of your fucked up plan. You always did. You showed me the photo of the other girl just to drag me in. Then you took Sophia and made it look like Murphy had done it.'

Laughter. It was always laughter that did it for him. Rick ran at Whitey just as he fired off a bullet. Rick braced himself for the impact but felt nothing. He smashed into Whitey and sent them both sprawling to the ground. He spat out a wad of dirt and shook his head from side to side.

The light faded. A momentary stalemate, then darkness, then back into the light. He opened his eyes.

Had he been unconscious just then? Where was Whitey? He scrambled around on the floor, looking for the gun. But they were both gone.

He tried to stand but his head ached like a bastard. A hand reached down and pulled him up.

'You alright, Rick? We've gotta get out of here right now,' Murphy said.

'You're alive,' Rick said, barely able to get the words out of his mouth. 'He told me he killed you.'

'Rule number one. Monsters lie.'

Suddenly, the top of the tank blew off and a gaseous discharge seeped towards them. Somewhere in the confrontation with Whitey, Rick had lost the torch. They were in total darkness.

'This way.' Murphy held the unsteady Rick as they edged their way back to the entrance.

'Joe, the bones. He killed them all.'

'I know.'

'She's here, Joe. That bastard brought her here. I know it.'

He was sure he was right. Suddenly, another tank blew its lid and started to exude acid. It was like lava; every spot it touched it burnt black. It sizzled and cut across the entrance. Murphy stopped in his tracks. The path was blocked.

'We have to find another way.' He tried to pull Murphy away from the acid but he wouldn't budge.

'There's no other way. If we move quickly, we can make it.'

There was a small opening to the left. Murphy edged towards it.

The voice echoed from behind the sizzling vat of acid. 'I wouldn't move if I were you.' Whitey was waiting for them.

He stood on a raised platform next to the vats. 'Both of you together. How convenient,' he said.

He levelled the gun at them.

'Be realistic now, Anthony. You won't get both of us,' Murphy said.

Whitey pointed the gun at Murphy then at Rick, seemingly unable to choose.

This time it wasn't Rick who lunged. Murphy sprang forward. A muffled gunshot ripped through the dark and dingy basement.

Suddenly, an explosion sucked the air right out of the basement and sent Rick flying toward the bottom of the stairs. An envelope of flame nearly consumed him as he struggled upwards. At the top, he turned and tried getting back down to help Joe but he knew it was hopeless.

'Joe… JOE!' His screaming voice echoed throughout the empty house.

The gaseous discharge had now seeped upwards into the house. Rick's reflexes were now working on memory alone. He had a sinking feeling in his chest. He knew that the whole place was going to blow at any moment. He stumbled.

He gripped his chest and felt for his heart. Was this it? Was this the feeling that his dad felt all those years ago when his heart gave out? He was just about to give up and fall to the ground when he felt something grabbing his arm, pulling it out of its socket. All he wanted to do was to collapse on the ground and close his eyes.

'Come on, Rick. One more breath. Come on, pally.'

That voice. It was Caruso. He knew it wasn't possible, Caruso was dead, killed by that bastard. He staggered through the corridor and collapsed in front of a wall. He had Caruso's voice in his head.

'Look where you least expect a room to be,' Caruso had said.

Then Rick saw it. A door that had been hidden from him when they'd entered now looked more than obvious. Behind him, smoke was billowing up from the basement. He wondered how long he had before it all went up.

He tried the handle but it was locked. He had no energy left. He thumped the door with his hand. It was metal. He slumped down to the ground his back against the door. He promised himself only a moment to catch his breath. He knew he was fading. Suddenly, he heard a noise from inside the room. A cry? A sob? He pushed himself up and thumped on the door. He called out and then listened but there was nothing. The hallway was now filling with noxious smoke. He could hardly breathe. Again, he charged at the door but it hardly moved.

Another explosion rocked the room behind him. A large piece of metal flew past his head and embedded itself into the wall. He tore his jacket off and used it to take hold of the heated rod. He pulled as hard as he could. He felt it give way. He attacked the door with the rod, levering the sharp end under the door jamb. He could think of nothing else he could do. If this didn't work, he was sure the fire would consume him along with everything in its path. He mustered all his strength and pulled the rod downwards. He heard a cracking sound as the plaster around the door began to give way. He watched as pieces flew behind him and a hole gradually open up over the door frame.

Then the smoke overwhelmed him and he dropped the rod. It echoed through his head as he slipped down the wall. He tried to latch onto something with his hands but there was nothing there, a bare wall. This was it. He knew it.

For a moment, his body lay on the floor then he felt a sudden urge to stand. He pulled himself up. He tried opening his eyes but the smoke was too thick. He gripped the edge of the ragged hole that had opened up above the door and dragged himself through it and onto the other side. He could now see just a little. The room was remarkably bright. Decked out in wild colours it seemed to be a page out of a fairytale. Lots of pinks and reds, blues and purples – a children's room. A light was swinging from the ceiling. Something was going on above him, a hole in the roof. Smoke poured into the room. He dragged himself a few metres then fell to the floor. He recognised this room. This was the room he had seen on the security camera back in the cottage.

A small figure lay curled up on the floor. She was dressed in blue jeans and a white top.

'Sophia?' he asked as calmly as he could.

Suddenly, another explosion rattled through the room, shaking it to its very core. He couldn't wait. This place was about to come down. He lifted her into his arms then stood and faced the door. There was no getting out there.

The girl whimpered as the ceiling began to fall away. He looked at her. For the briefest second, he could see Jody staring back at him.

'You came for me,' she said.

Then the sidewall fell. He saw a gap open up. He made for it.

*

The street was ablaze. Lights were flashing on and off. Sirens sounded over the chaos of explosions and the crackling of fire. There was a thought at the edge of his mind wanting to get in, he ignored it. He clutched Sophia even tighter. She clung to him even as a paramedic tried to take her from him. He resisted. A man began to talk to him but all he could hear were explosions going off in his ear.

'Don't let me go,' said Sophia into his ear.

He held her tighter.

Hendriks put an arm on his and made him relax his hold on the girl.

He looked up at her as she was taken by a paramedic. Then she was gone.

Something cleared his foggy mind. One of Hendriks men got a blanket and put it around his shoulders but he shrugged it off.

'Sally rang and told me you were coming for her,' said Hendriks. 'It's okay, Rick. She's safe now.'

'I need to go back. Joe's in there, and Ian…' Rick said, trying to think things through.

'Take it easy, Rick. Leave it to us. We'll get him out. And Ian's right here,' said Hendriks as he stood, ready to rejoin his men.

'Ian?' Rick lurched up and grabbed his friend in a bear hug. 'You're alive.'

'Course I'm alive. Why wouldn't I be?'

'Whitey…' Rick began but Ian interrupted him.

'I didn't see anyone. Heard the explosion so I rang Hendriks,' Ian said. 'He was already on his way.'

'You didn't see him get out?' Rick said.

'Whitey? No. I didn't see anything. I would have texted you if I'd seen anyone. Rick, what did you see in there? Who set off the explosion? Did Joe? He looked pretty burnt up when they dragged him outta there.'

'It was Whitey.'

'Nobody got in after you. I'm sure of that. He must have had the girl in there all the time. One of the neighbours thought that whoever owned the place kept a collection of dead animals in there as it stank to high heaven all the time. They complained to the council. But of course, nothing was ever done about it.'

'There was a collection in there but not dead animals. We saw it, both Joe and myself. Whitey was there. That's where he took the children. They're in there…'

'Shit, Rick, how many did you see?'

For a moment, Rick was unsure of himself.

'Hundreds. There were hundreds of bones. I saw the acid tanks. That's what blew. He had them set so that if it was breached it would destroy the cavern.'

'It's alright, Rick. If they're in there, they'll find them.'

'No, that's just it, Ian… they won't find anything. Those bones will be destroyed. He won, Ian. That bastard won.'

'No, he didn't. You got the girl out. You got Sophia.'

Suddenly, a thought so terrible crossed his mind. He scrambled to his feet and made a move back to the house. Ian, stunned for a second, ran after him. 'Don't be a bloody idiot. You can't go back in there. Shit, Rick, don't be bloody STUPID.'

Rick turned toward his friend and grabbed him. 'Ian, did anyone else get out of here?'

'You think Whitey got out?' Ian looked around, scanning the whole area.

'How did they get Joe out? Tell me… Joe was with Whitey. He saved me, he jumped on him when he was going to shoot me. Ian?'

'Rick, nobody else got out. They got Joe out from a window at the side of the house. There wasn't any other way out.'

'There must have been, Ian. There must have been another way out. One only Whitey knew.'

A cackling noise. They looked up. A dark shadow stood before them.

'You thought the girl was the one I wanted.' The voice was hoarse but Rick recognised it straight away.

Whitey moved into the half-light. He had Caruso's gun in his hand. He levelled it at the two. 'Actually, I lied. I did want the girl but I knew you would come looking for me. I knew you would make mistakes, and you did. The first mistake was involving your friends in this. I killed the cop.'

'You're a liar. They got Joe out,' Ian said.

Whitey laughed. 'You think I would let him go like that? He's as dead as his wife.'

'You're lying. He's alive, they pulled him out,' Ian said, stepping forward angrily. He waved his fists at the dark shadow.

Ian and Rick looked at each other. They knew what they had to do.

'You can only get one of us,' said Ian.

Just like they had rescued Caruso at the Picture Theatre, Rick and Ian attacked Whitey. The blast from the gun echoed through Rick's head. Then he saw Ian freeze and drop to his knees. Laughter from Whitey infuriated him but there was nothing he could do but hold Ian up from collapsing to the ground. Ian clutched at his stomach then pulled his hands away, showing Rick the blood.

'He fucking shot me,' he said, whimpering. Rick saw the colour fade from his face. 'I'm dying, Ricky. I'm too young, and I've got kids…' He was rambling now. The night sky was playing tricks on them both. Time slowed. Tiny drops of rain were hitting them both as Rick supported Ian on the ground. Ian's face paled and his eyes started to droop.

'Stay with me, pally.'

The smell of smoke wafted through Rick's nostrils. He wasn't sure whether it was the gunshot or the fact the house behind them was exploding in flames. Rick looked up to see Whitey had stepped a little closer. He could see his face now. Pale and withered. He smiled down at Rick and held up the gun again.

'Three outta three. First, I got your little wog friend. He was easy. Made it look like suicide to the cops but you didn't believe it, did you? I had to make you think I was still around. Couldn't get the three of you unless I got you interested, eh? Then the little trick with the girl. Made them all think that there was a copycat out there but you knew all along, didn't you? That's why I took the girl, someone close to you, made it all real for you, didn't it? That's why we're here. That's why I could get your buddies,' Whitey snarled.

'Ricky, I'm sorry I didn't believe you,' Ian kept rambling. His body was slipping and Rick knew he was drifting away. He looked up at Whitey.

'Go on then, shoot me. Sophia got away, she's safe.'

Whitey gave a little snigger. 'But she'll remember this all her life, won't she? She'll be damaged goods, just like her mother.'

'I'm dying, Eric,' Ian said. Under duress, he reverted to Rick's boyhood name. Rick put his hand under the back of his neck and laid him down on the ground gently.

'You're not dying,' Rick said with a falter. There was so much blood.

'That bastard killed me,' said Ian deliriously.

Rick looked back up at Whitey. The gun levelled at his head.

'Next,' Whitey said. 'I'm not as young as I once was. My aim is a little off,' he said, cocking the gun again. 'I used to be a dead-eye dick.' He shrugged as if saying he was sorry he hadn't killed Ian outright. 'You were smarter than I thought. I was used to running the cops around including your former partner, Murphy. They were easily fooled. I mean, no one even checked to see if my body was in the casket. Stupid if you ask me. No matter, I've got what I want. You three kids. You can join my troop.'

Rick looked around for the cops. They were away in the distance dealing with the fire. No one had heard the sound of gunfire against the exploding scene. He was on his own. By the light of the fire, he could see Whitey come closer.

This was it. This is how he died, Rick thought. Caruso wouldn't have known what was coming. He forced himself to try and stand to face Whitey. He was almost to his feet when he felt a sudden gust of wind from behind him. The flash of the gun took him by surprise. When he looked up, he saw a cloaked dark figure launch at the gun and the person holding it. It seemed like a bad dream. A scream from someone alerted him to the fact that the gun had gone off again.

The dark figure slammed into Whitey, sending him sprawling backwards. Behind him was the window he had escaped the house from. Both figures landed in the broken glass and another scream pierced the night sky.

The blaze from the house had erupted into the room directly behind the window. Fire and smoke were pulsating out of the only escape hole. The flames caught hold of both figures as they embraced in deadly combat. They were gradually being drawn back into the inferno.

Rick recognised the back of Joe's trench coat. He launched

himself onto the brawling pair and tried to pull Joe back. His hands were burnt and sore and they slipped off easily. They were now in danger of all three of them being sucked back into the fire. He took another breath and pulled at Joe's collar.

It was then Rick noticed that the gun Whitey shot Ian with lay on the ground. He tried reaching it, still hanging onto Joe's coattails. He knew if he let go, Whitey would succeed in dragging Joe inside the hell hole. He strained to pick it up but it was just outside of his reach.

Suddenly, an explosion rocked the whole building. It looked like the vats were finally erupting. The gaseous discharge seeped up through the floor and into the room. The flames reached the ceiling.

Rick wrapped his arms around Joe and tried pulling him back onto the ground but he felt a greater pull from Whitey. How could someone so old be so strong?

'Let me go,' shouted Murphy over the roar of the fire. 'Get the goddamned gun, and shoot the motherfucker.'

Rick knew that if he let go, there was no guarantee Joe would be there when he reached for the gun. He was talking seconds.

'NOW,' screamed the former detective.

Rick let him go and flung himself onto the ground. For a moment, he couldn't find the gun. It was dark and he was tired. His hand hit metal. He brought the gun up and levelled it at the window.

Whitey and Murphy had disappeared inside the raging fire.

Suddenly, a dark figure launched himself at him through the window. The scorched face of Whitey appeared like a ghost. He threw his hands around Rick's neck and started to drag him back into the inferno. Murphy had disappeared into the dark and Rick was on his own. He felt himself being dragged into the flames.

The heat was overpowering. He felt his strength leave him. If he closed his eyes, he would be gone. He fought that inclination.

He could see her eyes now. His mind was doing crazy things. He could see Jody as plain as day. She stood there and smiled at him. She whispered into his ear.

Then he heard the screaming. He looked up at Whitey and pulled him close to him. He lifted the gun and stuck the barrel into his forehead.

'SHOOT,' yelled Murphy who had dragged himself up and was hanging onto Whitey as he tried to pull back.

Whitey grinned like the monster he was.

Rick pulled the trigger.

The back of Whitey's head blew out.

Rick fell to the ground. Blackness engulfed him.

27

Endings and Beginnings

THE ICU OF THE hospital was remarkably calm. Rick sat alone in the waiting room, waiting! It was early. The morning sun was just poking its head from the west where it had been hiding all night. Two police officers were sitting on the bench seat opposite him, bored and sleepy. They, too, had been there all night. Rick had been checked and double-checked. A neurologist had even been called when the presiding doctor found out about his past. All checked out. A slight case of smoke inhalation and singed hands were all they could find. He had been discharged but still, he needed to stay.

Suddenly, the double doors burst open and a wheelchair-bound Ian was pushed towards his friend. His arm in a sling, he lifted his good arm slowly and smiled at Rick.

'Thought I'd never get out of there,' Ian said. He made a motion to rise from the chair but the nurse put a restraining hand on him. 'I'm fine, never better.'

'Not what you were saying when he shot you. You were screaming blue murder. Turns out he only winged you.' Rick smiled.

Through the glass windows, Ian could see his family arrive en masse. Ian sighed. 'I'm just glad he was a bad shot. How's Murphy?'

'Lucky to be alive, I guess. His hands were burnt but he's remarkably resilient for an old bastard.'

'I guess it got pretty real in there. I mean, you had to shoot the bastard's face off to kill him.'

Suddenly, Rick remembered what had pushed him to fight back.

'I saw Jodie. I saw her face. And then I heard screaming. It took me a while before I realised it was me who was screaming.'

'What did you tell them? The cops, I mean.'

Rick pursed his lips. 'I wasn't listening. Hendriks said something about finding a body. I guess he meant Whitey. He said it was hard to ID but forensics were working on it. I made a mess of him, Ian. The funny thing is I've never even fired a gun before. When I was aiming it at him, I wasn't sure what would happen when I pulled the trigger. Murphy knew. He kept on yelling at me to kill the motherfucker. It was weird, hearing him swear like that. An old dude swearing like a teenager.'

'Hilarious,' Ian said. 'He doesn't strike me as the type.'

'I thought Murphy was dead. Whitey told me he'd killed him, shot him with the gun he'd killed Caruso with. He thought it was a big joke.'

'Turns out the joke was on him,' Ian said, smiling. 'Did they find anything else in the house?'

'House was burnt to the ground. The firies couldn't save anything. Ash, just ash. The sulphuric acid did its job.'

'You think they'll find anything? You know, bones.'

Rick feared they wouldn't.

*

Rick, Joe and Ian stood in Hendriks office, waiting for the detective to finish a press conference he was currently presiding over on the steps of the station.

All the TVs were tuned to different news broadcasts and they all seemed to be congregated on the steps of CID. Rick couldn't hear any of what Hendriks was saying but he could get the gist of it.

A girl had been found. And yes, she was safe. A fire had destroyed a northern suburbs house where she was found and at the moment, forensic scientists were going through the remains for clues. An announcement on suspects will be forthcoming in the next few days. The usual fare.

Questions from the press would be allowed but not much information was expected to be given.

Hendriks eventually entered his office. His face was drawn and grey but he walked with a sure step of a cop that had gotten away with something monumental.

'I have to thank you, Rick, for what you did in there. It could have been much worse.' Hendriks closed the door behind him. 'As you can appreciate until you've been fully debriefed, I will ask you not to talk about it, even amongst yourselves.'

'You won't stop trying to identify the remains? Even if it becomes too difficult, will you?' Rick said. 'I mean, I know they're there.'

'I can confirm that we have found the remains of an elderly male along with some other ashen bones. But there is something else.'

He pulled open a drawer under his desk. From it, he took out a large plastic bag. He lay it gently on the desk. He looked up at Rick. 'Go ahead, open it. Be careful to hold it with the plastic.'

Rick unfolded the bag. He slid out a carefully wrapped handkerchief.

'Open it,' Hendriks began. 'It seems he also liked to keep personal trophies. We found this in a metal safe in the basement next to a series of bones we suspect are that of Jody Milburn, Hilda Milburn and Peter Milburn. It would seem to be the only things that survived the holocaust.'

Rick unfolded the dainty cloth. Inside was a little money and a note. He carefully took out the note. On it was a list of purchases Jody had made with her mother's money and a few words that said 'hoping to see Robert Dean from school at the beach'. Also, two long cords were coiled up carefully.

'These were the contents of the purse Caruso sent to you,' Hendriks said. 'The perpetrator kept them.'

Rick picked up the two coils and unfurled them. He recognised them straight away. They were the cords originally on Jody's purse.

'We've had them tested. They were used to tie the children up,' said Hendriks quietly.

Sadness engulfed Rick. He fingered the cords before carefully rolling them back up and placing them back on the desk.

Ian tried changing the subject. 'Who is Robert Dean?'

'It turns out that Robert Dean went to the same school as she did although in a higher class. We were able to speak with him and he confirmed that he knew Jody Milburn from school. He swore that he had no idea he was the apparent boyfriend. It would seem that Jody wished she had Robert as a boyfriend,' said Hendriks.

'And you're sure of that?' Ian said.

'As sure as we can be. He certainly got a shock when we told him that Jody considered him a boyfriend,' said Hendriks.

'So how do we prove that Whitey was the culprit? I mean, we all know but if it has to go to a coroner, we have to have actual proof,' Ian said.

Hendriks thought about that for a second. He looked at Joe, then at Ian and Rick. 'It looked to me to be a suicide thing. He probably thought he'd never make it out, so he went out with a bang, so to speak,' said Hendriks. 'DNA will give us the answer to his identity and guilt in these matters.'

'We might not need DNA to prove the case against Rutherglen,' Murphy said.

Hendriks looked at Joe and raised his eyes. 'You know something, Joe?'

'More like found something,' Murphy said.

'Conclusive?' asked Hendriks.

Murphy reached into his trench coat pocket and pulled out a cloth hanky. It was folded into a small square and stitched along one side, forming a pocket. He reached in and pulled out a photo.

It was a black and white photo of the three children sitting, squashed together on a bed. Whitey sat next to them with his arms spread wide. Rick recognised the room. It was the one he had just rescued Sophia from. His heart leapt. As he stared at the photo, her eyes seemed to lock on his.

'Jody,' whispered Rick.

'Found it in the basement near the vats. He wanted us to find it,' Murphy said. 'Probably taken by his brother Paul Stanley Elliott.'

'Bastard,' said Ian.

'Monster like his brother,' said Rick.

Hendriks sighed deeply. 'We have taken Paul Stanley Elliott into custody. We believe he was complicit in the abductions of the three children but getting a conviction will be problematic as he has an advanced case of dementia. And as we speak, border police have picked up the gardener. He says he knows nothing but he had to have known something.'

'And the commander, Judge Renly Shaw?' asked Ian. 'He had to have known something too. If it weren't for Joe here, he might have gotten away with it.'

Hendriks looked down at his notes. 'I have asked my boss, the commissioner, to bring charges against the judge and of course, the AVO against Murphy here is dropped but for now, we won't know about resolutions until we've finished the investigation,' said Hendriks.

'As it should be. If it weren't for Joe, we wouldn't have found the place and Sophia would be dead,' Ian said. 'Just so you know,' he added.

Joe looked at Ian and Rick and gave a small smile. For once, his hands remained still.

'Thanks, guys. I'm just glad that none of us died. Big bonus, I'd reckon,' Murphy said.

Hendriks shook each one of them by the hand. When it came to Rick's turn, he said, 'Just one last thing before you go, Rick. There is someone next door that wants to say thanks.'

He opened a side door.

Sally and Sophia sat on a wide bench seat.

Sophia stood and took a step toward Rick. Then she ran the last few steps and jumped into his arms.

Sophia with blue eyes.

Sally smiled at him.

*

St Julien's Cemetery was empty but for three men. Ian with his arm still in a sling, Murphy with his bandaged hands, and Rick with a bunch of sunflowers wrapped up in plain brown paper. They stood in front of the newly erected headstone at Gino Caruso's grave.

It read:

Here lies our friend Caruso.

'Everything can find a way home.'

The sun was out. It was going to be hotter today. Maybe summer this year will be a good one.

'Can we drop you anywhere, Rick?' Ian said. 'My wife's going to get the car.'

'Nah, one of Hendriks boys went and got my Jag from the scene. I might just take a run...'

'To the beach,' Ian finished.

'You know, Rick, it's not too late,' Murphy said.

Rick looked at the former detective curiously.

'You should go get her. Tell her you love her. Life's too short and all that. I had a good life with Sarah, made me the man I am today. You need a woman to do the same for you.'

Rick coughed into the palm of his hand. Ian laughed.

'You won't get him to admit it, Joe. He can be an insufferable arsehole at times. Can't admit that he needs anybody.'

'Everybody needs someone, sometimes,' Murphy said softly.

Rick laughed.

It was good to laugh.

POSTSCRIPT

THE BREEZE BRUSHED AGAINST his cheek. It was definitely getting warmer. More kids on the jetty now. Dogs too. An unfettered one just ran past, its owner a distant figure holding the animal's halter. It had escaped. He thought of Nero. He'd had a phone call earlier. An old mate had some funds available to do a recording and he wanted Rick and the Anchormen to do an album. He was slightly amused. Maybe he would. He could probably dredge up a few songs to do. Maybe if they recorded it here at the beach. That would be a good idea. Then he could see Sally and her daughter, and Vince and Molly and Ian and possibly Murphy. He could see himself living back here now.

He leaned over the jetty railing and watched as the circle lady finished her latest grand offering. As usual, it baffled him. She looked up at him then waved her stick. This time, she seemed happy to see him. She smiled. He smiled back.

She was by his side. He hadn't seen her approach. She stood next to him, staring down at her work.

'Did you find what you were looking for?'

A gentle breeze swept down the beach. On its waves, Gammy the gull squawked and landed on his lookout post.

He thought about that question. Yes, he had found the children and the monster who had taken them. Yes, he had found his old love. Yes, he had found his friends. Three yes's.

'Did you know that I lost my dad right down there? Right in the middle of your circles.'

'The beach knows all. It has a memory, you know. That's what I draw. The beach is at peace now. I can see it in your face.'

'Are you a psychic? How do you know these things?'

'The beach tells me. I am a storyteller, that's all.'